Naughware to Run

Book 1 of the Peter Naughware Chronicles

Jaz Primo

RUTHERFORD LITERARY GROUP

Novels by Jaz Primo

The Peter Naughware Chronicles

Naughware to Run
* *Feeling the Burn*
* *Damned Luck*

* Additional Titles Forthcoming

* * *

The Sunset Vampire Series

Sunrise at Sunset: Revamped
A Bloody London Sunset
Summit at Sunset
Wicked Sunset
Sunset Rising
* *Sunset Burning*

** Additional Titles Forthcoming

* * *

The Logan Bringer Urban Fantasy Series

Bringer of Fire
Bringer Unleashed
Bringer's Law *

* Additional Titles Forthcoming

* * *

Gwen Reaper
(A Young Adult Paranormal Romance)

* * *

All titles published by Rutherford Literary Group

This is a work of fiction. Names, characters, places, and incidents either are the product of the author's imagination or are used fictitiously, and any resemblance to actual persons, living or dead, business establishments, events, or locales is entirely coincidental. The publisher does not have any control over and does not assume any responsibility for author or third-party websites or their content. Any trademarks mentioned herein are not authorized by the trademark owners and do not in any way mean the work is sponsored by or associated with the trademark owners. Any trademarks used are specifically in a descriptive capacity.

Published by:
Rutherford Literary Group
1205 S. Air Depot, PMB #135
Midwest City, OK 73110-4807

Cover art by Katrina Curry, Crimson Phoenix Creations

Title Page Artwork: "Angel and Demon on Shoulders" by Gunay Aliyevs

Edited by Laura Matheson

ISBN 978-0-9968813-1-9 (Trade Paperback)
ISBN 978-0-9885690-9-6 (E-Book)

DEDICATION

I appreciate the encouragement and support of my friends and loved ones, as well as the valued readers who enjoy my creations. As I've grow older and matured as a writer, I'm especially grateful for the fortunate circumstances that my life provides so that I may focus on my creative endeavors. And though it may sound strange, my heartfelt thanks to Dungeon and Dragons as a source for stretching my imagination both during my youth and throughout my adulthood, and for the welcome escape it provides while spending time with my friends and loved ones. Special thanks to that charming lady in my life whose love and influence is both positive and nurturing. If she's not the stuff that heroes are made of, I don't know who is…

CONTENTS

Naughware to Run

CHAPTER 1

The best birthdays aren't celebrated over dead bodies.

Detective Peter Naughware stepped into a floristry warehouse called the Bouquet Corral that was strewn with blood, gore, corpses, and shredded pieces of assorted flowers and plants. The assortment of crime scene investigators and police officers pouring over the area reminded him of a flock of vultures picking over road kill.

"Lucky me," Naughware said, loosening his necktie. "Not everyone gets a massacre for their thirty-third birthday."

A patrol sergeant approached him. "Mornin', Detective."

"Is the entire precinct here, Wilson?" Naughware asked.

"Yep," Wilson said. "Whoever could find an excuse."

"Most of them should leave."

Wilson gave Naughware a sober look. "You don't see something like this every day in Abaddon, Detective."

"Nobody should have to see this," Naughware said while scanning the area. "On any day."

"True enough," Wilson said. "Just so you know, Lieutenant Dawkins has already taken site command."

"Figures," Naughware said.

He walked over where the lieutenant stood beside a young woman he didn't recognize.

"Detective Naughware," Dawkins said. "Let me introduce you to your new partner, Detective Alicia Keane."

Naughware looked at Dawkins with disdain. "New partner?"

The detective eagerly offered her hand in greeting. "Pleased to meet you, Detective."

Naughware reached out to shake. "Detective Keane."

He thought her grip felt firm and confident, while the look in her eyes said, "*I'm professional, but don't fuck with me.*"

"I'm eager to begin working with you on this case," Keane said.

Naughware politely nodded but longingly looked past her at the crime scene beyond.

"You'll pardon the rather unusual place and timing of the introductions, Naughware," Dawkins said. "Keane transferred in from the department in Peoria a few days ago. She finished our department orientation, and HR just cleared her for duty this morning, so it seemed fitting for her to meet you at the start of this case rather than back at the precinct after the fact. This way she won't need to catch up on anything."

"Hm," Naughware said. "Makes sense, I suppose."

The last thing he wanted was a new partner. He still missed his former one.

"Any questions before I leave you two?" Dawkins asked.

"Yes, Lieutenant," Naughware said. "Could you please clear my crime scene of half of these nonessentials on your way out?"

Dawkins gave him a wan look. "I'll look into it."

"I'd appreciate that," Naughware said.

"For now, the scene's all yours, detectives," Dawkins said. "At least until Vigoda and Levitt arrive. They're handing off their current case to Yemana in order to run point on this one."

"Wait, what?" Naughware asked.

Dawkins adopted a wry expression. "Naughware, you know very well that Vigoda's Senior Detective Sergeant since your partner retired. This is one of the biggest body counts in decades, and the mayor will want our most experienced detectives on it."

"If this is Vigoda's case, why am I even here then?"

"Not my idea," he replied. "That was Captain Gunderson."

Naughware frowned.

"I don't know. Maybe the captain figured Vigoda and Levitt have their hands full and need some extra help on a case this size," the lieutenant said. "Anyway, from my perspective, this is a good one for Detective Keane to cut her teeth on."

"Listen—"

The lieutenant held up his hand. "Take it up with the captain later, if you want," he said before turning and walking away.

"Cocky sonofabitch," Naughware muttered under his breath.

Keane glanced over at him and then watched the lieutenant walk away before returning her attention to Naughware. The tension in the air between the two men felt palpable to her.

"So, Detective, would you like for me to start—" she asked.

"Feel free to look around until Vigoda and Levitt arrive," Naughware interrupted her. "All I ask is a quiet scene until I have a chance to look things over."

He didn't wait for a response and instead withdrew a pair of stereo earbuds from an interior pocket on his sports jacket and walked away from her.

"All right then," she said while resting her hands atop her hips. Just her luck to get saddled with a detective who was on the outs with his supervisor. She only hoped his bad aura wouldn't extend to her by association.

Naughware seated the earbuds and withdrew a small digital player from his pocket. He glanced down at its screen, which uncharacteristically flashed.

New song added, it displayed.

The revelation stopped him in his tracks.

He frowned and scrolled down the short list of songs in the root folder, expecting to see the usual eleven songs. Instead, he counted twelve.

"'The Gospel of John Hurt' by alt-J?" he asked. "Where the hell did you come from?"

No time for that now, he thought. *Not much time left before Vigoda and Levitt arrive.*

A din of voices echoed through the warehouse.

"How about some quiet on this scene?!" he yelled.

A tense hush fell over the warehouse as he walked over to the nearest corpse and looked down at it.

"What have you got for me today, I wonder?" he whispered, shifting his gaze to his digital player's small screen.

He selected the random play option and "Long Cool Woman (In a Black Dress)" by The Hollies began to play.

* * *

Only a few minutes had passed, and yet, Detective Alicia Keane was already regretting being assigned to Naughware. She knew from experience that warming up to new partners was difficult, but he had already exceeded her worst expectations.

For one, she wondered what she had done to deserve the initial cold shoulder from him.

She looked across the warehouse to study Naughware. He made a slow stroll of the crime scene, reminding her of a predator stalking prey.

"Welcome to the Fourth Precinct, Detective," Sergeant Wilson said. "You must be the new Robbery-Homicide transfer I heard about at roll call."

Keane turned and reached out to shake the sergeant's hand. "That's me. Alicia Keane."

"Sergeant Wilson," he said. "Word has it you transferred in from Peoria."

She nodded her head. "Yeah, just finished my HR orientation, in fact."

"I've got a sister who lives in Peoria," he said. "Nice town, she says. The sort of place she said she'd never want to leave."

Keane appeared reflective. "I've found that people and places are like puzzle pieces. Everyone doesn't fit everywhere."

His eyebrows rose. "Well, glad to have you here, just the same."

She glanced over at Detective Naughware, who slowly perused the crime scene. "Thanks, Sergeant. If only everyone felt the way you do."

The sergeant followed her gaze. "Are you partnered with Naughware?"

"So it would seem."

He reached up to scratch the back of his head. "Rough start?"

"More cool than rough, really," she said. "Might just be some tension I sensed between him and the lieutenant."

"Well, you might do well to know, and it's no secret, there's no love lost between Lieutenant Dawkins and Naughware. Since his former partner retired, he and Dawkins have frequently argued at crime scenes. Around two months ago, they ended up in a shouting match over Naughware wanting a search warrant," he said. "I wouldn't worry about Naughware. It may just take some time for him to get to know you. He's a good sort. Of course, he's not your typical sort."

"Typical sort?" she asked. "Sort of what?"

"Sort of anybody," he said. "Or anything, for that matter."

She stared at him. "Care to elaborate?"

"Begging your pardon, Detective," he said. "Naughware's a solid cop. Most just find him to be a bit eccentric. He has a reputation for unorthodox approaches to investigation."

"Ah, lucky me," she said while watching Naughware. "What's with the earbuds?"

"That's just his thing," Wilson said with a shrug. "I think it's music or maybe even white noise or something. Seems to help him focus on the crime scenes."

"Mm," she said. "Unusual, huh?"

The sergeant gave her a tentative look. "If you'll excuse me, Detective," he said. "I'd better finish securing the scene."

Keane watched Naughware for a few moments longer before turning to apply her own deductive skills to the litany of bodies lying around her.

* * *

Naughware slowly surveyed each body and evidence components no less than twice while replaying The Hollies song again and again.

Eleven bodies, he thought.

Most of the corpses were scattered around a periphery of boxes and crates. At the center of the chaos was a metal table that had a centerpiece of two opened, blood-covered, and bullet-riddled packages of a white powdery-looking substance and a tote bag filled with bundles of newly minted cash, of which he saw one-hundred-, fifty-, and twenty-dollar bills.

Beside the bag of cash was a wooden crate containing perhaps a dozen more bags of the white substance.

Two bodies lay astride the table, opposite each other.

Naughware considered the scene. *A drug exchange gone bad?*

It looked clear-cut, and yet, something felt off about it. There was something missing.

Including whoever may have survived this bloodbath.

He licked the tip of his forefinger and reached down to tap it against the white powder before him. He smelled it and then touched his tongue to the substance.

An overpowering bitter reaction was followed by a metallic-like aftertaste.

"Shit," he said, spitting onto the floor. "Not coke."

Rubbing his fingers against the side of his pants, he

caught the disapproving gaze of one of the crime scene investigators.

"That's not what you might think it is, Detective," the investigator said, annoyed to see Naughware touching the evidence. "Though what it is precisely has yet to be determined."

Naughware ignored him and stood surveying the area for quite some time, carefully taking time to reexamine each body in the warehouse as he listened to the song.

As to its lyrics, a woman was a key figure in the tune, and yet, Naughware didn't see any female victims at the scene.

Perhaps it was just an element to ignore, or … something more.

It was too early to tell, but the digital player rarely led him astray. He merely had to determine which pieces of the song to keep and which to discard.

Eventually, he wandered over to where Detective Keane was talking to one of the CSIs.

"Any survivors at the scene?" Naughware asked.

"No," replied one CSI, a woman he thought he recognized.

"McCool, isn't it?" he asked.

She smiled and nodded. "That's right."

"Any witnesses? And was anything moved before I arrived?" Naughware asked.

"No to both, Detective," replied McCool. "Everything's just as the responding officers found it."

"Thank you," he said, turning to Keane. "Any thoughts?"

"You mean, other than a perfectly nice floristry warehouse was turned into a war zone?"

"War zone?" he asked. "Nah, I've seen those. This is more like an abattoir."

Keane and McCool appeared perplexed by his choice of words. He pointed over to his right.

"That guy over there had his arm severed with a machete that's lying over there," he said, pointing in the opposite direction.

Then Naughware vaguely gestured to somewhere across the warehouse. "And the fellow over there nearly had his head cleaved from his body with what I surmise was the same blade."

The two women stared at him blankly.

"Your point?" Keane asked.

The edges of his mouth upturned. "Who brings a machete to a gun fight?"

Keane and McCool gave him an odd look.

"More to the point," he said. "What sort of person bothers *using* one in the midst of a shootout?"

CHAPTER 2

Detective Sergeants Hal Vigoda and Ron Levitt arrived on scene a little over an hour after Naughware and Keane. They quickly assessed the scene and did a cursory review of each of the bodies, as the medical examiner's staff was eager to remove them from the scene. Then they met with the two junior detectives to go over the evidence being processed.

Relegated to lesser duties, Naughware and Keane spent a couple of hours questioning onlookers and nearby businesses, turning up neither witnesses nor credible leads. Before leaving the scene, one of the Assistant Medical Examiners estimated the time of deaths around two o'clock in the morning.

Detective Vigoda took Keane and Naughware aside.

"Any thoughts," Vigoda asked.

"Drug deal gone bad?" Keane asked.

"We'll have to ask the survivors," Naughware said. "That is, once we find them."

Vigoda nodded. "I think I only recognize a couple of the perps' faces in there," he said. "I'm willing to bet a number of them aren't locals."

"It'll be helpful if we can get IDs on them," Naughware said. "Keane and I can check with some local informants. Something this scale should generate a conversation on the streets by now,"

Vigoda nodded. "Good idea. You two can handle that."

"Though I'm equally curious as to what sort of drug that is over there," Naughware said, pointing over to the packages of white substance.

Vigoda looked back across the warehouse in the direction he pointed. "What? That's not cocaine?"

"Nope," Naughware said. "Though the techs aren't sure what it is, only what it isn't."

Vigoda frowned. "Something new on the streets?"

Naughware shrugged. "That happens over time, doesn't it?"

Vigoda merely grunted in agreement.

"What's next, Sergeant?" Keane asked him.

"Levitt and I will look around a bit more," Vigoda said. "You two can return to the precinct to start working on the mountain of documentation and reports associated with the case."

"Yeah, thanks. You're all heart, Vigoda," Naughware said.

Vigoda gave him a self-satisfied look. "First-responding detectives get first crack at the bureaucracy."

As Naughware drove the department-issued sedan, he mulled the facts around in his head, even while recalling the lyrics to The Hollies tune.

Then he recollected the new song that was added to his digital player.

Gotta remember to check that out, he thought.

"So, what's the deal with the tunes, Naughware?" Keane asked.

Naughware's train of thought immediately derailed.

"What?" he asked.

"The tunes," she said. "Are you listening to meditation tracks? You know, one of my instructors at the police academy used to teach meditation techniques. He swore that it helped officers center themselves during stressful conditions."

"It's not like that," Naughware said. "Why? Are you into meditation?"

"Nope," she replied. "That stuff never worked for me like it does others. Turns out, I'm more of a power-through-the-stress sort of woman. And you're avoiding answering my original question."

"Yes," he said. "Yes, I am."

She looked sidelong and gave him a hard look. "You know, if we're going to work together with any hope of success, it might behoove both of us to try to get along. Are you feeling me here?"

"Seems like a reasonable request," Naughware said dryly. Though, rather than get along, he preferred to find her another partner altogether.

"Good," she said. "So, what's the story with you and the lieutenant, if you don't mind me asking?"

He glanced over at her.

"No mystery, just oil and water," he said. "For the record, my former partner didn't get along with him, either. After seeing the way the lieutenant treated him, it soured me on Dawkins pretty quickly, too."

Keane nodded. "What happened to your previous partner? Finally lost their mind after working with you? Maybe jumped from the top of a tall building? I'm seeing either heavy medication or a mortuary there."

He couldn't help but crack a smile.

"See? I knew there was a smile just waiting to get out," she said.

He had to credit her for trying to get along.

"To answer your question, my partner retired less than a year ago," he said. "And he's still very much alive."

"Was he a good detective or one of those jaded old guys counting down the days?" she asked.

"Jaded? Nah, Sarge is the best," he said. "He taught me everything he knew about being a detective."

"Sarge?" she asked.

"Yeah, as the story goes he reached Detective Sergeant

earlier in his career than most," he said. "Besides, he's a former Marine sergeant, which may have more to do with it, now that I think about it."

Keane deliberately looked out the passenger window. "Sounds like you really respect him."

"Yeah," he said. "We were well-matched. We understood each other."

The two fell silent, and Keane decided to take her small victory and not press further.

"So, partner," she said. "You want to clue me in on where we're going?"

"Unless you've got some other ideas to run down, back to the precinct," he said. "Tell me, what did you take away from the crime scene this morning?"

She considered his question, silently recounting the details that stood out in her mind.

"A whole lotta ammunition was expended," she said. "A shootout on an epic scale. I'm thinking a drug deal went sideways. Though it was strange that whoever walked away from the scene didn't want either the drugs or the tote bag full of cash. Who the hell doesn't at least take the cash?"

"Yeah, that struck me as odd, too," he said.

"Unless they were wounded and just desperate to get away," she said. "We should double-check area hospitals and clinics."

"Good idea, though I didn't see a blood trail either leading to any exits or outside anywhere."

"Who knows? Maybe they had a getaway car waiting outside," she said.

"Possibly," he said.

Once they arrived at the investigative offices of the South Precinct, a passing officer caught Naughware's attention.

"Captain's looking for you," he said.

Naughware nodded. "Thanks."

He turned to Keane. "I'll meet you back at the desk."

"Sure thing."

Naughware bypassed what he considered the world's slowest elevator and headed toward the nearby stairwell door.

As Keane entered the detectives' office area, she saw an older-looking clergyman standing beside Naughware's desk talking to Detective Garcia, whom she had met earlier that morning.

She liked Garcia. He had politely introduced her around the precinct before the lieutenant took her out to the crime scene.

She quietly walked to her newly assigned desk, which was opposite Naughware's, and spotted a tall insulated mug with a decorative white bow taped atop it.

She picked up the mug and noticed a Post-it Note stuck to it.

Welcome to South Side, Detective Keane.

The department seal was emblazoned on the mug's facing.

"… would let Peter know that I stopped by," the clergyman said.

"Will do, Father Ash," Garcia said. "Hey, this is his new partner, in fact."

"Father Thomas Ash is the Head Pastor of the Ascension Episcopal Church," the detective said. He turned toward Ash. "Father, this is our newest detective, Alicia Keane. She just transferred in from—"

"Peoria, Illinois," Keane said. She reached out to exchange a firm handshake with the clergyman. "Pleased to meet you, Father Ash."

"Welcome to Abaddon, Detective Keane," Ash said. "Peoria, eh? Your home town?"

"No, born and raised in Ames, Iowa," Keane said. "I started my police career in Peoria."

"Ah, so working your way back closer to home, then," Ash said with a warm smile.

"Yes. Something like that," she said. "Closer, anyway."

"Well, I was just telling Detective Garcia about Peter's birthday dinner tonight," he said. "And, as you're his new partner, I insist that you come, too."

"Birthday, eh?" she said, looking around. "You'd never know it was someone's birthday around here."

"I'm fairly certain nobody around here even realized his birthday was today," Garcia said.

"Ah, well, Peter's not overly observant of them," Ash said.

Keane noticed a twitch to the man's brows when he said that.

"At any rate, dinner is at Stringfellow's at seven o'clock tonight," he said. "I certainly hope you can make it."

"I'll try," she said.

"Good day to you both," he said with a nod.

After the clergyman exited the office, Keane turned to Garcia.

"There goes a priest that really looks after his flock," she said.

"Well, Father Ash is a good pastor, but also Naughware's father, so—"

"Oh," Keane said. "Father and *father*."

For reasons she couldn't explain, that revelation surprised her.

"Ha, I love the look on your face," Garcia said. "I think I probably had that same expression back when I found out."

"So, his dad's a priest," she said, lightly tapping one of her fingers atop her desk.

"Actually, Father Ash is his adoptive father," he said.

"Oh?"

Garcia looked around and lowered his voice. "Rumors say that he was unceremoniously dropped off on the church's front doorstep when he was only a newborn."

Keane appeared shocked. "Abandoned? That's terrible."

"Yeah, a pretty shitty start in this world, if you ask me."

Keane frowned. "Hold it. So then, why isn't his last name Ash?"

Garcia smiled. "Ah, you picked up on that pretty fast, too."

"Wait," she said. "You used the word *rumors* a moment ago."

"Well, Naughware doesn't talk about any of it, and his adoption records are sealed, but word gets around from here and there," Garcia said. "So, basically, he was a no-name as a newborn, but somehow ended up with the surname Naughware. Someday, I'm going to start a lottery around here on the theories to that."

Keane chuckled. "I'm surprised somebody hasn't already."

Garcia adopted a sober expression. "Nobody would dare. Not openly, anyway."

* * *

As Naughware ascended the stairs toward the third floor, something stirred in the back of his mind.

He paused to withdraw his digital player from his pocket, inserted his earbuds, and navigated to the root directory.

He scrolled down to the newly added tune, "The Gospel of John Hurt" by alt-J.

Happy birthday to me, he thought. *The question is, where did this new song come from?*

New songs randomly played on his device as a matter of routine. But this was the first song to be added to the root directory of the original eleven tracks since he received it on his twenty-second birthday. He had never seen a new tune appear on its own before.

He pressed play and slowly resumed his stair climb.

The song was completely foreign to him, and he had never even heard of the group alt-J before.

The lyrics sounded ominous and weird.

Of course, weird was something he had become acutely accustomed to during his lifetime.

The five-plus-minute song was scarcely halfway finished by the time he exited onto the third floor. He walked over to a nearby waiting area that was thankfully devoid of visitors and stared out the window.

Many elements of the song's lyrics confused him.

What did John Hurt have to do with anything? And what, precisely, did exiting a forest signify?

The song caused an eerie sensation to wash through him.

The whole day rang peculiar to him from the very start. It began when he woke that morning feeling … strangely different. Although he couldn't articulate fully quite why, or to what degree, to anyone, if he had been pressed to. All he knew was that his internal compass was spinning off its normal heading.

However, his body felt both refreshed and energized, which in and of itself was strange because he was never much of a morning person. He believed there was a sense of newness to him.

In addition, he sensed something new simmering just below the surface inside him, though he couldn't put his finger on what, exactly.

It was an odd, rather unnerving perception for him.

His bizarre day continued with the new song appearing on his root listing.

Add to that, he had a new partner he really didn't want, or entirely like, for that matter.

And it all had to happen on his birthday, already not his favorite day of the year.

He took a deep breath and let it out slowly as he stared out a large window looking out onto the city.

"Peter?"

He turned to see Betty Penney, the captain's administrative assistant, staring back at him.

"I thought it was you who I glimpsed exiting the stairwell," she said. "Are you all right?"

He nodded and removed his earbuds. "Sure, Betty. Right as rain."

She arched her brow at him. "Well, as someone who's known you all your life, I'll believe that when I see it. But I suppose wonders never cease, do they?"

He gave her a sour look.

"Best you hurry on, then," she said. "Captain Gunderson's waiting to see you."

"Any idea why?" he asked.

"As if I knew," she said.

"Betty, you know damn-near everything around here," he said, walking past her.

"Be nice, young man, or I'll tell on you to Father Ash," she said, following after him. "And happy birthday, Peter."

He tried not to wince at that.

"I hear Father Ash has a nice dinner planned for you at Stringfellow's tonight," she said, walking briskly beside him to keep up.

"Yep, he even called me last night to remind me," he said. "I'm surprised he hasn't shown up in person this morning, too."

"Well, it all sounds lovely, if you ask me," she said. "I'm looking forward to being there."

Naughware stopped and turned to her. "Wait, this isn't a party, is it?"

"Oh, Peter," she admonished, slid past him to sit behind her desk. "It's probably just a dinner gathering. You should be both glad and thankful for it. As Father Ash always said, 'Let us rejoice in today's blessings.'"

Yep, he had heard it said a million times since he was a boy. He continued toward the captain's office and managed not to roll his eyes.

He knocked once on the closed door but didn't wait for a response before opening it.

Captain Freida Gunderson looked up at him from her desk. "Ah, Naughware. I wondered when you'd finally drop by. Sit down."

"Captain, I didn't even know you wanted to see me until I returned to the precinct just now," he said, taking one of the chairs placed before her desk.

"Well, I did email you this morning," she said.

"After receiving the call from dispatch, I went directly

from home to the crime scene," he said. "Besides, I don't usually read email until later in the day."

"If ever, so I'm told," she said.

"Dawkins is exaggerating … yet again," he said, shaking his head.

"What makes you think it was Dawkins?"

He remained silent for the sake of valor. She knew that he and the lieutenant didn't get along well.

"Grisly business down in the warehouse district this morning," she said. "I don't like wanton shootouts taking place in our city, much less in my very own district."

She stopped and studied him for a moment. "Dawkins sent me a message about your taking umbrage with Vigoda and Levitt running lead on the case."

"It's fine," he said. "I understand that you'd probably want sergeants leading this one."

"True, as a matter of procedure on a case this size," she said. "But I also wanted to make sure that one of my most talented detectives was part of the mix."

Naughware nodded. "Thank you. I appreciate that, ma'am."

She frowned. "Something else on your mind today, Naughware?"

"Just the case, Captain," he replied. "Why do you ask?"

"I don't know," she said. "Just something I thought I picked up on when you entered. Maybe you seem distracted. At any rate, you'll need to put aside any other open cases you have."

"But Dawkins—"

"I'll make sure the lieutenant reassigns them to other detectives," she said. "This is a public relations nightmare for us. This precinct has dedicated more than three years of effort in both funds and manpower to eliminate the drug runners and gang activity in the warehouse district, and I'm not going to see it all go up in smoke over this."

"Understood. Don't worry," he said. "I'm focused on this, Captain."

She nodded. "Very good. See that you stay that way until it's solved."

Naughware lightly tapped his fingers against the chair arms while the captain observed him.

"Peter, you may be young compared to most of your peers, but you're already an exemplary detective in your own right, and frankly, you've got a keen sense for leads on investigations," she said. "I'm counting on you. Don't screw this one up. And, for God's sake, if you feel you're getting in over your head, let me know immediately. I can't let this turn into a fiasco over one man's false sense of pride."

"Yes, ma'am," he said. "And thank you for your confidence in me."

The corners of her mouth upturned slightly.

He knew the captain wasn't a person prone to smiling, so he viewed it as a positive response.

He started to stand. "If that's all, Captain?"

"Actually, there's one more thing I want to talk to you about," she said.

He sat back down and waited.

"Detective Keane comes highly recommended from Peoria's department. She was a detective for only a year before earning a commendation for breaking up a major drug ring," Gunderson said. "I hope you're committed to working as a team with her on this case. Based on what little I've already heard about the crime scene, Keane should have insights and experience that are bound to prove useful."

"Yes, ma'am," he said, albeit ruefully.

"Naughware, I know that you and Detective Sergeant Taylor were close," she said. "After all, he was your mentor when you first became a detective."

"And my only partner from that point on," he said.

"True enough," she said. "However, Taylor's been retired now for nearly a year, and it's time for you to move on. And that means taking on a new partner."

"It was bound to happen," he said. "However, and as I recently told Lieutenant Dawkins, I've worked well on my own since Taylor retired. Surely, my performance assessments—"

"Your performance ratings are not in question here," she said.

He quietly waited as she stared back at him.

"Dawkins wanted to assign you to either Sergeant Vigoda or Levitt," she said.

"Neither of whom likes me," he said. "Besides, I'd hate to break up such a cute couple."

She arched one brow at him. "Now you're sounding like someone who doesn't like to play nicely with others."

He gave her an innocent look. "I play nicely with others," he said. "And hey, a good portion of the precinct doesn't dislike me."

She gave him a flat look. "Or so you believe," she said, arching one brow as the edges of her mouth turned upward. "Naughware, do you know why we pair detectives together in this department?"

"So that if something happens to one investigator, the other can immediately take over the case," he said.

"Yes, but also so there's backup, if needed," she said. "You know better than most the South Precinct isn't the tamest part of the city."

"Yes, ma'am," he said. "You may recall that I grew up on the south side."

"Oh, I remember that well," she said. "However, just because it's your backyard doesn't mean you're invincible in it."

He nodded. "I'll try to remember that."

"And give Keane a chance," Gunderson said. "I think you'll find she's a competent detective. And you might actually end up appreciating a partner again."

"Maybe so," he said, though he seriously doubted it.

"Now, I'm tired of looking at you," she said. "Get back to the case … and your new partner."

He stood. "Yes, Captain."

CHAPTER 3

Naughware spent the remainder of the day working alongside Keane on reports and going over evidence. They worked together amicably enough, though he couldn't help getting the feeling that she was scrutinizing him.

In truth, she was.

"Naughware," she said.

He looked up from a preliminary ballistics report to see her glance over at him with an arched brow. She appeared to be studying him.

"Something on your mind?" he asked.

"Just that I don't see too many people still carrying a wheel gun these days," she said. "What is it?"

"Ruger Super Redhawk," he said, patting the holster with his hand. "Forty-four caliber."

"Are you Old School for a reason?"

"You mean, besides that it never jams?" he asked as the corners of his mouth upturned.

"Smart alec," she said, crinkling her nose. "I just figured it had sentimental value or something."

He nodded and patted the leather holster under his arm. "This is one of a matching pair that's seen me through battle when I was in the Army," he said. "And a forty-four will do wonders compared to those nine millimeters the department issues."

"Yeah, maybe if you're trying to shoot through people instead of at them," she said, frowning. "But then, I guess that must've been the idea in the Army."

"Something like that," he said with a faraway expression. He momentarily seemed lost in thought before abruptly returning to the present. "You know, you're always welcome to go out to the range sometime and try it out."

"Nah, thanks just the same," she said with a shake of her head. "My Glock gets the job done just fine, and besides, it's just reassuring to carry something that I can share rounds with the rest of the team on."

Her eyes narrowed a bit, as if reassessing him.

"You know, my former partner, Evan Taylor, carried a forty-four caliber, too," he said. "It worked out nicely for us because we could share ammo."

She gave him a sober look and shook her head. "Still, boys and their toys, I suppose," she said fleetingly. "I'll stick with my nine, and you can just get used to carrying around extra ammo. How's that sound?"

He shrugged. "Suit yourself. No harm either way," he said, deferentially inclining his head toward her.

Toward the end of the workday, Detectives Vigoda and Levitt met with them to share information and discuss how to proceed with the investigation.

"The best lead we've managed is gaining IDs on the eleven bodies at the scene," Vigoda said, handing out typed lists to each detective. "Two of them are locals, Travis Carr and Elijah Hansen. Both have long rap sheets, and have histories as thugs for hire."

"However, we've also got Liam Bailey," Vigoda said. "He's the middle brother of the Boston Bailey Irish Mob trio that runs their family business."

"What's the biggest Irish Mob on the east coast doing way out here in Abaddon, Iowa?" Keane asked.

"Good question," Naughware said. "Let's not forget that Sal Bianchi and two of his thugs out of Chicago are on the list."

Keane shook her head. "Haven't heard of Bianchi."

"No reason you should. Small time, for the most part," Levitt said. "But for even more local flair, three of these victims were known associates of Decebal Lungu."

"Also, new to me," Keane said.

"Decebal Lungu. They call him 'The Lion' in Abaddon," Naughware said. "He's a Romanian mobster, who supposedly still maintains ties with the Volkov Domen out of Eastern Europe."

Keane's eyebrows arched. "Now *them* I've heard of."

Vigoda nodded. "Well, fortunately, they've stayed far away from Abaddon."

"Any word on the white substance on the table?" Keane asked.

"Not yet," Levitt replied. "Their preliminary readings weren't conclusive. The lab said that all their test results won't be completed for at least a few days."

"Any word back from area hospitals or clinics on walk-in gunshot victims?" Vigoda asked.

"Nope," Naughware said. "Keane and I already contacted every one within a sixty-mile radius of here. Even checked with veterinarians."

"All right, then," Vigoda said. "Let's knock off until the morning. There's bound to be enough late nights in the near future for us as it is."

Keane stacked two piles of files in an orderly fashion on her desk while Naughware watched Vigoda and Levitt return to their side of the forty by thirty foot office.

"It's been quite a first day," she said.

"Yep, and congratulations on that," he said. "So, are you ready to request a reassignment for another partner yet?"

She thoughtfully rubbed her chin with her fingertips. "Hm. Not yet, but I filled out the transfer form just in case."

He smiled before wondering if she was joking or not.

Suffice to say, Naughware was happy that their shift officially ended on time. However, the very nature of their case suggested that Vigoda was probably correct that both overtime and late nights were forthcoming.

Never mind that the case was already a high-visibility and potentially politically charged affair.

He detested all things political. Office politics were partly behind the rift formed between him and Vigoda and Levitt. Naughware's former partner urged him to let his reputation as a detective be formed by solving cases instead of office politicking to curry favor with the brass; essentially, to spend more time showing than telling. He long since learned that Levitt and Vigoda weren't above brown-nosing, or playing other detectives off each other, to get their way.

As he and Keane walked down the hallway together, he ruefully remembered his evening event.

"Listen, Keane, I know this is only our first day working together," he said. "But there's, uh, a special dinner tonight for me, so—"

"Oh, I'll be there, partner," she said.

"You will?"

"Sure," she said. "Your father and I met while you were meeting with the captain, and he invited me. In fact, he seemed pretty insistent about it."

"My father," he said. "You mean, Father Thomas."

She gave him an odd look. "Yeah, Thomas Ash. Who else?"

He appeared reflective, but nodded. "Good, then," he said. "I'll see you there."

She watched him walk away, and muttered, "You're an odd one, Naughware."

***

There were more than two hours before the dinner started, but instead of going home—and after the day he'd had—Naughware needed some liquid courage.

He stopped by one of his favorite dives.

Beers to You was the bar owned by his best friend, Glenn Bacardi.

Naughware's mood improved as soon as he entered the establishment. The bar had a comfortable, inviting feeling to it. It reminded him of some he had seen in old movies. The generous use of polished wood accented with tarnished brass and a large mirror on the wall behind the bar was a throwback to simpler times; traditional without feeling either antiquated or pretentious.

He walked to the bar and sat on an available stool. There were only a handful of patrons around; most of them Naughware recognized as regulars.

Glenn was manning the opposite end of the counter and immediately walked over to him.

"Hey, bestie," he said. "Happy birthday!"

Naughware gave him a wan look. "Thanks."

"The usual?" Glenn asked.

"Sure," Naughware said. Then he held up his hand. "No, wait. Give me something different."

"Really?" Glenn asked with a surprised expression. "You're serious?"

"Surprise me," Naughware said. "It's been that sort of day."

Glenn looked down into the cooler beneath the bar.

"Your birthdays are always that way, as I recall," Glenn said. "And I've known you since I was four."

"Yeah, but this one's different," Naughware said. "I've had a *really* strange day."

"Then I want to hear all about it."

Glenn pulled out a bottle of beer, uncapped it, and presented it to his friend.

Naughware glanced at the label and gave him a curious look. "Midnight's Call?"

"No questions, just drink."

Naughware picked up the bottle, took a moment to sniff the bouquet, and took a big swig. The cold liquid felt wonderful going down, and the aftertaste was smooth.

"Oh, I like," he said.

Glenn winked. "New brew."

Naughware frowned. "Good blend, weird name."

"Weird day, right?" Glenn asked.

"True."

"Tell me all about it," Glenn said, leaning against his side of the bar. "We've got some time before the rush hour starts."

Naughware took another swig of beer and gathered his thoughts.

"I felt good, but odd, from the moment I woke this morning," Naughware began. "Energized, yet ominous. Does that even make sense?"

"You rarely do when you talk about your feelings," Glenn said. "Continue."

"I get assigned a God-awful crime scene first thing this morning," Naughware said. "Bullet-ridden bodies sprawled around a warehouse over on South Clark Street called, get this, the Bouquet Corral."

"Sounds grisly enough," Glenn said. "Wait, I think I've driven past that place."

"Yeah, looked like a drug buy gone bad, but something still feels wrong about it."

"Hey, you can call it 'The Shootout at the Bouquet Corral'," Glenn said, fanning his hands wide before him. "That sounds totally kick-ass."

"No, it really doesn't. And nobody in their right mind's going to call it that," Naughware said. "This is a real political volcano waiting to erupt. The captain already gave me personal marching orders this morning."

"I thought Lieutenant Dawkins was your supervisor—"

"This case went up the ladder fast," Naughware said.

Glenn nodded. "Good times, huh?"

"But there's more," Naughware said. "I get on scene and I'm handed a new partner."

"Oh, joy," Glenn said.

Naughware nodded and took another swig of beer. "You know, this brew's really good. I think it's my new favorite."

"Great, but forget the beer," Glenn said. "I want to hear

more about the new partner. I thought you'd finally convinced Dawkins you didn't need one."

"Yeah, well, Captain gave me this whole speech about needing backup," Naughware said. "But anyway, her name's Alicia Keane and she's out of the Peoria department."

"She? As in, female?" Glenn asked. "Wow, is she cute?"

Naughware gave him a disgusted look. "*She* usually means female, doesn't it? And as for cute? Crap, I don't know. I mean, what the hell do I care? I don't want a partner. Period."

"This all goes back to your bad dating streak," Glenn said.

"Shut up. This has absolutely *nothing* to do with dating," Naughware said. "You don't date fellow officers. Or anybody you work with, for that matter. Big no-no. There's this whole thing called policy and procedures."

"I try not to let things like that stand in the way of a good match," Glenn said, absently wiping the top of the bar with a towel.

"Yeah, well, you're only one borderline lawsuit away from sexual harassment about every six months," Naughware said with a grin.

Glenn stopped wiping and looked up at him with a mock-insulted expression. "Hey, strong words, friend. Too strong, in fact," he said. "But what can I say? If a match feels good, there's nothing wrong with shopping close to home."

Naughware shook his head. "Are we talking about your day or mine now?"

"Sorry," Glenn said. "There's more?"

Naughware paused to drink. "Oh, this shit-fest just keeps getting better."

Glenn frowned. "Okay, what else?"

"So, I pull out my digital player this morning and there's a new track," Naughware said.

Glenn stared at him. "So? You've said it plays new songs all the time."

"Yep, but those just pop up … this one's appearing in the *root* directory," Naughware said.

"Uh-huh."

Naughware leaned forward. "Not *uh-huh*. That's something special. You can't even delete what's in that directory, much less add songs to it. Those other eleven are the originals, remember?"

Glenn's eyes narrowed. "Okay, yeah. I remember you saying that. So, a new song in the root … that's never happened before, right?"

"Not since I first got it," Naughware said.

"Hm. What tune?" Glenn asked, leaning across the counter toward him.

Naughware withdrew the player from his left pocket and navigated to the root folder.

"'The Gospel of John Hurt' by alt-J," he said.

"Who's alt-J?" Glenn asked.

"I certainly had never heard of them," Naughware said. "Although I did some searching after lunch, and it's a legitimate rock group. Had a number of hits over in Britain and then here in the US, apparently. But not this particular tune."

"Can I listen to it?" Glenn asked.

Naughware handed the player to him.

Glenn was the only person with whom Naughware had ever shared information about his digital player. In fact, he confided in Glenn more than anyone, including Father Thomas.

Although, while he trusted Glenn with his life, there were still things that Naughware wouldn't even tell him; subjects that were forbidden with anyone.

At any rate, Naughware considered the mystery of his little player as far too weird for most people to grasp, much less accept on face value.

He continued drinking his beer while Glenn listened to the song. After a few minutes, he removed the earbuds and handed the player back to Naughware.

"Never heard that one," he said. "Sort of ominous sounding. Interesting lyrics, too."

"Yeah, I haven't had much time to mull those over fully yet," Naughware said. "Especially about John Hurt."

"Oh, the actor from *Alien*," Glenn said.

"Which one?"

"The first one, way back in the 1970s," Glenn said.

Naughware frowned. "How did you know that?"

"Whadda you mean?" Glenn asked. "You know I'm a huge sci-fi nut, and Hurt showed up in a lot of sci-fi movies over the years. He once played an incarnation of Doctor Who, in fact."

"So, John Hurt was in, *Alien*, was he?" Naughware asked, deep in thought.

"Yeah, one of the alien creatures burst out of his chest," Glenn said. "Man, that was harsh. Blood sprayed all over everybody on set. It really set the trend for all of the sequels after that, too. I watched those over and over again as a kid."

Naughware gave him a hard look. "Wait, it burst out of his chest?"

"Yep. Great shock value," Glenn said. "Loved that."

Naughware visibly blanched. "Loved it? Buddy, that's only because you haven't suffered through gory crime scenes day in and day out."

"Yeah, probably so. But why do you think that particular new song showed up today?" Glenn asked. "I mean, it's pretty much out of the blue, right?"

Naughware shrugged. "Well, it is my birthday."

"Yeah, but today's only number thirty-three for you," Glenn said. "It's not one you'd typically consider a milestone or anything."

Naughware considered that for a moment. "Not so much to me, anyway."

"Man, you've been mulling over those—what was it, eleven?—songs for years," Glenn said.

"Twelve songs now," Naughware said. "And it was eleven years ago today that I got it."

Glenn frowned. "Eleven songs for eleven years," he said. "Okay, so twelve songs now. But hey, it's just tunes. Why get worked up over it. It's a music player … it plays music, right?"

"A music player that picks tunes out of the air at random?" Naughware asked. "I never even loaded most of the crap that comes out of it. Hell, I've never even heard most of the songs before, either."

"Yeah, but they're real songs," Glenn said. "It's not like somebody's making them up. It's pushing out music randomly, that's all."

"From where? Wireless pushing to devices didn't start until years after I got it," Naughware said. "And why do the tunes that I listen to on crime scenes end up being meaningful?"

Those questions had burned in him ever since he had joined the police force.

Glenn's eyebrows arched. "Coincidence? What did it play at the Bouquet Corral?"

"Stop saying Bouquet Corral," Naughware said. "It sounds corny. Even the press are starting to wear the name thin."

"Nope," Glenn said. "I'm rockin' this for all it's worth."

"You would," Naughware said. "So, today it played 'Long Cool Woman' by The Hollies."

Glenn adopted a far off expression. "That's an oldie; one that I've probably only heard a couple of times. You get anything from it yet?"

"Yeah, an oldie, for sure," Naughware said. "I've got some ideas, but I'll have to listen to it a few more times before I'm ready to venture anything useful. Hell, like you said, it may just be a coincidence."

"Never has before," Glenn said. "Just like out of a sci-fi movie."

"Look, maybe it's like those Nostradamus predictions," Naughware said. "People look to divine meaning from them. They find creative ways to make reality fit the portents. In fact, it's just like the Bible, right?"

"Oh, this again," Glenn said. "You're like the city's chief agnostic. And you were adopted by a priest, for God's sake."

"I don't fault Father Thomas, but religions come, and religions go," Naughware said. "Human history is replete with them. Look at the Egyptians, the Greeks, and the Romans. Nobody on the planet today still thinks their gods were real. Give it another thousand years and they'll say the same about who and what everyone's worshiping today."

"Hm, maybe," Glenn said. "But I'd like to think there's more to it than that. It's like we keep trying to find the answer, but maybe we're just misinterpreting the formula."

"You're a philosopher now? However, I do like that," Naughware said. Then he held up his digital player. "But let's be real. This is very likely just my imagination feeding me wild-ass ideas."

"Peter, since we were kids, you and I have talked about a lot of bizarre shit," Glenn said. "So, maybe this particular shit's for real."

Naughware drank his beer, nearly draining it. "Yeah," he said. "Only, maybe that's what I'm afraid of."

He wondered what Glenn would think if he was completely honest with him about everything he had experienced since childhood. But there were secrets that even his most-trusted friend could never know.

That realization tortured him time and again, and he frequently felt a sense of guilt over it. Yet, silence felt to be the better part of valor to him. If he told Glenn … of so many strange things he had experienced … would his childhood friend not think him insane?

Worse yet, if not insane, the onus would be upon him to prove what he claimed. And he wasn't prepared to do that yet.

Yet? If ever.

A young woman wearing an apron with the bar's name blazoned across the front of it walked by.

"I'm on-shift, Glenn," she said.

Glenn glanced over at the clock on the far wall. "Good timing, Trudy," he said. "Peter and I have a dinner to go to."

Naughware gave him a long look. "You heard about that?"

Glenn smiled. "Buddy, I'm not only your best friend, I'm also a bartender. I hear most everything."

"You mean Thomas called you," Naughware said.

"Hey, I hear things over phones, too," Glenn said. "Oh, wait, before we leave I want you to hear one of the songs I'm trying out in the bar. It's part of my big new push to stimulate more drinking."

"Oh, no," Naughware said. "Friend, when are you going to realize that it's booze and atmosphere that brings in the crowds? Not music."

"Well, *friend*, I'm the one with the marketing degree," Glenn said. "And I happen to know that music can be a bait for attracting new customers."

He reached beneath the bar and "Bikini Girls with Machine Guns" by The Cramps started up, and he bobbed his head to the tempo.

Naughware adopted a sour expression. "Seriously, no."

"Should really draw in the college crowd," he said.

Trudy rushed over to the bar. "Glenn, that crap's lame!"

A series of groans and curses rose up from most of the patrons. Glenn finally reached down to turn off the music.

"Okay, so I'll keep looking," he said.

A tall man wearing a bar apron exited the back room to stand beside Glenn.

"Yo, what was that shit about?" he asked.

Glenn slowly turned to look up at him. "Thanks for the support, Mackie."

Naughware smiled before turning up his bottle to finish the last two swallows of beer.

Glenn reached down below the bar and crisply placed a small, wrapped gift before his friend.

Naughware looked down at it and then back at Glenn. "What's this?"

"Oh, well, that's what in Western civilization we call a 'gift.' It's generally bestowed among friends and loved ones at least once a year," Glenn said.

"Smartass."

"Better that than a dumb ass," he countered.

Naughware removed the heavily taped blue wrapping paper to reveal a set of high-quality earbuds.

"Thanks, Glenn," he said.

"You're welcome," Glen said. "It seems rather prophetic, doesn't it? I mean, you get a new song with new earbuds for fresh new tunes."

Naughware couldn't help feeling he might be right about that.

CHAPTER 4

Naughware dreaded the impending dinner during his entire drive to Stringfellow's.

It wasn't that he didn't like the idea of celebrating birthdays. And it wasn't that he didn't have friends and loved ones to celebrate with him. That much he was grateful about.

Rather, it was that, as an adopted child, each birthday left him wondering who his real parents were. More importantly, he wondered what sort of parents would drop their newborn baby off on the doorstep of a church and just leave him there.

As they pulled into the parking lot, Glenn looked at him.

"You all right?" he asked.

Naughware nodded. "Let's get this over with."

Inside, they were directed to the banquet room in the back of the restaurant, where nearly two dozen people mingled and chatted.

Naughware put on a civil face and spied Keane off to the side of the room by herself with a half-filled glass of wine in hand. He motioned to Glenn and walked over to where she stood.

"Hey, Keane," he said. "Nice of you to come."

She smiled and lifted her glass. "There's worse ways to get to know people, I suppose."

"Glenn, this is my new partner, Alicia Keane," Naughware

said. "Keane, Glenn's been my best friend since we were kids."

Glenn eagerly reached out to shake her hand. "Glenn Bacardi. Happy to meet you."

Keane's eyebrows rose. "*Bacardi?* Are you related to—"

"Nah, I wish," Glenn said. "My clan hails from the poorer side of the Bacardi family tree."

"Oh," Keane said.

"Glenn's just being modest," Naughware said. "He owns a well-known bar here in Abaddon."

"Beers to You," Glenn said. "That is, it's my bar. Beers to You."

Keane chuckled. "Catchy name."

"Nice place," Glenn said. "You should drop in sometime. All the booze that's fit to choose, I say."

"You never say that," Naughware said. "And don't start now."

"Hater," Glenn said.

Keane grinned.

"Peter, you made it," Father Thomas Ash said, approaching the group. "Detective Keane. Glenn. So happy both of you could join us."

"Father Thomas," Glenn said, shaking the elder priest's hand.

"Glenn," Thomas said, before turning to Keane. "When Glenn was a boy, he spent nearly every weekend and most of the summers at his aunt's house just down the street from us. He and Peter were nearly inseparable."

"Speaking of which, Glenn, I haven't seen you in church recently," Thomas added.

"Well, living across town now, and what not," Glenn said, shifting nervously. "Of course, I don't make it over to my aunt's as often as I used to. The days just roll by, you know."

"Of course," Thomas said. "Though perhaps you should stop in to see your old aunt now and again. She speaks often of you and your mother."

"Er, thanks for putting this whole dinner thing together,

Thomas," Naughware said, changing the subject.

The elder clergyman turned and embraced him in a warm hug.

"Happy birthday, son," he said. "I stopped by the precinct this morning, but you were away. I understand it was quite a grim case you were handed today."

They parted from each other, though Thomas grasped the top of Naughware's shoulder with one hand as they stood there.

"Thank you," Naughware said. "Yep, this case is ugly. But with a high body count, drugs, and money abound, who could ask for more?"

Thomas looked at him with a hint of disapproval and released his grip on the younger man. "Honestly, Peter, your sense of humor sometimes …"

"I know," Naughware said. "But it gets me through the day."

The elder man gave Naughware a supportive look before turning to address the small banquet room filled with people.

"All right, everyone," Thomas said. "The man of the hour has arrived, so let's move to the chairs around the table. But don't sit yet … I want to say a prayer before we start. Peter, you're at the head."

Naughware curtailed a sigh as he moved to stand behind the chair at one end of the series of tables all lined up end-to-end in a single row.

Father Thomas stood immediately to his right, and Glenn to his left.

"Let's bow our heads," Thomas said. "Dear Lord, we come here today to honor my son, Peter, and partake in a bounty of food and fellowship. But we also ask your blessing on all those brave first responders who stand to protect and serve Abaddon …"

Naughware's mind wandered as he stood with his head bowed. He wasn't one for prayer, despite being raised by Father Thomas and the parishioners of the Ascension Episcopal Church.

Honestly, he wasn't entirely confident that there was anyone—or anything—aloft to hear those prayers.

It wasn't as if he didn't believe in spiritual things. He'd had his own brushes with the bizarre. He merely doubted that the human race understood what little mysticism it was exposed to; not that he understood any of it himself, much less where it was derived from.

"… continued blessings upon Peter as we celebrate his special day. In the Lord's name we pray, amen," Father Thomas concluded.

Naughware looked sidelong at Thomas and smiled. Despite the question of his biological parents, he was nevertheless grateful for the only real paternal figure he had ever known. Unmarried as Thomas was, the priest had done his best to raise Naughware in both his own home and the church, which even Naughware acknowledged was an atmosphere of affection and support.

He loved the old man, despite his own misgivings about Thomas' faith in a God he could hardly fathom himself.

"A toast to Peter," Glenn said, raising his wine glass. "Happy birthday to the best friend a guy could have."

Naughware smiled before drinking in response.

* * *

Naughware thought the dinner went well all the way through dessert, at least until the moment he was discreetly handed a note from one of the waiters, who then stood off to the side of their table.

He unfolded the note, which read:

Detective Naughware,

A moment of your time, if you please.

We have mutual interests to discuss.

M. Rowe

Father Thomas leaned over to him. "That's not the check, is it? I told them to bring it to me."

"No, just someone who wants a quick word," Naughware said.

Thomas frowned. "Who?"

"Work-related," Naughware said as he rose from the table.

He motioned to the waiter, who led the way from the banquet room. They walked to the opposite side and the opposite end of the restaurant, where three men and a woman were seated in a corner booth devoid of nearby patrons.

Two of the men looked like thugs in suits, while the other man was stocky like a football lineman and wore his Italian-made suit like a second skin.

That man, Naughware recognized.

Mosqos "Skeeter" Rowe.

The waiter gestured toward the booth and made a hasty departure.

"Detective Naughware," Rowe said. "So sorry to interrupt your gathering. But needs must, you see."

"Skeeter Rowe," Naughware said, raising the note in his hand. "What mutual interests could a cop like me have with a repudiated Abaddon gangster? I'm not on your payroll, as I recall."

"Naughware, there's no need for a tone, friend," Rowe said, gesturing with a hand that hosted chunky gold rings on most fingers. "I'm a businessman. All that gangster stuff left Abaddon when Prohibition ended and Capone and his boys cleared out."

Naughware shook his head. "Liquor may have come into the light, but there's still lots taking place in the dark around this town, Skeeter."

Rowe gestured to the two men with a nod and turned to the lady at his left. "Maybe this would be a good time for a powder room break, honey."

The woman quietly scooted from her seat beside Rowe and walked away while both bodyguards rose from their seats and flanked the sides of the booth.

"I didn't ask you over to argue, Naughware," Rowe said.

"I've been charged by one of this city's finest residents to find out more about the senseless violence taking place on the south side of town."

"Which resident, in particular?"

"Actually, it's better for everyone involved if I don't say who," Rowe said.

Naughware shrugged. "Then I'm leaving."

He turned to walk away.

"All right. Midas Hyde, if you must know," Rowe said. "But let's keep that between us. Mr. Hyde prefers discretion."

Naughware turned back around. "Hyde?"

That surprised him. Midas Hyde was the controlling heir to one of the richest, most prominent founding families in Abaddon, and he wondered why Hyde would seek the services of someone like Rowe.

"None other," Rowe said.

"Why?" Naughware asked. "And moreover, why tell me about Hyde?"

"It's important that you don't discount what I'm trying to accomplish here," Rowe said. "The Bouquet Corral was one of Mr. Hyde's investments, you see."

"Did he happen to know there were drug exchanges going down there?" Naughware asked.

"Oh, now, Mr. Hyde would never sully his hands with such nasty business," Rowe said. "In fact, he personally asked me to look into why something like that went down there the way it did."

The edges of Naughware's mouth upturned. "The way it did, eh?"

Rowe stared back at him with a flat look. "You wouldn't happen to know who, if anyone, might have managed to walk away from that—sordid business—would you?"

Naughware met the man's gaze eye for eye. *They don't know for sure who was there that night.*

"Well, lots of bodies didn't leave that night," Naughware said. "And I may, or may not, know who did. But you'll understand that's not something I'm supposed to talk about.

You see, my captain's got this funny thing about off-the-record leaks and what not."

"I know how grateful Mr. Hyde would *personally* be if our city's finest were to make a gesture of good will," Rowe said, leaning forward. "In fact, I wouldn't be at all surprised that Mr. Hyde would remember such a gesture, which may be handy at some unknown future time. One never knows where life's path will lead."

Rowe leaned back against the back of the booth seat while the hint of a smile formed. He appeared quite pleased with himself.

"You sound a little like Father Thomas now," Naughware said.

"Well, I, too, am a man of faith," Rowe said.

Naughware wagged his forefinger at him. "Oh, but faith in who or what, I wouldn't venture to say."

Rowe didn't appear amused. "No need to go and challenge a man's faith."

"Isn't that what faith's all about?" Naughware asked.

Rowe's icy demeanor promptly softened, which surprised Naughware a bit.

"I hope you'll give my, rather Mr. Hyde's, request further consideration, Naughware," Rowe said, once more adopting a diplomatic expression. "One way or another, information going to come out. I'd be one to want the benefits of that, versus feeling left out in the cold."

"Fortunately, I have a really good coat for when things get cold," Naughware said.

"Oh, but the winds in Abaddon can cut right though a man," Rowe said, "shredding even the best of coats that I've ever seen."

"You have a good night, Rowe," Naughware said, turning to leave.

"Hey, Naughware," Rowe said.

Naughware stopped, but didn't look back.

"I hear a cold front may be coming soon," Rowe said. "Better button up your coat before it arrives."

Naughware calmly walked away, but his mind buzzed with thoughts over the exchange he'd just had with Skeeter Rowe. The problem was, he didn't think that it really helped him with the case all that much.

At least, not yet.

The conversation suggested that Midas Hyde had an interest in what happened at the warehouse. But, if so, what was Hyde's interest, specifically?

The idea that Hyde might have a hand in what had taken place there was unsettling.

If so, was Hyde betrayed, or merely wanting to take advantage of the turmoil left in its wake?

More to the point, Naughware wondered why the people who escaped the crime scene were of interest to Hyde. Were they accomplices or merely business opportunities?

Or rivals?

As Naughware walked past the various booths and tables, he noticed a cute young woman sitting at a nearby table looking quite shaken as she talked to a waitress he recognized.

At first, he started to walk past them.

"There's no way my card could be denied," the woman said. "Please, it's less than thirty dollars, so if you'd just let me make a quick run back to my shop—"

"I'm sorry, ma'am," the waitress said. "I'm afraid I'll have to call the manager over."

Naughware stopped just beyond the table and turned around to look back at them. The pleading expression on the woman's face touched him.

He walked over to the table. "Sorry to interrupt. Any trouble, Sue?"

"Oh, hi, Detective Naughware," the waitress said. "It's a payment issue …"

The young woman looked up at Naughware. "Detective?"

Naughware reached into his back pocket and the young woman's eyes went wide.

He pulled out his wallet, extracted one of his credit cards, and handed it to Sue.

"I'll cover it," he said.

Sue took the credit card and quietly walked away.

"But—" the woman said. "Why would you do that?"

Naughware shrugged. "It's my birthday."

The woman's eyes narrowed. "But doesn't that mean *you* receive the gift?"

"Sometimes the gift comes in strange forms," Naughware said, remembering something that Father Thomas told him time and again. Though he'd thought often enough that was just a mysterious way to convey the idea that one should make lemonade out of lemons.

He reached out to shake her hand. "Peter Naughware."

She returned his handshake. "Eva Shyne."

"Pleased to meet you, Eva Shyne," he said. He liked the way her name sounded when he said it.

Sue returned with two receipts and his credit card and handed them to him.

He signed one of the receipts and conveyed it back to her. "Thank you, Sue."

She nodded back at him. "Detective."

Eva nervously adjusted her trendy-looking eyeglasses as Sue walked away. "Uh, I can repay you after I retrieve some cash from my shop."

"Nah, karma will take care of it," he said. "Pass it on. Do something nice for someone else someday."

"You believe in karma, Detective?"

"Believe is a strong word," he said. "But life is both strange and funny at times. That much I'll admit."

She appeared amused by his response and fished inside her purse to retrieve a business card, which she handed to him.

"Well, if you ever want to know more about either strange or karma, let me know," Eva said.

He looked down at the card.

Eva Shyne
The Spooky Word

"Your Occult and More Store"
1122 Hyde Street
Abaddon, Iowa

He stared down at her.

"Hyde Street?"

She appeared surprised by his tone. "Um, yes. Is something wrong?"

He paused, reaching up to thoughtfully rub his chin.

"Sorry," he said. "Just ironic how some names repeat themselves in short order, that's all."

She tentatively smiled at him, and he found himself smiling back.

"Well, I'd better get back my party," he said. "Good evening to you, Ms. Shyne."

"Thank you again, Detective," she said. "And happy birthday."

He inclined his head toward her and returned to the banquet room, absently strumming the edge of the business card against his knuckles.

CHAPTER 5

Later that evening, back at his apartment, Naughware lay atop his bed thinking about the day's events. The morning's crime scene had been one for the ages. His new partner was a surprise, though he thought perhaps he should give Keane a chance, at least. And the dinner had gone well, and was much appreciated by him, in the end.

He withdrew his digital player and rolled it around in his hand. As he had done at least a thousand times or more since turning twenty-two, he stopped to read the inscription on the back of the unit.

Happy Birthday, Peter. -- Music is a doorway to your soul.

He often wondered if the songs placed in the root directory were especially for him? And, if so, why?

He pondered that there were many mysteries behind that gift, the least of which was, who had anonymously left it for him?

The only other information on the outside of its metal shell was scant, at best.

Manufactured by Keuze Pad

Serial #: DL112233

His mix of excitement and curiosity over the new song on the player once more played across his thoughts. He had long ago grudgingly considered that the device was comprised of more than mere electronics.

In fact, he had spent many hours wondering about that strange, remarkable device.

The possibilities were endless and, many times, unnerving.

However, the day had drained his mental and physical energy, and he was happy just to be home.

He needed quiet time and space to take in all that had transpired.

The muffled sounds of traffic from the street outside his apartment mixed with the noise of dance music and footfalls or television sounds emanating from the apartments above and beside his.

He wanted a respite; somewhere tranquil to think things through.

As he had done time and time again when such moments arose, he closed his eyes and concentrated on darkness and nothing.

Complete emptiness.

His Nowhere Place.

It was only a single moment of light-headedness that followed; like the subtle shift in gravity via a short fall. Then he felt a cool, hard surface beneath him.

He had arrived.

He sat upright and gazed into complete, penetrating darkness. The ensuing feeling of sensory deprivation generated a momentary wave of dizziness that threatened to overwhelm him.

With practiced grace, he removed his smartphone and turned it on. At least the dim light emanating from its screen generated a small parcel of comfort.

However, the device's aura of illumination barely pierced the darkness around him.

Despite years of experience, the place unnerved him each and every time he came. His first voyage had been a complete mistake; an emotional upheaval when he was only eleven.

Since then, he called it many things.

The Nowhere Zone.

Nowhere Space.

The Nowhere Place.

The void.

Even after all those years, he still didn't understand what or where it was. For one, his mobile phone lost its communication signal in that place.

However, he was convinced of three truths about that place.

First, it was a real location. It was no mind palace; no imaginary hallucination. It was as real as normal reality was when he wasn't there; only it was much emptier.

Second, it seemed boundless. To date, he had never found a border, even after hours of walking in what he thought was a single direction.

And third, it was the eeriest and ominous place he had ever trodden.

As such, he only visited when he desperately needed to completely escape the regular world. In a weird way, it sort of calmed him.

It helped him center and focus his thoughts.

Naughware took a deep breath through his mouth and let it out slowly through his nose. Even the air he breathed in held a heavy quality to it.

The inescapable silence was almost deafening. And yet, it was completely peaceful.

He often wondered if a sensory deprivation tank was similar.

There were no structures other than the seemingly impenetrable surface, or floor, for lack of a better term. The air was still and not entirely fresh, like one might expect from a long-shut vault.

For what must have been the hundredth time, he wondered where the air even came from.

Add to that, the temperature of the place was neither cold nor hot. The best term he could think to describe it was *completely neutral.*

There were no people or any other living creatures that he knew of; at least, that he had ever seen, heard, or detected.

And yet, on rare occasions, he couldn't help feeling like there might be a distant presence there. That was the truly eerie part.

Naturally, he had told nobody about the Nowhere Zone.

Who would have believed him?

He couldn't prove it since he had never tried bringing anyone there. He wasn't even sure that he could, really.

At first, Naughware thought himself crazy, even as a child. And yet, he *knew* he was no longer on *terra firma.* It was someplace else.

But the "where" of where he was remained a complete mystery.

Once, years ago, just to make sure he was actually leaving the world behind, he had recorded himself with Thomas' video camera while lying on his bed. After he disappeared and later returned to his bed, he rewound the video and replayed it in real time.

He had watched as one moment his body was lying on the bed, and the next moment it disappeared from view. He fast-forwarded a time until his body reappeared on the bed.

Naughware only recorded himself one time. After that, he was too unnerved to keep doing it.

Besides, what would someone say if they had discovered such recordings?

Despite the oddity, the strangeness of the place, it was where he would come when he needed to escape everyone and everything.

He looked at his watch.

Eleven fifteen.

Time seemed to pass normally when he was there. Upon returning to the normal world, the time on his watch always matched other real-world time sources.

When he was sixteen, and had just had a major disagreement with Father Thomas, he came to the Nowhere Zone for nearly a day. When he returned, which was after his supply of flashlight batteries ran out, Father Thomas had long since sent out notices to search for him, including calling the police. Thomas was concerned that he had run away from home.

In a sense, Naughware supposed he had.

He still felt guilty over that. And after seeing the fear in the priest's eyes, he had never again remained in the Nowhere Zone for very long.

In truth, the place sort of unnerved him.

He glanced at his mobile phone screen.

Yeah, still no signal. Surprise, surprise.

"Hello! I'm back!" he shouted.

His voice didn't even echo.

Of course, it never did. The oppressive darkness smothered sound, as well as light.

And, per the norm, there was no response.

At least he was somewhere where his thoughts wouldn't be interrupted.

He slipped his phone into his shirt pocket and sat down on the hard surface with his legs crisscrossed before him.

Naughware inserted his earbuds and played the newest song in his root directory.

As "The Gospel of John Hurt" by alt-J began to play, he closed his eyes and let his thoughts drift.

* * *

Father Thomas sat on his worn sofa with a distant expression on his face, nursing a glass containing a modest portion of Irish whiskey.

It was one of his few indulgences.

He looked over at the end table, which sported a photo of Peter, the one taken at a local lake when he was only twelve. The boy hoisted up a huge bass fish that was nearly a quarter his own height, a proud grin adorning his face.

Thomas smiled.

"My son's thirty-three today, Lord," he said, raising his glass in a toast and then sipping from it. "As good a son as any man deserves, I suppose."

His features darkened as he silently reminded himself that Peter wasn't truly his son, merely the boy whom he had been charged to raise. Although Peter was as much of a son as Thomas would ever have during his own lifetime.

Thomas thought that through his ministrations and love, Peter had grown into a good and honorable man with a kind heart.

He sat the glass aside on the end table and lightly massaged his closed eyes with his fingertips.

"God, forgive an old man for sins of omission," he whispered. "It was for the best, after all."

It was a practiced-enough entreaty on his part.

A wave of doubt washed over him, yet again, as the old arguments resurfaced. Such recurring self-doubt was his most formidable enemy.

His personal demon to slay.

Thomas reflected upon how, when Peter was younger, each birthday he would ask Thomas if he could tell him anything at all about his real parents.

And each time, Thomas replied in what he felt was the noblest manner possible, "Nothing at all, Peter. I'm sorry."

However noble the gesture was, ultimately, he lied each time.

Thomas reached out to take the fishing photo in his hand and stared down at it. "You're better off not knowing what little truth I know, my boy. It's better this way … for both of us."

The mere recollection of whom he had encountered at his doorstep that day sent a shiver down his spine.

The priest didn't particularly want to ruminate over the actuality of Peter's arrival in his life. In fact, after so many years passed, he had begun to wonder if it had ever been real in the first place.

However, obsessions being what they are, they rarely left one in peace.

He mused they were merely memories glossed over with too much imagination and emotion; mere figments of the reality of what had really transpired.

Embellishments from flawed memory recall.

Only he knew that wasn't entirely true, either.

He held the photo in one hand while reaching over to grasp the whiskey glass with his free one. The glass shook unsteadily in his hand as he drank nearly half its contents.

Thomas stared into the bottom of the remaining whiskey.

"Am I just getting too old and emotional?" he asked. "Or is my sense of guilt finally winning out?"

He looked up at his living room ceiling with glistening eyes.

"Your promise, Lord, is to share the heavy weight of our burdens in this world," he said. "It was *Your* will be done that day …"

He frowned. "Wasn't it?"

For years, and with practiced grace, he regularly assured his parishioners that God heard their pleas and prayers, even if He never responded directly.

It was at times such as this that he doubted the veracity of those assurances.

"It was your heavenly couriers that brought Peter to me, wasn't it, Lord?"

Distant thunder sounded, and a shiver ran through his body as long-suppressed memories resurfaced.

It was thunder that had preceded Peter's arrival that fateful September day thirty-three years prior.

Fateful, because of Peter, and likewise fateful because Thomas had experienced a shift in both faith and responsibility that irrevocably altered his life.

It was enough to shake even the world's most devout priest's faith.

The old man looked down at his trembling hand gripping the glass, and he quickly brought the rim to his lips and drank.

CHAPTER 6

Peter abruptly woke to the sound of the alarm on his phone going off, only then realizing that he was back in his bedroom lying atop his bed.

As his thoughts cleared, he vaguely remembered transporting back to his room sometime during the night.

He yawned while reflecting back upon the new alt-J song he had played over and over again while in the Nowhere Zone. Of course, he was no closer to divining any meaningful information from his reflections.

However strange the song lyrics were, they had grown on him to the point that he was beginning to like the tune.

"Maybe someone's trying to tell me I'm an alien," he said while stretching. "Or something's coming out of the woods to get me?"

Another aspect of the song bewildered him, and he frowned as he walked to the nearby bathroom to shave. "But what's John Hurt have to do with it?"

Glenn's information about John Hurt occurred to him.

"I hope nothing's going to burst from my chest."

During his brief journey to the precinct, he reflected on the prior night's birthday event and the meeting with Skeeter Rowe, followed quickly by pondering the Bouquet Corral case.

After everyone raided the coffee pot at least once,

Naughware huddled around Detective Sergeant Vigoda's desk with Levitt and Keane to discuss their next steps on the case.

"First of all, I've got an important announcement from the lieutenant, which he said comes straight from the upper brass," Vigoda said. "Everybody's working weekends, and maybe weeknights, if needed, until we crack this case."

"You've got to be kidding! Today's Friday," Levitt said. "I've already got tickets for the movies tonight, and this weekend I'm going to the—"

"Well, find somebody who can use them, and reschedule your weekend plans, Levitt," Vigoda said, cutting him off. "This is priority one until further notice, straight from the top."

"The little woman at home ain't gonna like this," Levitt said.

"The little woman?" Keane asked.

"Yeah," he said. "You know, the wife."

"Seriously, are you straight outta the 1950s or something?" Keane asked.

Naughware bit back a grin.

"What?" Levitt asked. "It's just an expression. My dad used to say that all the time."

Keane shook her head. "Oh, it shows."

"All right, pipe down. Everybody knows working Robbery-Homicide means we may have to work weekends and holidays, as cases require," Vigoda said. "Now, what new information do we have?"

Perturbed, Levitt held up a manila folder. "Scarcely ten minutes ago, we received a preliminary report from ballistics on the weapons found at the scene."

"Anything helpful?" Vigoda asked.

Levitt flipped open the folder. "Maybe," he replied. "All the weapons had prints matching each of the bodies at the scene, except one."

He withdrew a color printout of a small-frame revolver with pearl handles.

"This thirty-eight was found beneath a crate in the

warehouse," Levitt said.

"Somebody tried to hide it?" Keane asked.

"Nah," Levitt replied. "Looks like it might have been dropped and then kicked, based on the scratches along one side of it."

"Did we get a hit on the prints?" Naughware asked.

"Sort of," Levitt. "That is, it's not what I would've liked."

"Christ's sake, Levitt. What the hell is that supposed to mean?" Vigoda asked. "Whose prints were on it?"

"According to the FBI database, a twenty-four-year-old woman by the name of Jenny Vance from Sioux City," Levitt replied. "No felonies, but she has some misdemeanors for disorderly conduct and other minor infractions. There's a couple of possession charges that were dropped, out of both Sioux City and New York City."

Vigoda frowned. "That's it?"

Levitt shrugged. "That's what the database said, anyway."

"Maybe she was just arm candy for one of the thugs there," Keane said.

"Maybe," Vigoda said, though he didn't sound convinced. "Naughware?"

Naughware shook his head. "I'm not buying that ... sounds too tidy."

Vigoda grunted. "More like half a story."

"False identity?" Keane asked.

"Or an alias," Vigoda said. "Say, maybe someone from witness protection?"

While the detectives threw out other random ideas, Naughware considered the topic while draining his coffee mug. Then he walked across the room to the coffee pot.

He slipped his earbuds in and hit random play before refilling his mug with fresh java.

The Hollies' "Long Cool Woman (In a Black Dress)" played.

The first verse of the song struck him like a bolt of lightning.

Pocketing his player, Naughware walked back around to

where the detectives sat.

"Undercover agent," he said.

The three looked at him with blank expressions.

"What?" Vigoda asked.

Naughware took his time at a swig of coffee. "The woman. Maybe she's undercover."

"Undercover with who?" Levitt asked.

Naughware shrugged. "Don't know. FBI, DEA, or maybe Iowa State Bureau …"

"Hell, she's twenty-four," Vigoda said. "That's barely enough time to cut her teeth as a street officer. Maybe a snitch, at best."

"Just saying," Naughware said. "At least until we've got something more solid."

"All right, people. Sitting around here on our asses shooting blanks ain't good for hunting," Vigoda said. "Naughware, you and Keane go and dig up anything else you can find on this Jenny Vance. Be sure to take color copies of her DMV photo with you. Maybe take a drive up to Sioux City to check out her last-known address."

Keane didn't look particularly enthused about that idea, but Naughware motioned for her to follow him.

"You don't mean to tell me we're actually driving to Sioux City?" she asked as they walked back to their desks.

"What? Hardly," Naughware said derisively, rifling through his center desk drawer for something. "We'll have one of the uniforms do that."

"And as for us?" she asked.

"We're going to go talk to someone local who might have some insights."

"Who?"

He withdrew a silver coin from the drawer and flipped it over in his hand before pocketing it.

"You'll see," he said.

***

The northern side of the city was populated with upscale shops and restaurants, and served as the bustling heart of the financial district. It was where the wealthy and powerful weaved business dealings and summarily celebrated their accomplishments.

When Naughware parked the sedan in front of a designer clothing boutique on Commerce Street, Keane whistled.

"Naughware, you sure do know how to take a girl to all the right places," she said with a smile. "I already like where you get your insights from."

"Sorry, no shopping trips today," he said.

They walked down the street past more shops until they arrived at the entrance to a coin collector's shop called The Prescott Exchange.

Inside, the shop was adorned with display cases and cabinets arrayed with precious metal coins and a small variety of paper currencies. A security guard stood just inside the door, watching them.

They were greeted by a fashionably dressed woman standing before an elaborate glass display cabinet.

"Welcome to The Prescott Exchange," she said. "How can I be of assistance to you today?"

"We'd like to visit with Mr. Prescott, please," Naughware said, removing his police badge to display it toward her. "Official business, you understand."

"I'm sorry, but Mr. Prescott isn't available just at the moment," she said. "Perhaps if you'd like to leave your contact information, I'll happily forward it to him."

Naughware removed the silver coin from his pocket and held it up before her.

She stared at the coin, though made no visible reaction at seeing it.

"Follow me, please," she said, turning to walk toward one of two doors at the back of the shop.

Keane observed the exchange with interest but said nothing.

She unlocked the door, and Naughware and Keane

followed her through, into the small room beyond. It looked like one might expect a typical manager's office to look, complete with bookshelves adorned with volumes on coin collectibles and various appraisal-related texts.

The woman went to one of the bookshelves and pulled a book halfway from its place, at which the bookcase swung inward to reveal a short span of dimly lit hallway.

She quietly led the way to a metal door at the other end and pressed a button seated into the door jamb.

A quick series of clanking noises sounded within the metal door, and it gave way when the woman pressed it inward.

She gestured with one hand and waited to shut the door behind them.

"Where are we going?" Keane whispered to Naughware.

"You'll see," he said.

Soft light illuminated the interior room, which was approximately fifteen feet in depth and one end was lined with more glass displays holding a variety of collectibles, including precious coins, paper currency, and other historical knickknacks.

The opposite end of the room sported a large oak desk where a broad-shouldered man sat with his fingers steepled before him. A nearly ceiling height, imposing-looking metal vault door stood shut behind him.

"Detective Naughware," the man said, rising from his seat and stepping around his desk to greet them. "An unexpected surprise so early in the morning."

"You would have expected me in the afternoon?" Naughware asked.

The tall man smiled and chuckled before turning his attention to Keane. "And who is the lovely lady you've brought with you today?"

He extended his open hand toward her. "Thaddeus Prescott, at your service."

Keane stepped forward to shake hands with him and displayed her badge with her free hand. "Detective Keane."

Prescott gently gripped her hand and placed his other

hand over the top of hers. "Pleased to meet you, Detective."

He momentarily closed his eyes. Keane gave Naughware an indignant look, but he shook his head and held up his hand in a halting manner.

Prescott opened his eyes and smiled again. "Congratulations on finding and embracing yourself, Detective. Far too many people live their entire lives out and never do."

Keane frowned and gently pulled her hand free of his grasp.

"Keane's my new partner," Naughware said.

Prescott's eyebrows arched in amusement. "A new partner. This is already a day of revelation."

"Yeah," Naughware said. "And that's why we're here, actually. We could use a tall order of revelation … to go."

"I'm not reading tea leaves here," Prescott said, wagging his finger.

"One could always hope. I like tea now and again," Naughware said. "However, information of any kind is always welcome. Especially right now."

"Welcome is a strong word, depending upon what one learns," Prescott said, gesturing to two chairs placed before his desk. They sat as he returned to his high-backed chair opposite them.

"Tell me more about what you're seeking," he said.

"There was a shootout on the south side," Naughware.

"Yes, the florist warehouse," Prescott said. "Such a terrible business. So much death in one place."

"True," Naughware said. "Which is why we're interested in learning more about the motive and any parties associated with the event."

"This is still fresh," Prescott said. "And, as you well know, information can take time to surface."

"Has anything helpful surfaced yet?" Keane asked.

"When opposing factions vie for resources, it's typically about power and control," Prescott said. "Both are predictable and understandable. But what if there were more at stake?"

Naughware frowned. "Such as?"

"Principalities."

"You mean, principles, don't you?" Keane asked.

Prescott shook his head. "No, Detective. I mean Principalities."

"As in—" Keane said, motioning upward toward the ceiling.

"The fifth highest order of the nine-fold celestial hierarchy," Prescott said, looking first at Keane and then at Naughware, who stared back at him with a flat expression.

"Woah, okay," Keane said, holding up one hand. "Let's stop at the metaphysical and return to the realm of reality here."

"Take a time out, Keane," Naughware said.

She turned toward him with an incredulous look on her face. "Time out? Are you kidding me? Mumbo jumbo ain't going to solve this case."

"Naughware knows what I'm saying isn't mere … mumbo jumbo," Prescott said, staring at her. "He was raised by a priest. He should know that the spiritual world has power."

Naughware massaged his forehead with his fingertips and stared down at the floor. "Thaddeus, you know I don't talk about that stuff."

"Your disbelief doesn't alter the reality," Prescott said. "Eventually, you're going to be forced to confront that."

"Yeah, well, some things I believe in," he said. "Others, not so much."

Keane stood up and looked at her partner. "Naughware, what are you thinking?" she asked. "Bringing us downtown to see a coin-dealing soothsayer."

"Because you're with Naughware, I will choose not to take offense to that," Prescott said.

Keane turned her attention back to him and held up a color photo. "Mr. Prescott, returning to the physical world of here and now, perhaps you've seen or heard of this woman? She's going by the name Jenny Vance."

He shook his head. "That's not a name or face that I'm familiar with, Detective."

"Mm," she said, turning toward Naughware. "I'll wait for you at the car. Don't be long … we've still got real detective work to do today."

"Detective," Prescott said, respectfully rising from his chair.

But Keane had already walked out of the room by the time Prescott stood. He looked down at Naughware.

"Well, that was enchanting," he said.

"Oh, she likes you," Naughware said, standing. "I can tell already."

"By her disposition, I could say the same for you, Naughware," Prescott said, arching one brow.

"Yeah, you might say it's a slow start with us," Naughware agreed. He handed Prescott his own printed photo of Jenny Vance. "Listen, take this and call me if you happen to get any hits on this woman's whereabouts. It's important, or I wouldn't trouble you with it."

Prescott nodded and reached out to shake his hand. "Fair enough."

Naughware looked down at the man's hand. "Let's skip the handshake this morning."

"Humor me," the tall man said.

Naughware slowly held out his hand.

Prescott closed his eyes, gripped the detective's hand firmly.

After a moment, he released his grip and stared directly at the detective.

"What?" Naughware asked, though he wasn't sure he really wanted to know.

"I sense you're going through changes, my friend," he said. "Some things have already changed, in fact."

"Everybody's changing," Naughware said. "Every day."

"No," Prescott said. "*You've* changed. And you've *felt* it. It's a new world for you now, isn't it?"

Naughware felt unnerved. "What the hell do you mean by

that?"

Prescott gave him a patient look. "Heard any good music lately?"

Naughware's heart skipped a beat, and he felt the muscles in his throat tighten.

"How did—"

"You be careful out there, Peter," the tall man said. "A storm's coming to Abaddon, and big changes that will take time to understand. But time may not be your ally."

"Why Abaddon?"

"Why anywhere," Prescott replied. "Or *Naughware* in particular."

Naughware stared back at him in stunned silence, too unnerved to ask anything further. Instead, he turned to leave.

As he walked through the doorway, he reached back to grab the door handle and swing it closed behind him.

Before the door closed completely, he heard Prescott say, "Come back when you're ready to see all sides."

Naughware quickly pulled the door shut. As he proceeded down the hallway, he paused, removed his earbuds from his jacket pocket, and inserted them.

He hesitated and then activated random on his digital device.

The Doors' "Break on Through" began to play.

"Aw, hell."

CHAPTER 7

Detective Keane leaned back against the hood of their sedan as she waited for her partner, still fuming over what she viewed as a fruitless visit.

She spied Naughware as he exited the coin shop, discreetly removing his earbuds.

"Great," she muttered. "First, mumbo jumbo. Now, Detective Jukebox and his magical mystery tour."

Naughware didn't say a word as he walked toward her and unlocked the doors with the key remote.

She didn't waste any time getting into the vehicle.

"You look pissed," he said, pulling his door shut.

She turned sidelong in her seat to confront him. "You bet I'm pissed. You want to tell me what that shit was all about back there?"

"In addition to being a successful businessman, Thaddeus Prescott has a reputation as someone who acquires information for a price," Naughware said.

"And?" she asked.

"They call him The Monk in some circles because it's said he may also have psychic visions and insights."

Keane shut her eyes and took a deep breath, then exhaled slowly.

"Seriously," she said. "I don't need this crap today. We'd have been better off driving to Sioux City."

"Hey, he's panned out with vital information on a number of prior occasions," Naughware said. "He's helped me, anyway."

She nodded. "Yeah, yeah. I know all about the value of informants. And normally, people like that have a price. And since I didn't see you flash any cash, I've got to wonder why Prescott is so forthcoming to you? You two seem chummy enough."

Naughware shook his head. "You might say, he owes me. But not to worry … it's all on the up-and-up."

She frowned. "Oh, really?"

"Yep," Naughware said.

"You want to share with me how that works, exactly?" she asked.

"Maybe someday," he said, staring out through the windshield. "Being in the right place to help Prescott's family nearly cost me my life. Little did I realize at the time what would spring from that."

He produced the coin and held it out toward her.

"See the eye imprinted there?" he asked. "That's a seer's coin, and it gets me immediate access to The Monk whenever I need it."

"Yeah, whatever," she said. "Action movie theatrics aside, don't you think that's a little squirrely, going in there like he's some sort of fortune teller or something?"

"Many claim he sees things other people don't," Naughware said. "And he occasionally does acquire useful information on the darker elements operating in the city."

"Seems to me he's playing on your spiritual background," she said.

Naughware's features hardened. "And just what is it you think you know about my *spiritual background*?"

"It's only logical. Who wouldn't be impacted spiritually by that, even more so if they had a background for it?" she said. "I met Thomas. Your father's a priest."

He glared back at her. "Just for the record, and I'll only say this once," he said. "Sure, I may have been raised by a priest, but you don't know *one damned thing* about either my father or my faith."

She was taken aback, and she stared back at him in silence.

"All right," she said. "Let's just keep it professional and stick to standard police investigative procedure, okay?"

Incredibly angry, Naughware decided not to tell her about Prescott's parting ominous portent. Instead, he quietly started the car and pulled back into the flow of traffic.

* * *

Naughware's temper had cooled by the time he and Keane walked into the office, and he had no sooner headed toward the coffee pot when Lieutenant Dawkins walked out of his office with Detective Vigoda in tow.

"Levitt, Naughware, and Keane," Dawkins said. "The captain wants to meet with us ASAP."

Naughware gave the coffee a last longing look before following Keane out of the office.

Upon exiting the elevator on the third floor, Betty Penney was already standing in the hallway to direct them to the nearby conference room.

They entered the room to find the captain waiting along with men and women wearing business suits, as well as District Attorney Jorge Abasolo and Police Commissioner Rhonda Ellery. Nobody appeared particularly pleased to be there.

"Come in," the commissioner said. "And don't bother taking a seat, this won't take long."

The detectives exchanged suspicious looks, but remained silent. The commissioner cleared her throat.

"This morning, DA Abasalo and I were approached by FBI SAIC Denise Warwick and DEA SAIC Todd Langdon regarding our investigations into the Bouquet Corral incident," Ellery said. "Due to the sensitive nature of this case, I'm not permitted to elaborate beyond saying that both the DEA and FBI have active ongoing investigations related to some of the victims, which included an undercover DEA agent who was using the alias Julio 'Glam' Bonilla."

Naughware caught the wholly surprised expressions on both Vigoda's and Levitt's faces, which likely matched the one on his own.

"... and as federal agencies take precedence, the Abaddon department will stand down from the investigation. Your case files should be turned over to Agent Warwick by the end of the day, and you will be reassigned to other outstanding investigations."

"Thank you for your service and professionalism," Ellery said. "That will be all. Dismissed."

Vigoda shrugged and shook his head, but quietly left the room with Levitt close at his heels.

"Good end to a bad start," Keane said before turning to leave the room.

Naughware stood with his arms folded before him and caught Captain Gunderson's attention as she was walking past him.

He glanced over at the commissioner, DA, and federal agents across the room.

"Captain, that's it?" he asked, exasperated.

"That's it," she said.

"This isn't right or fair," he said. "We're just getting started. Damn it, we were first on scene."

"Naughware, everybody knows federal agencies take precedence when investigations conflict with local authorities," Commissioner Ellery said. "The FBI is taking lead on the investigation, so just drop it and move on, Detective."

Gunderson gave him a sympathetic look and walked out of the room.

Naughware trailed her and proceeded into the hallway where he took out his smartphone and dialed.

"Hey," he said. "Do you have lunch plans today?"

***

Naughware sat in a booth at one of the city's most popular locally owned cafes, Hamburger Hill.

He looked up just in time to see a friendly face slipping into the booth seat opposite him.

"Hey, kid," Evan Taylor said. "I just saw you at dinner last night. You're missing me already?"

"Yeah, well, I didn't catch enough hell from you about getting older," Naughware said. "So, now it's time for round two."

Taylor chuckled. "Yeah, well, you're always going to be a youngster in my book, no matter how gray your hair gets."

The two of them perused the menu.

"I guess I'll get the usual," Taylor said.

"You order the same thing practically every time," Naughware said. "Spread your wings; there's lots of great things on the menu. And your colon just might appreciate a change from all that red meat."

"Don't give me any shit about my colon," Taylor said, pointing his finger at him.

"You know, that sounds pretty funny when you say it like that," Naughware said.

Taylor gave him a wan look from over the top of his menu.

Naughware grinned. After his tumultuous beginning with Keane, he missed his former partner so badly he practically ached.

"You buying today?" Taylor asked. "As an old retiree, I'm on a fixed income now, you know."

Naughware looked over at him with a surprised expression. "What?"

"Gotcha," Taylor said, winking at him. "When the day comes that I can't pay for my own meal, you can damn well shoot my ass."

"Glad to hear a year of retirement hasn't made you soft-hearted."

They exchanged small talk until a waitress stopped by to take their order. As she walked away from their table, Taylor's expression turned serious.

"Something's on your mind beyond pining for your old partner," he said. "What's up?"

"You mean, aside from being pulled off the biggest case in my career by the feds less than a day into it?" Naughware asked. "Or the fact that in less than twenty-four hours I've managed to alienate my new partner?"

Taylor pursed his lips. "You are in a world of shit, aren't you? All right. Tell me about it."

By the time Naughware recounted the basic details on both issues, their meals had arrived, and each fell silent for a time.

"Your new partner, Keane, just needs to get the lay of the land," Taylor said. "She'll come around as your leads start panning out. Remember, you and I aren't … I mean, weren't … the poster children for procedure."

"Yeah," Naughware said. "Just so long as things don't get any weirder than they already are."

"The Monk episode from this morning," Taylor said. "I've never known what to make of all that mysticism stuff. He's a bit odder than most, but his tips are solid the vast majority of the time. Again, Keane will see that eventually. Be patient."

"*You're* telling *me* to be patient?" Naughware asked. "I recall you tearing into the lieutenant's ass a time or two just for foot-dragging on warrants. And what about the time you threatened that records clerk within an inch of his life."

"Aw, Dawkins was always stalling," Taylor said. "And hell, I had a suspect dead to rights based on what was in that file from Records."

"Some example you are on patience."

"Take good advice for its value, not the source," Taylor said. "So, quit your bitching. I nurtured you into the respectable detective you are today."

"Nurtured? I remember you throwing down on me from

day one," Naughware said.

"Hey, it was the hard-love sort of nurturing. You were a candy-ass greenhorn, just outta patrol," Taylor said. "I had to break you in fast before you went sideways on me. You had all those enlightened notions about detectives swooping in like those ridiculous TV crime dramas."

"And just how is that so different from Keane?"

"Keane's not a greenhorn," he said. "Didn't you say she was a detective back at the Peoria department?"

Naughware started to protest, then stopped.

Taylor paused to take a swig of his cola. "Now, if you're through whining, let's go over the case again, but this time in more detail," he said. "There's gotta be a loophole somewhere."

Naughware recounted everything again, including giving Taylor a photo of Jenny Vance.

"Wait a minute," Taylor said. "You said you got her prints off a revolver?"

"Yep," Naughware said. "Hers only showed up on the pistol, nowhere else at the scene, so far as we've found."

"What did ballistics say about the revolver?"

"Not much on the preliminary report. Thirty-eight, pearl-handled," Naughware said. "There may be more, but the final report won't be done for days, if not a couple of weeks."

Taylor snapped his fingers. "That's it. Pearl-handled."

Naughware frowned.

"That's an expensive mod," Taylor said. "So, either it's special to her, or maybe someone else."

"Maybe a gift?" Naughware asked.

Taylor gave him a sour look.

"Or maybe stolen," Naughware said.

"Exactly, now you're thinking," Taylor said. "Run it through local, state, and federal robbery databases, and if you get a hit, you can pursue it as a stolen property case. That's outside the scope of the federal murder investigation, and it gives you local legal justification to pursue."

Naughware grinned. “Old man, you just earned lunch.”

“Damn straight,” Taylor said. “Now, pay the tab and cross your fingers. If this pans out, you go teach those sons-a-bitching feds a lesson that they don’t mess with the Abaddon PD.”

CHAPTER 8

Naughware felt re-energized when he returned to the precinct.

Keane noticed his enthusiasm as soon as she saw him burst through the office door in a manner suggesting a cat pursuing a mouse.

"Ready for our new case?" she asked when he stopped at his desk to drape his sports coat over the back of his chair.

"A new one?" he asked.

"A south side jewelry store was broken into last night, and the security guard was assaulted and knocked unconscious, but only a handful of items were actually taken," she said. "Could be interesting."

"Maybe later," he replied. "First, I'm headed to Records."

Upon his return from the records storage room, Keane watched as he poured over a mix of physical case files and computer records. Meanwhile, she gathered information to review on their latest assignment before heading out for field interviews.

"Anything interesting there?" she asked.

"Stolen property issue," he said. "Probably nothing serious, but I wanted to wrap it up before we go out on the jewelry case."

She gave him a curious look. "Is that also fresh pickings?"

"Nah, formerly picked," he said, flipping through pages on

a case file.

Her eyes narrowed, and she wondered what he was up to. Instead, she returned to her efforts on the case they were actually assigned.

By late afternoon, the information Naughware had been waiting for still hadn't arrived, so he conceded to going into the field with Keane on the jewelry case.

The south side of Abaddon had been established during the city's founding and, while appearing every bit the oldest portion of the city, it nevertheless had a well-maintained historic district.

Keane eyed the street sign they passed.

"Ascension Avenue?" she asked. "You have the weirdest street names in this town."

"Seriously? The town is named Abaddon," Naughware said. "Of course, the founders were a bunch of spiritual and religious nuts, so that may have as much to do with it as anything."

"Oh, then you fit right in here, don't you?" she asked with a smug expression.

"You're hilarious," Naughware said as he parked their vehicle at the front of the exclusive shop called Karatopia Jewelry.

Upon entering, Naughware was surprised not to see any broken glass or crime tape. However, he did see a security guard, sitting on a nearby stool, intently watching them.

A woman standing at the jewelry case looked over at them while talking to a gentleman wearing a business suit. A younger male clerk walked over to greet them.

"Welcome to Karatopia," he said. "Are you two looking for something special today? Perhaps wedding sets?"

Keane gave him a near-horrified look as she withdrew her badge. "Are you kidding me? Not even on a dare."

Naughware gave her a dry sidelong look before holding up his badge and addressing the clerk.

"Detectives Naughware and Keane, Robbery-Homicide," he said. "Your shop was robbed last night?"

"Yeah, um, perhaps you should speak to—" the clerk said.

"Oh, detectives, over here," the woman standing to their left said while motioning them over to her.

"Gemma Stephens," she said. "I'm the proprietor. This gentleman is Mr. Dwight Peevish. He's with the insurance company."

The man nodded politely. "Detectives."

"We've read the police report you filed, but it would be helpful if you could describe everything from the beginning," Keane said.

"Yes, well, when I came in this morning around nine o'clock to open the store, I was shocked to find the alarm turned off and my security guard lying unconscious on the floor," she said. "Of course, I immediately called the police. They left a couple of hours ago, in fact. This afternoon, I finished inventorying our complete lines of merchandise but still only found a pair of items missing."

"Is he the security guard who was injured?" Keane asked, pointing to the nearby guard.

"Oh, no. He's one of our daytime security," Stephens said. "Benny Hilliard was the guard on duty last night. Nasty business. The poor man's face was all bloodied and swollen, and he's still in the hospital for observation."

"Are you certain that all the doors were secured after closing time?" Keane asked.

"I should say so," Stephens said. "Detective, we lock the store at closing and set the alarm, even with on-site security throughout the night."

"I see. So, did the alarm go off during the robbery?" Keane asked.

Stephens frowned. "Erm, not exactly."

"But wasn't it a forced entry?" Keane asked.

"Well—yes, but—"

"But?" Keane asked.

"Benny said he never heard the alarm actually go off," Stephens said.

"Uh-huh," Keane said. "So, the door wasn't actually

forced, then?"

"Well, it wasn't damaged, but there were nicks on it, as if it were picked or something," Stephens said. "Though I'd think Benny would have seen or heard that taking place, which seems odd. He's a very reliable, long-term employee, you see. Of course, if he had blacked out as he said—"

"Wait, blacked out?" Keane asked.

"Yes, before he was taken to the hospital, Benny said something about blacking out and then waking to find intruders inside the shop," Stephens said. "That's when he said he was assaulted by them."

"I see," Keane said, furiously scribbling on her notepad.

Naughware listened, though after everything that had happened over the Bouquet Corral case, he was less than enthused about their current robbery case.

Sounds like more of an inside job, he thought. *Keane should be able to cut her teeth on this well enough.*

He casually scanned the arrays of rings, watches, and pendants on that side of the store.

"Benny has worked for us for many years and has even thwarted numerous attempted thefts during that time," Stephens said. "He has a distinguished military record, as well. I can't think of more to tell you at the moment."

"That's fine for now. Thank you," Keane said. "Naturally, we'll interview Mr. Hilliard at the hospital in the near future."

Stephens nodded. "Of course. Though the entire affair was strange. I found everything in place initially, or so I thought once I scanned our normal inventory repository," she said. "That changed once I looked in the special collections holding safe."

"Special collections?" Keane asked.

"Yes, it's where the non-traditional or exclusive items are kept," Stephens said. "It's double-locked with its own multi-sensor alarm."

"What was missing?" Keane asked.

"Here, let me show you," Stephens said, arranging color photographs on the countertop before her. "These are both one-of-a-kind items."

"Oh, my," Keane said.

When Naughware looked up to see Keane's surprised expression, he returned to where she stood. Mr. Peevish quickly gave way to him and stepped aside.

Naughware attention darted downward at the photos, which comprised a bracelet affixed with a gold dragon wrapped around a red gem, and a gold ring with a scary-looking face with black gems for eyes emblazoned atop it.

"Where did those come from?" Naughware asked.

"The wrist bracelet is gold with red rubies. Definitely Chinese, and documented to be from the time of the Xia Dynasty," Stephens said. "I have my own doubts about the era, especially given some usual markings on the piece, though I can't be certain without further research."

Keane and Naughware raised their eyebrows in unison.

"The ring is yellow gold with black hematite eyes, and documented as Turkish," Stephens said. "While not formally classified to a particular era, I'd venture Ottoman Empire."

"Documentation aside, your own assessment of these pieces sounds remarkably well-informed. If you don't mind me asking, how is it you're so knowledgeable?" Keane asked.

"I'm a former archeologist and was assistant curator of antiquities at the Newcastle University Museum in England," Stephens said.

"And now you're running a jewelry store in Abaddon?" Naughware asked.

"Detective, I don't care what you've seen in the movies," she said. "While curating antiquities is fascinating, jewelry is a far more lucrative business."

Keane and Naughware exchanged glances.

"More money in jewelry than antiquities," Naughware said. "Imagine."

"Yeah, I heard her," Keane said, quickly returning her attention to Stephens. "Estimated value of the merchandise stolen?"

"Both items only just arrived but were prepaid prior to

conveyance," Stephens said. "Owner transfer was scheduled for later this week, in fact."

Keane's eyebrows rose. "Value?"

"Together, in excess of ten million dollars," Peevish replied.

"Woah," Keane said.

That caught Naughware's interest, and he leaned across the counter at Stephens. "*Who* were the buyers?"

The woman appeared taken aback by his directness. "W-well, the ring was purchased by Joseph Fyre and the arm bracelet by Luna McDoom."

Naughware frowned.

"You said, *Fyre* and *McDoom*?" Keane asked.

"Tell you all about them later," Naughware said. "If you like power and intrigue, you'll love them."

Keane gave Naughware a wan look and returned her attention to the proprietor. "Ms. Stephens, why don't you show us the safe where the items were stolen from."

"Certainly," she said. "This way."

Keane followed Stephens and Peevish into the back room while Naughware stared down at the jewelry photos.

"You're both rather dire-looking, aren't you?" he muttered while removing his smartphone from his pocket to take quick photos of the images. "In fact, you match up nicely with your prospective owners."

His phone buzzed, and he read the text message.

Your report is ready. - AW

***

On the drive back to the precinct, Naughware remained silent, deep in thought.

"You awake over there?" Keane asked. "Since you're driving, I hope so."

"Hm," he said. "Yep, awake."

"You giving me the silent treatment now?" she asked.

"Nah," he said. "We're good, I suppose."

"I'll settle for polite and professional for now," she said. "But Naughware, we're far from good."

He recalled what Taylor had said to him at lunch and had to crack a smile over that. "Well, you're not wrong there."

She looked over at him. "Listen, I know you had your heart set on that Bouquet Corral case," she said. "But that's off-the-rails-strange for a homicide, in my opinion. I'm craving a little normality again, so this jewelry theft is more my speed. And there could be interesting angles to it."

"Mm."

"Now, you want to tell me about these McDoom and Fyre characters?" Keane asked. "With names like that, they've got to be keepers."

"Two of Abaddon's elite founding families," he said.

"Just how many founding families does this place have?"

"Quite a few," he said. "And, often enough, too many."

"I see."

"These two are of the powerful sort, too," he said. "Moreover, I'm fairly certain they're not going to be happy that their jewelry was stolen."

She sighed and shook her head. "Great. You know, Naughware, I think you're just a crap-load of bad luck for me."

He chuckled. "I hope you don't mind, but I have to make a stop on our way back to the office."

Upon their return to the precinct, Naughware carefully cradled a sub sandwich wrapped tightly in butcher-block paper as he walked down the hall in the direction of the records room. He anxiously anticipated what he would discover.

He noticed one of the CSIs from the warehouse crime scene, Patti Drew, walking toward him, and he stopped her before she passed by.

"Hi, Patti," he said. "What brings you back over to south side?"

"Picking up evidence for testing," she said, holding up a small black specimen case.

"Say, do you know if the lab ever figured out what those packages of white powder contained at the Bouquet Corral?"

She frowned. "Yeah, some pretty weird stuff."

"Oh?" he asked. "Like what?"

"25C-NBOMe, but with some strange additives," she said.

He shook his head. "*What?*"

"It's a psychedelic drug, derived from the psychedelic phenethylamine 2C-C by substitution on the amine with a 2-methoxybenzyl group," she said.

"Impressive," he said. "But really not helpful."

"On the street, they commonly call it N-bomb or Smiles."

"Oh," he said. "Okay, I may have heard of that, after all."

"Anytime," she said. Then her expression brightened. "Oh, yeah. And someone said you actually tasted it on the scene. As in, dipped your finger in it."

His expression soured. "Had the crappiest bitter taste ever."

"Idiot move, Naughware. And, just so you know, users usually snort it," she said with a chuckle before continuing her way down the hall.

He spun on his heels and reached out to gently grasp her elbow. "Hey, hey, one more thing."

"Yeah?"

"You said there were additives in it," he said.

She adopted a perplexed expression. "Yep, freaky level stuff … human bone powder, reptile bone powder, and ground rose thorn."

His eyes narrowed. "*Human bone powder?* What for?"

She shook her head. "Beats the crap outta me. It's one thing to cut a substance with something neutral, like talc or flour, to bulk it up and stretch it. It's something entirely twisted to do what they did; though it wouldn't have affected the 25C-NBOMe's properties any."

"Strange enough," he said. "Anything like that ever turn up before?"

"N-bomb? Sure," she said. "But those additives? Not in Abaddon … not that I've ever heard of, anyway. I have read that additives like bone powder was used in some ancient rituals."

"Okay, thanks," he said. "Pretty weird, eh?"

"No doubt," she said. "Good luck to the feds on that, right?"

He matched her mischievous expression. "Yep, it's their nightmare now."

As soon as he turned around from her, his expression sobered as he hastened his way down the hallway.

* * *

Naughware placed the wrapped sandwich atop the desk of the records clerk, who looked at it with anticipation.

"How do you feel about an early dinner, Anastasia?" he asked. "Turkey and bacon club, just as you like it."

"Well, well, my TGIF just got even better," she said, looking up at him. "Naughware, you are always so sweet on me."

"Because I appreciate you and all you do," he said with a warm expression.

She smiled while handing him a manila folder. "Final ballistics report on the Bouquet Corral case. Fresh from the lab."

"That was epic levels of fast," Naughware said.

"Must have worked around the clock specially for the feds," she said. "And, most importantly, I never handed it to you."

"Oh, thank you, dear lady," he said.

"It's a copy, so no need to return it," she said.

He leaned against a nearby unoccupied desk while she unwrapped her sandwich.

"Don't you be reading that in here, honey," she said.

"Oh, sorry," he said, lurching forward and heading for the door.

He went directly to his desk and looked around to make sure nobody was watching him before opening the folder and reading.

A sense of hope welled inside him.

"Back in the game," he murmured.

CHAPTER 9

On Naughware's evening drive to his apartment, he felt so encouraged that he didn't even mind the traffic jam that he was stuck in for twenty minutes.

His phone rang, and he smiled when he read the caller ID.

"Hello, Monk," he said. "Good news, I hope."

"I've got a hit on your missing woman," Thaddeus Prescott said. "I have it on good authority that the lady was seen at this location multiple times over the past couple of weeks."

"That's great," Naughware said.

"And if I were you, I'd go there *right now*."

"All, right. Keep your pants on," Naughware said. "Where exactly?"

He reached for a blank pad on his console and started scribbling.

"You're kidding," he said with exasperation. "Where the hell is *that* at?"

"You do realize you can Google it, right?" Prescott asked wryly.

Within the hour, Naughware drove to the far north side of town and pulled into the parking lot of a place he'd never been to, much less ever heard of.

He stared up at the gaudy purple neon sign prominently

placed at roof level.

"The Velvet Taco," he said. "Bar and Taqueria?"

At first, he started to get out of his car, but then stopped. He reached into his jacket pocket and withdrew his earbuds, slipped them into place, and selected random on his player.

An odd-sounding, but peppy, tune played, and he looked down at the player's display.

Wall of Voodoo: Mexican Radio.

"Oh, you're hilarious," he said. "Where do you get these songs from?"

He shook his head as he walked across the parking lot toward the entrance as the song continued.

* * *

Detective Keane was relieved when the work day had finally ended. She felt tired, and her feet ached, but she was happy to be home.

Her evening got even better when she discovered that she had special dinner plans out on the town for the evening.

At the restaurant, Keane smiled and stared across the table at the one person who managed to steal her heart.

"Thank you, baby," she said, reaching out to hold hands. "After the day I've had, you can't imagine how wonderful it is to be here with you."

"Tell me all about your day, Lesha."

Keane paused long enough to sip the cold margarita that had just been placed before her.

"Oh, that's so good," she said, momentarily closing her eyes. "Everyone's heard horror stories about being saddled with a nightmare partner, but I've got to tell you, I'm suddenly the poster child for it."

"Maybe you just need to get to know him better."

"I tell you, Naughware's a complete nut case," Keane said.

"He can't be all that bad, can he?"

"Bad? I mean, certifiable cray bucknutty," Keane said.

"Cray buck-what?"

"Look…at first, he just seemed quirky," Keane said, shaking her head. "But the man practically seeks out all things mystical for leads in cases. Honestly, after only two days, I'm already thinking about requesting a partner reassignment."

"But, Lesha, you've only just started."

"I know," Keane said. "It might not look good to ask for reassignment, but I'm thinking there's just no fixing this. Come to think of it, one of his prized contacts claims to be a psychic. The guy said the weirdest thing to me today, and almost had me doubting my own good sense."

"A psychic? Oh, that sounds intriguing. What did he say?"

Before answering, Keane felt as if someone was standing behind her. She quickly turned around in her seat.

"Keane? I thought that was you sitting over here," Naughware said. "What are the odds?"

Keane's shoulders stiffened, and her expression soured.

"Me? I was here first," she countered. "What in God's name are *you* doing *here*, Naughware?"

"Well, I—" he said. "Er, tacos?"

Her eyes narrowed. "Tacos? Do you have any idea what sort of place you've walked into?"

He gestured grandly. "It's a bar and taqueria, or so the sign outside says."

Keane chuckled. "Well, forgive me, but you just don't seem like the sort of guy who knows his way around a *taco*."

"Hey, I like tacos," he said.

"So, I'm betting this is your new partner?" the woman sitting across the table from Keane asked.

Keane groaned. "Naughware, this is Brooke McDonough," she said. "She's my SO."

He stepped past Keane's chair to gently grasp and shake the woman's hand. "Pleasure to meet you, Brooke."

Then he turned back to Keane and frowned. "Wait, SO? Your sobriety officer?"

"*Significant other*, fool," she said, squinting at him. "Were you dropped as a child?"

"Oh, sorry," he said. "And yeah, maybe one or twice … or, so I'm told. Though I was assured that both times were accidents."

Brooke stifled a laugh.

"Don't encourage him," Keane said to her before returning her attention to Naughware. "Did you even bother to look around this place first?"

Everything was beginning to take shape in his mind. "Oh, I'm getting the sense that it's 'ladies' night,' right?"

"Naughware, I'm pretty much betting every night here is ladies' night," she said dryly.

He took a moment to scan the room and took stock of all the women who appeared to be mostly paired off with each other. However, he did finally spot two men sitting together … and kissing.

"Yeah," he said. "Ah, *tacos*."

"You're an idiot," Keane said.

"*Sweetie,*" Brooke said. "Too strong."

"Dear, you don't understand, this guy specializes in stretching patience," Keane said before looking at him. "Honestly, tacos, Naughware."

Brooke gave Keane a hard look. "And somebody else might not be getting a taco tonight, either, wearing that attitude."

Keane's cheeks flushed, and she fell silent.

Brooke stood up and gave Keane a cool look. "I'm going to the ladies' room, and I do hope things have simmered down by the time I return."

Keane and Naughware watched her walk away.

"Of all the places for you to walk into," Keane said, massaging her temples.

"Yeah, a weird coincidence on a grand scale, don't you think?" he asked.

"Not as weird as seeing you here tonight," she said. "At least Brooke and I are equipped for it."

Naughware adopted an unimpressed expression.

"And thank you for killing the Friday-night mood with my girl," she said.

"Look, Keane, sorry to crash your party," he said. "But I seriously wasn't expecting to see *you* here."

"Seriously?" she asked. "You don't know me."

He nodded. "True enough, it seems."

"Wait a minute," she said. "Precisely, who the hell were you expecting to see?"

"Just following a lead," he said.

Her eyes narrowed. "A lead," she said. "Please tell me you're not still working the Bouquet Corral case."

"Actually, a stolen property case," he said.

"And to think, I thought we were working a jewelry robbery case," she said.

"You could say I'm doing this one on the side," he said.

Naughware turned around and scanned the faces in the room. He stopped at one in particular.

"Holy crap," he said, spinning around to face Keane.

"What?" Keane asked.

"The woman in the back of the room to the right," he said. "Correct me if I'm wrong, but she looks a helluva lot like FBI SAIC Denise Warwick."

Brooke returned to her seat. "Looks like things are much calmer, I'm happy to say."

Keane discreetly looked in the direction Naughware had indicated and then stared adoringly over at her girlfriend. "Yep, sure does."

"Sure does?" he asked. "You mean Warwick, or Brooke?"

Brooke frowned. "Who's Warwick?"

"Naughware, sit down," Keane said before turning to Brooke. "Sweetie, Warwick's an FBI agent we met today."

"Wow, she's into tacos, too?" Brooke asked. "Small world."

Naughware took a seat beside Keane and hunkered down slightly to block Warwick's view of him.

"You were looking for Warwick on a stolen property

case?" Keane asked dubiously.

"No, but it's just as interesting a development," he said, peering around Keane. "She looks like she's waiting for someone."

"Yeah, but who were *you* expecting to find?" she asked.

He gave her a furtive look. "Maybe Jenny Vance?"

Keane stared daggers at him.

"Look, the revolver was flagged on the final ballistics report as stolen," he said.

"You saw the final report? What part of the term 'federal investigation' confuses you?" Keane asked. "You could get written up, suspended, or even fired, over this."

"Technically, I'm running down a perpetrator in stolen property," he said. "It's about justice for the woman who owned the revolver."

"What justice?" she asked. "And precisely what woman?"

"Sue Blevins," he said. "Or was it Blevings?"

Keane sighed. "Why can't you just let this go like the rest of us? I'm more than ready to go in a different direction for the time being."

Naughware clenched his jaw and stared back at her. "You don't get it, do you?"

"Look, I'm trying to understand you here," she said. "Help me … meet me half way."

Naughware considered matters and gathered his thoughts.

"You know, at first it was just about pride," he said. "Not wanting to give a big case up to the feds."

Keane nodded as Brooke scooted her chair closer and leaned in to hear better.

"But then there's the drugs they found," he said, eyebrows raised. "And things feel … wrong," he said with a distant look in his eyes as he rubbed his chin between thumb and finger.

"What drugs?" Keane asked. "You mean, that pile of whatever we found at the scene?"

"Yeah, only remember there was also a crateful of it beside the table," he said. "That 'whatever' was something I can't even recall, but its street name is Smiles or N-bomb."

"Okay," Keane said, nodding. "I've heard of that. Pretty bad stuff. Hallucinogenic, right?"

"Right," he said. "Only this stuff had additives in it."

Keane's brows rose. "Such as?"

Naughware noticed Brooke's intense expression and he deliberately paused for effect. "Human bone powder, serpent bone powder, and ground rose thorn."

"What?" Keane demanded.

"Eww," Brooke said, making a sour face.

"That's twisted shit right there," Keane said. "What's all that supposed to do?"

Naughware shrugged. "Not sure yet. But between that, the warnings from The Monk, and an unexpected conversation with a mobster named Skeeter Rowe at Stringfellow's—"

"You met with a mobster?" Keane asked.

"Oo, who's The Monk?" Brooke asked.

"Tell you later, sweetie," Keane said, lightly touching her arm. "Mobster, Naughware?"

"Yeah, he took me aside at my birthday dinner," he said. "Apparently, another powerful mover and shaker, Midas Hyde, has interests in the Bouquet Corral shootout. The Hydes are another founding family, you see."

"Again with the powerful family names today. And you're just now telling me about this one?" Keane asked with a penetrating look. "Some partner you are."

"Baby, getting strong again," Brooke warned.

He held up his hand. "Nah, Brooke. I actually deserved that one."

"You're damn right, you do," Keane said. "Partners don't keep shit like that from each other."

"So, you're saying we're still partners, then?" he asked, brows arched.

"Would you like something to drink, sir?" interrupted

the waitress who had stopped by the table. "And are you ladies about ready for fresh margaritas?"

"Oh, definitely," Keane said, alternating pointing between hers and Brooke's glasses.

"I'll just have what they're having," Naughware said.

"Coming right up," the waitress said.

Keane gave him a sidelong look. "Margaritas *and* tacos? Aren't you just full of surprises tonight."

Naughware ignored her and instead peered around her to check on Warwick.

"Damn it," he said, standing from his seat. "Warwick bolted."

* * *

Naughware and Keane both walked through the restaurant, and he even walked twice around the building and through the parking lot, but they found no trace of Agent Warwick. They also consulted the manager on duty to review security camera footage, but Warwick had gone to particular trouble to sit at a table outside of clear camera viewing.

When they returned to Brooke, she was eagerly delving into a guacamole appetizer.

"Well, that cinches it. No big break tonight," Naughware said, plopping down onto *one of the* table's empty chairs. He reached out to the appetizer platter and used a tortilla chip to shovel some guacamole.

"Still … Warwick," Keane said, staring into her margarita. "That's something more to go on."

"Yep. Definitely unexpected," Naughware said, munching on another chip. "Interesting that The Monk received word from one of his contacts that Jenny had been seen here multiple times in the past couple of weeks. Makes me wonder if Warwick was part of that mix, too."

"I thought the feds just arrived on scene?" Keane asked.

Naughware shrugged. "Maybe, maybe not. At this point, anything's possible."

"Speaking of contacts, that Monk of yours must have some reach," Keane said with a frown. Then she recalled what he had told her when he held her hand earlier that morning, and she wondered if there wasn't more to the man than she had first thought.

"It's too coincidental that Warwick would happen to show up some place somewhere Jenny had been seen," Naughware said.

"You think Warwick was here looking for Vance, too?" Keane asked.

"Yeah, perhaps," he said, deep in thought. "But maybe not for the same reason."

"Surely, the FBI has access to a lot of informants," Keane said. "Who knows, maybe even men like Thaddeus Prescott."

Brooke adopted a puzzled expression.

"Prescott; he's The Monk," Naughware said to her.

"And we are going to stop calling that man The Monk," Keane said.

"But it sounds so mysterious," Brooke said, wide-eyed. "This is better than the movies."

Keane shook her head and looked up at the ceiling, to which Brooke poked her shoulder.

"Hey, be nice," Brooke said.

"Oh, I'll be real nice later, sweetie," Keane told her with a mischievous expression.

"Mm-hm," Brooke said.

Naughware grinned.

"Well, it looks as if we're still in the dark almost as much as we were when you came in here tonight," Keane said.

"Maybe not," Naughware said.

"Oh?"

"We know that Agent Warwick is still hanging around town," he said. "Which suggests that maybe Jenny Vance is, as well. And if Jenny's been seen here recently, perhaps there's more to the case than a mere drug deal gone bad."

"Hm," Keane said. "Let's talk about this more Monday

morning. For now, it's my date night."

"Monday?" Naughware asked. "I thought maybe we'd meet up at the office tomorrow morning. Remember? Vigoda said to get ready for overtime and weekends."

Keane gave him a dirty look. "Uh, I don't think so. That was the Corral case. Our active case is the jewelry heist, and I don't recall hearing any orders to work weekends on it. Besides, Brooke and I already have plans."

"Ugh, some plans," Brooke said. "Still unpacking from our move here."

Keane looked at Brooke warily. "Baby, we don't give up to others about our plans."

"Fine," Naughware said. "We'll talk first thing Monday morning, then."

He stood to leave and gave his regards, but Brooke urged him to stay, and even Keane reluctantly nodded her assent.

They ate dinner together, and with the help of Brooke, managed to talk about topics other than the job or their caseload. At least the conversation was light-hearted.

In the end, Naughware thought perhaps there was a sliver of hope for both he and Keane. He only hoped that extended to the Jenny Vance case, as well.

CHAPTER 10

Naughware began his Saturday morning continuing his research into the Jenny Vance case.

Though officially pulled from the case, it didn't keep him from leaking word to some key underground resources that he wanted a meeting with one of the city's repudiated mobsters, Decebal "The Lion" Lungu.

He thought perhaps there was a way to justify his boon by looking into two cases at once; one official, one less so. Unfortunately, by early afternoon and despite his efforts, he had arrived at a bit of an impasse on either, and wasn't sure how to proceed until one of his resources panned out to contact Lungu.

His own sense of urgency aside, he couldn't help feeling like he was running out of time. For all he knew, it might be too late to find Jenny, who may have already fled town.

While eating lunch at a deli near his apartment, he received a text message from Thomas.

Don't forget poker night or your dish.

"Damn," he said, having forgotten about Thomas' monthly poker night gathering.

He stopped by a bodega on the way back to his apartment to pick up some groceries before preparing a baked macaroni and cheese casserole for Thomas' evening event.

While cooking, he listened to the new alt-J song on his player, and tried to divine further meaning. His thoughts soon turned again to how differently he felt since his birthday on Thursday.

As surreal and bizarre as the timing of his digital player's music for crime scenes and personal insights, he could scarcely believe the new tune could have anything to do with the subtle changes he was feeling inside him.

Yet, its appearance was undeniably suspicious.

He mulled over the eleven-year-old message engraved on the back of his player.

Happy Birthday, Peter -- Music is a doorway to your soul.

The memories of countless Sunday morning sermons from Thomas about souls flashed in his mind.

"My soul," he said.

The problem was, he simply wasn't certain that a soul was real. Rather, over time, he had come to believe it was merely a concept conjured by mystics and believers who yearned for something eternal in themselves, something that existed beyond their physiological mortality.

Nobody liked the idea that they existed only in finite terms and for only a brief period in time.

Despite his Judeo-Christian upbringing, he didn't view the world narrowly from that perspective. He was no stranger to diverse cultures. During his youth, he had traveled outside the country both alone and with Thomas or other church parishioners; mostly on pilgrimages to help destitute people living in areas of Central America. However, during his four years in the Army, he had also experienced a tour of duty overseas in the Middle East, where cultural diversity and religious tumult went hand in hand.

His experiences there taught him everything he needed to know about the basest nature of humankind, as well as humanity's potential for both compassion and extreme violence.

And if there was one thing he realized during his journeys around the world, it was that people clung to all manner of beliefs and mysticisms.

Many people spent their lives searching for answers to their existence, their purpose, and hopefully, an afterlife.

Naughware wasn't sure the afterlife even existed; no matter the religion, faith, or fervent belief system by which it was measured or informed.

And yet, he held in his hand a complete mystery wrapped in a little metal shell. It was merely a small device, but one that threatened to uproot his former stoicism about all things supernatural.

The problem was, even if he believed that small device held some ounce of cosmic truth or power within its construction, it left him just as confused and befuddled as the rest of the human race about what was true, much less plausible.

He was dislodged from his musings by the smell of burning macaroni.

"Shit!" he exclaimed as he rushed into the kitchen.

* * *

Naughware juggled a casserole in one arm and a paper sack filled with beer in his grasp while pressing the doorbell at Thomas' house with an elbow.

Zelda Woosley, Associate Pastor of the Ascension Episcopal Church, answered the door.

"Peter, you made it just in time," she said, holding the door open for him. "Do you want any help?"

"Nope, just fine," he said. "Thanks, Zelda."

Naughware made his way toward the kitchen, which was filled with people who were practically extended family to him and Thomas.

Rabbi Isaac Horowitz stood at the counter chopping fresh vegetables. Standing beside the oven, Father "Chance" Kleisterman, head clergyman at St. Seton's Catholic Church, opened plastic containers and removed foil-covered pans of food.

Zelda's husband, Pat, sliced a brisket atop the counter next to the stove.

Thomas removed flatware from a drawer and looked up at Naughware and grinned. "Ah, my boy," he said. "I was worried you'd be late again."

"Not today, Thomas," Naughware said.

He sat the casserole on one of the few open spaces along the kitchen counters as Zelda took the paper sack from him.

"Everyone, apologies ahead of time," Naughware said. "You'll want to avoid the outer edges of the mac and cheese."

"No worries," Zelda said. "But happy to find these beers are chilled already."

"Of course," Naughware said. "Burned casserole, we can overcome, but who wants warm beer?"

"Germans?" Pat asked with a grin.

"Who cares about beer when I've got a nice bottle of Shiraz already opened and breathing?" Rabbi Horowitz asked.

"You can have your Shiraz," Father Chance said.

"Or, you can have some of each," Thomas said, as he squeezed past Naughware with handfuls of flatware.

"Thomas, ever the diplomat," Horwitz said.

Naughware helped Thomas set the dining room table, and he noticed that his adoptive father kept looking over at him, though he said nothing.

"What?" Naughware asked.

Thomas shrugged. "Not sure. I can't quite put my finger on it, really."

"Finger on what?" Naughware asked, catching Zelda's curious expression as she placed food onto the table and returned to the kitchen.

"Ever since Thursday, you've been in my thoughts," Thomas said.

"Oh?"

Thomas finished setting the places and clasped his hands thoughtfully before him.

Then he looked up at Naughware. "Are you feeling well?"

Naughware frowned. "You're not the first person to ask me that this week."

Thomas arched one brow. "Well, then, what did you reply to anyone else when they asked?"

"I feel remarkably good for the rollercoaster sort of week I've had," Naughware said. "To be honest, since Thursday, I've actually felt unusually energized."

"Hm, perhaps turning thirty-three agrees with you, after all," Thomas said.

"Sure, but what's the difference between thirty-two and thirty-three besides twelve months?" Naughware asked.

Thomas stared at Naughware as he thought about that. "Well, no matter," he said. "I'm just glad you're well. And most of all, I'm happy you were able to come, particularly given the big case you're working on."

"Yeah, about that," Naughware said. "The feds pulled it out from under us yesterday morning."

The sounds of preparation in the kitchen ceased, and Thomas looked up with surprise.

Naughware glanced toward them and saw a host of curious expressions staring back at him as people crowded into the doorway.

"What happened?" Zelda asked.

"Ask the feds," Naughware said.

"The feds took over your case?" Chance asked, snapping his fingers. "Just like that?"

"One of the people killed was an undercover federal agent, and the FBI already had an outstanding operation underway, so they claimed jurisdiction over us," Naughware said. "Of course, there's more to it than that, but I'm really not at liberty to say."

"Sort of a buzzkill, wasn't that?" Pat asked.

"*Pat,*" Zelda said.

The edges of Naughware's mouth upturned slightly. "Well, it was a disappointment, that's for certain."

Thomas regained control of the situation by clapping his hands. "Come now, everyone, let's finish getting the food in here before it gets cold."

Though he hated to admit it, Naughware appreciated the distraction from his investigations, and he enjoyed the company of those gathered around the table.

After dinner, he helped clear the table and assisted Pat at the sink with dishes while the others prepared the cards and poker chips in the other room.

As Naughware dried dishes, his mind returned to mulling over details surrounding the Bouquet Corral case.

"Peter, aren't you playing?" Thomas called from the dining room.

"Helping Pat with the dishes," Naughware said. "Be there soon."

Pat nudged his elbow. "Go on. I've got this."

"Are you sure?" Naughware asked. "You'll never make the game with all this remaining."

"Yes, yes, go," he said. "Besides, Zelda's the poker player between us. I'd just end up losing next week's lunch money."

Naughware grinned and made his way into the dining room.

"Jokers are wild," Thomas said, shuffling the deck. "And everyone must declare which charity effort they're playing for before we begin. I'm for the Abaddon Orphan Children's Network."

Naughware took a seat to Thomas' right, saying, "Mine's the Police Department's Survivors Fund."

"Just so you know, Thomas, you're not going to guilt us into letting you win by picking an especially needy charity," Father Chance said.

"Frankly, you can pick most any charity these days, and you'll find they're all in need," Zelda said. "I'm choosing the church's food pantry."

"Excellent choice," Thomas said.

Small talk ensued among them throughout the first two hands of poker. The first round went to Father Chance, and the second to Zelda. Before the beginning of the third round, Pat finished with the dishes and pulled up a chair beside his wife's.

Halfway through the third hand, Rabbi Horowitz groaned.

"Oh, these cards," he said. "Thomas, your dealer skills are a crime tonight."

"Speaking of crime, Peter," Pat said. "Really tough luck on the Corral case. It's got to be the biggest event in Abaddon since Prohibition."

"Yeah," Naughware said, rearranging the cards in his hand. "Big case. To be honest, I'm still miffed about being pulled off of it."

"What will you do now?" Pat asked.

"My partner and I have already been reassigned to a jewelry store robbery," Naughware said.

"Speaking of your partner, how is Detective Keane doing?" Thomas asked. "How are you two getting along?"

"Keane is doing well enough," Naughware said, removing two cards from his hand and placing them facedown before him. "And we're getting along okay, I suppose. There's some rough edges, but it takes time working in a new partner."

Zelda gave him an onerous look. "I'm sure she feels a similar challenge, as well."

Naughware gave her a long look. "Two cards, if you please."

Thomas dealt two cards to him. "Well, I have faith that God will see both of you through it to a good end."

"Perhaps," Naughware said. "Though, in my experience, God can't fix everything."

"But faith can move mountains," Zelda said.

"Or, we'd like to view the world that way, at least," Naughware said.

Chance looked up from his cards. "What do you mean by that, Peter?"

"Take our game tonight, for example," Naughware said. "The Jokers typically aren't used in card games, and generally, have the smallest value compared to the other cards. But tonight, Jokers are wild, which means they can be anything we want them to be. They can be as powerful as you need them to be."

"Okay, but honestly Peter, I don't see what that has to do with God and the nature of one's faith," Thomas said, shaking his head.

"Tonight, the Joker can be powerful because we decreed it to be," Naughware said. "We imbued the Joker with special abilities and influence above all other cards. Yet, it's just another card in the deck."

"So, you're implying that God is the Joker in life's deck of cards?" Rabbi Horowitz asked. "And we simply imbue him with power and influence?"

"Not strictly," Naughware said. "Though it seems that quite a few people approach God that way."

"Or, are you saying that parishioners only imbue God with power because they choose to worship him?" Zelda asked.

Naughware's attention shifted to her. "Well, not exactly, but that's a really interesting perspective," he said. "If God even exists, that is."

Thomas placed his cards facedown and massaged his temples with his fingertips. "Oh, Peter. Not this again."

"What?" Naughware asked. "We're just grown adults having a conversation over a friendly game of poker."

"Thomas, let the man speak," Chance said. "Personally, I find these sorts of debates invigorating."

Thomas took a quick swig of beer. "Well, you're a saint for saying so."

"Look," Naughware said. "I'm not saying there's anything wrong or misguided with someone having faith in God and seeking solace in that. I'm just not convinced it's all actually real."

"Faith or God?" Chance asked.

Thomas looked up sharply at Naughware, hesitant over his response.

"Oh, I'm not disputing a person's convictions or

beliefs," Naughware said. "Nor a person's commitment to faith."

"Well, I should hope not," Thomas said, somewhat relieved. "You were raised in the Church, for goodness' sake."

Naughware ignored him. "I'm just not convinced that God is real."

Thomas slapped his cards facedown onto the table and groaned.

Rabbi Horowitz chuckled. "Oh, well if that's your only concern, you're in good company, I can tell you."

"Isaac, please," Thomas said. "Don't encourage him."

"Now, Thomas," Horowitz said. "Our churches and synagogues are filled with those who fervently want to believe, who may even practice their faith, but still have their innermost doubts. It's a perfectly normal experience in one's journey of faith."

"The struggle to gain, and hold onto, one's faith is precisely why fellowship among fellow believers is so important," Chance said. "The flock struggles together, encouraging each other."

Thomas nodded. "Well, that's true enough, I suppose."

"Peter," Horowitz said. "Tell me, why it is you doubt God's existence?"

Zelda and Chance looked at Naughware with anticipation, while Thomas folded his arms before him and merely appeared livid with the whole affair.

Naughware stalled by taking a swig of beer. "Well, admittedly, I've seen my share of strange, sometimes inexplicable, things over the years."

Thomas' eyes narrowed.

"I've seen inspired acts of kindness from people," Naughware said. "And I've seen some of the worst that humanity can demonstrate against itself. But I have yet to see anything—feel anything—that convinces me that God is real."

He looked at the faces around the table and stopped

when he met Thomas' penetrating stare.

Horowitz nodded with a thoughtful expression, folding his arms before him. "Fair enough," he said. "And again, that's something I've heard said many times before."

"Peter, I'm curious about those so-called inexplicable things you referenced," Chance said. "If not God, then to whom or what do you attribute those things?"

Naughware considered the priest's question at length as each of them stared at him. His mind revisited a number of key issues such as the Nowhere Zone, his strange digital player, and the odd conversations he'd had with The Monk during the past couple of days.

Unfortunately, each of those things wasn't anything that he could easily confide in them, including Thomas, without his own sanity being called into question. And as for the Nowhere Zone, something dark and dreadful inside himself urged that he dare not reveal that to them, either.

Finally, Naughware leaned back in his chair. "That's the million-dollar question, isn't it?"

Everyone around him fell strangely quiet, though Horiwitz appeared contemplative.

Naughware frowned. "Or perhaps it stems from something altogether new."

"Something new?" Chance asked. "What 'new' could there be after thousands of years of well-established religious study?"

"Father Chance is right, my boy," Horowitz said. "There is little not already written about. Why, Judaism was founded over 3,500 years ago, largely predating both Christianity and Islam, of course."

"You just had to point that out, didn't you?" Chance asked him with a wry expression.

The corners of Horowitz's eyes crinkled as he smiled with amusement. "It is what it is," he said with a shrug.

"Ah, but there are more ancient religions out there than even Judaism," Naughware said.

Horowitz's expression sobered.

"Pagan religions are a fiction. Figments of the imagination," Thomas said. "There is but one true God."

"And yet, didn't the believers of those long-dead religions also feel the same fervent belief in their own deities?" Naughware asked. "What might humanity think of today's active religions another thousand or more years in the future? Maybe they'll see us today as pursuing figments of our imaginations."

"I'm pleased not to see such a future," Thomas said. "If what you propose may even come to pass."

He stared back at Naughware, wondering how the young man had fallen into such doubt about faith and God. He thought he had firmly seated and fostered the tenants of Christianity as he raised him from infancy.

Naughware, in turn, wondered what the man, who was like a father to him, was thinking at that moment. "Not trying to upset you, Thomas."

Thomas merely nodded as he pursed his lips.

Horowitz and Chance traded sharp looks with each other and then discreetly scanned the faces of those around them.

"Well, that was invigorating," Zelda said. "Now, whose turn was it again?"

***

Another hour had passed, and as Naughware studied the new hand of cards before him, he received a cryptic text message from an unknown number.

716 Mellett Avenue 11:15 p.m. Alone. Lungu

He noticed that it was already nearly ten thirty.

"Sorry, everyone," he said, laying his cards face down. "I've gotta run."

"C'mon, Peter," Zelda said. "It's the last hand, and I haven't taken all of your money yet."

Everyone, except Thomas, chuckled or laughed.

"What is it?" Thomas asked.

"Just working a case, Thomas," Naughware said. "Might be the break I've been waiting for."

"At this hour?" Thomas asked. "And it's Saturday."

"Every day's solve-a-crime day," Naughware said, picking up the small amount of his cash that remained and stuffing it into his front jeans pocket.

He said quick goodbyes and grabbed his jacket off the couch on his way out to his car.

While he might not risk missing a good contact, he also wasn't either careless or stupid. On his drive home, he considered calling Keane.

However, she hardly seemed in favor of his freelancing efforts. Thus far, she had behaved as a by-the-book sort of investigator, which strongly conflicted with his own style. At least, for most of the time. Procedures had their place, he conceded.

Instead, he called his former partner, Evan Taylor.

Unfortunately, Taylor didn't pick up, so Naughware left him a voicemail message.

"Hey, Taylor," he said. "Listen, just in case something goes sideways tonight, there's something I need you to know …"

CHAPTER 11

A quarter before eleven o'clock, Naughware parked along the street directly across from a large trucking repair facility on Mellett Avenue.

He watched as a lone man wearing a hoodie leaned against the brick wall beside the building's main entrance.

Naughware exited his vehicle and took a slow look up and down the largely deserted avenue before walking across the street toward the man.

He stopped two feet from the guy, whose face was hidden in the shadow of his hoodie.

"I'm Naughware."

The fellow chuckled. "Man, around here most everybody knows who you are. You badge types may as well have a sign hanging around your necks."

"Ah, the price of local celebrity."

The man stared at him. "You're early."

"I'm eager," Naughware said. "Where's Lungu?"

"Just slow your roll," the man said. "He's waiting. Follow me."

Naughware followed him inside the dimly lit shop, which had long since closed down for the day. Yellowish street lighting streamed in through the rows of elevated windows along the length of the shop.

They walked past large tractor trucks in various stages of

maintenance that were arrayed in stalls along both sides of the garage.

Near the back of the establishment, in an empty stall situated between two tractor trucks, stood Decebal "The Lion" Lungu.

He was short of stature, but carried himself like an animal poised to strike out at any moment. And while not afraid of him, Naughware found him somewhat unnerving. The man had a brutal reputation on the street.

No less than five other men sporting automatic weapons were arrayed in positions nearby. Naughware noted that the man in the hoodie stood not far behind him.

Naughware considered the strength of their presence surprising.

"I thought you used the word 'alone' in your text?" he asked.

"That's right," Lungu said in a thick Balkan accent. "For *you* to come alone, not me."

"Well, I just came for information, so I don't know what you're so worried about," Naughware said, spreading his arms wide. "Don't tell me you're worried over a friendly guy like me, Lungu."

Naughware had to hand it to him; the man maintained a poker-quality facial expression.

"Word's out all over town today about you wanting to meet with me," Lungu said. "And I don't crave any publicity right now. What do you want?"

"Can I show you a photo of something?" Naughware asked, slowly reaching into his pocket. "I just want your opinion, if you don't mind."

Some of Lungu's men cocked their weapons.

"Woah, it's just a phone," Naughware said, slowly extracting his smartphone and wagging it side to side.

He pulled up the jewelry photos from Karatopia and extended the phone toward Lungu, who cautiously stepped forward and reached out to take his phone.

"There's a couple of photos there, if you'd just swipe,"

Naughware said.

"You asked me here to look at jewelry?" Lungu asked.

"Sure," Naughware said. "I mean, there's not much going on in this city that you don't know about. I respect that."

Lungu looked up at him with a suspicious expression. "Don't play me for a fool, Naughware. I'm not in the mood."

"No fooling," Naughware said. "Seen either of those pieces around anytime recently?"

Lungu looked back down at the photos before handing the phone back to Naughware.

"Hardly," Lungu said. "That looks like gaudy costume jewelry, just like the tourists bought from street vendors back in Bucharest."

Naughware pocketed his phone. "Aw, well. Worth a try since I was here."

Then he snapped his fingers.

Two of the men leveled their weapons at Naughware.

"Crazy-man, are you trying to get yourself killed tonight?" Lungu asked. "What the hell is your problem?"

"I knew I was forgetting something," Naughware said. "Your trigger-happy friends just reminded me."

"You're certifiable, Naughware," Lungu said, shaking his head.

"Wilky Jean-Lunet, Jose Ramos, and Sonny Blevins."

Lungu's features hardened. "These names … I should know them?"

"Uh-huh," Naughware said. "They're *your* men. They were found dead at the Bouquet Corral warehouse, but I'm fairly sure you already know what I'm talking about."

"Bad luck for them, it seems," he said, shrugging. "But, you see, I am not their keeper. What they do on their own time is their business, no?"

"You want to tell me why it was merely bad luck?"

Lungu stared at him. "In truth? Not really."

As Naughware reached up to scratch the back of his head, the remaining men raised their weapons.

"Punchy bunch you've got here," he said. "Any reason for that?"

"Naughware, you bring a lot of whys in here tonight," Lungu said. "Too many questions can get a man killed."

"Or, are you afraid that so can too many answers?"

Lungu's features appeared frozen in place.

"How about if I said I was just trying to get justice for Jean-Lunet, Ramos, and Blevins?" Naughware asked. "Surely, you'd want that for your dedicated hired hands. Am I right?"

The tension in the air heightened, and a cool, electric-like charge ran through his body, unlike any he had felt before. His mind reeled over the strange sensation.

"Ah, but you don't give the two shits about Wilky, Jose, and Sonny," Lungu said, wagging his forefinger at him.

Naughware paused to steady himself. Fortunately, the moment of disorientation quickly abated.

"Crazy-man, are you even listening to me right now?" Lungu asked. "Maybe you are high on something, yes?"

Naughware refocused his attention on The Lion. "Listen, Lungu, when people turn up dead in my city, I want to know who did it and why. Who they were, or who they might have worked for, doesn't factor into it."

When Lungu glanced over at the men standing to his right, Naughware discreetly flexed his gun hand.

Lungu's gaze fixed back upon Naughware. "Sometimes things go bad, and there are no reasons," he said, shaking his head. "It happens. Life is full of bad surprises, no?"

Naughware considered that. "Okay, tell me something else," he said. "Any reason someone would want to add human bone powder, serpent bone powder, and ground rose thorn to a perfectly good batch of N-bomb?"

He noticed Lungu's right eye twitch.

"How they say? *Bad mojo*," Lungu said. "Me? I'm a simple businessman. I want nothing to do—"

The sound of nearby glass breaking barely preceded Lungu's head exploding in a shower of blood and gore.

* * *

After Lungu's body dropped to the garage floor, there was only a split-second pause, which Naughware used to crouch while drawing his revolver. The barrel had barely cleared his holster before gunfire erupted throughout the room.

He nailed the man directly across from him in the chest as splinters of concrete showered his own face and neck from the impacts of bullets around him.

The booming sounds of large-caliber handguns went off in concert with a host of automatic weapons.

Naughware dropped two more gunmen before realizing that someone else was drawing fire away from him.

The gunfire ceased as Naughware turned to see Evan Taylor standing with a pair of large, smoking black revolvers held aloft, one in each hand.

Both of them scanned the room for a few seconds before Naughware sighted a broken window on the side of the building opposite where Lungu had stood.

"Sniper," Naughware said, pointing to the window.

Taylor hurriedly leaned against the grill of a nearby truck for cover. "Well, don't just stand in the line of fire, numb-nuts!"

Naughware holstered his pistol. "The shooter's long gone by now. They'd have dropped me already if they'd wanted to."

He calmly withdrew his phone from a jacket pocket. "Thanks for the help, Taylor."

"You feeling all right?" Taylor asked. "Lungu was right about one thing. You looked a little out of touch there at the end."

"I'm fine," Naughware said. "I just felt—I don't know, strange for a moment."

His ex-partner took one last look around before settling his big revolvers into twin underarm holsters. "What the hell were you thinking, coming to this by yourself?"

"Who was I supposed to show up with? Keane's definitely not in," Naughware said. "Hell, I'm lucky she's not *turning* me in."

"You could've called me," Taylor said.

"I *did* call you!"

"Yeah, just to leave a message telling me where to find your dead body if things went south," the old man said. "You disappoint me."

Naughware gave him a wary look, but Taylor frowned back at him.

"Oh, shit-can the puppy dog eyes and call dispatch, hero," Taylor said, examining each of the bodies lying around the garage. "I'll be damned. We shot three a piece," he said with a chuckle.

Despite the adrenaline rush or the carnage around him, the corners of Naughware's mouth upturned as he called it in.

CHAPTER 12

It was well after two o'clock Sunday morning before Naughware finished his statement to the responding officers, including Captain Gunderson.

"You can't even take a weekend off, can you, Naughware?" Gunderson asked.

He shrugged.

"Well, I'm glad you're okay," she said. "In the meantime, go home and get some rest. We'll talk more about this on Monday morning."

"I'm a little surprised LT isn't here berating me," Naughware said.

"Oh, I called him," she said. "I told him I'd handle it. Now, head home."

Despite the captain telling him to go home, Naughware only stopped there briefly before spending the better part of Sunday morning and afternoon in the office preparing his report over Saturday evening's shooting.

Of course, he did take the time to let Thomas know what had happened, if only because he preferred to tell the old man himself versus Thomas hearing about it secondhand on the news.

First thing Monday morning, Keane sat at her desk sipping coffee and sorting evidence paperwork while she waited for Naughware to show.

When he walked into the office, everyone just stared at him.

He proceeded over to the coffee pot to fill one of the empty ceramic mugs.

"Hey, some people take the weekend to go fishing, Naughware," Levitt said. "You? You go shoot up the town and leave a pile of dead bodies to clean up. That ain't what 'paint the town red' is supposed to mean."

A detective sitting near Levitt chuckled.

"You're hilarious, Levitt," Naughware said. "So, tell me, how's *the wife*?"

"Hey, fuck you, too," Levitt said.

Naughware sat in his chair nursing his coffee mug and looked over at Keane, who stared back at him.

"Mornin'," he said.

"That's what you have to say to me?" she asked.

"What?"

"I don't recall getting a phone call Saturday night asking to back you up," she said, giving him a suspicious look.

"Hey, I'm respectful of your quality time with Brooke," he said. "Besides, it was a last-minute meeting. And how was I supposed to know it was going to turn into a bloodbath? Hell, it was some sniper who started the whole thing, not me."

She leaned across her desk toward him. "Listen, partners are expected to have each other's backs," she said. "So, I don't get a phone call from you, and what am I left to think? Are we partners or not?"

He sat his mug down atop the desk and stared into it.

"Yeah, I guess I should've called you," he said, sheepishly.

"Damn right you should've," she said. "And you're damned lucky, too. You could've gotten your ass shot to hell and back."

"Maybe. But if I *had* called you, I'm not sure you'd have liked what I wanted to meet with Lungu about," he said. "Aside, of course, from the stolen jewelry … which I actually did inquire about, just for the record."

"Like you care about the Karatopia case," she said, looking up at the ceiling.

He gave her an innocent look. "Hey, I even asked Lungu about both pieces of jewelry. He wasn't impressed."

"Look, I know you're the senior partner, so I'll likely get stuck with the bulk of our paperwork," she said. "But you're actually going to have to put in some legitimate effort to help solve our stolen jewelry case."

"Didn't you hear what I just said? That's what I'm doing," he said. "In fact, I'm working it right now."

"Seriously?" she asked.

He took out his phone and within a few minutes had texted photos of the stolen jewelry items to The Monk and a couple of other street resources.

She watched him with a dubious expression. "Looks to me like you're goofing off on your phone."

"You just might be surprised. I'll have you know I have access to some helpful street contacts," he said. "But speaking of goofing off, I sure enjoyed dinner with you and Brooke on Friday night."

She arched an eyebrow. "It turned out okay, I suppose. Mind you, not what I had in mind when the evening began."

He smiled at that. "You have a beautiful girlfriend," he said. "Brooke's also a real charmer."

"Oh, you best not be daydreaming about my girl," she said.

"Nah," he said. "Just saying."

"Yes, she's quite a lady," Keane said as the hint of a smile formed. "My little piece of sunshine in the world, anyway."

She paused and then looked at him. "You could probably use your own little piece of sunshine, too, you know."

He gave her a wry look and gulped a mouthful of coffee. He doubted there was enough caffeine left on the planet to fully deter the building exhaustion inside him.

"You know, you're awfully chipper for a guy who nearly died Saturday night," she said.

"On the contrary," he said. "I have a new lease on life because of it."

However, he pondered the unusually energized feeling he had. Far from stressing him out, his exploits on Saturday night only reinvigorated his resolve to dig further into the Vance case.

He was convinced there was far more to it than he had first believed.

Keane returned to her paperwork for only a few more minutes before stopping and looking over at him.

"Hey," she said. "You mind telling me something? Why are you having such a hard time moving past the case with Jenny-you-know-who?"

"Fair question," he said. "Too many and too much."

She gave him a perplexed look. "Try again, Captain Cryptic."

He leaned over his desk and lowered his voice. "Too many bodies. Too many unanswered questions. Too many weird clues. And too much interest from the feds, who decidedly don't want the aid of local law enforcement."

She considered his responses.

"The feds have more resources at their disposal, including crossing state and local jurisdictions, as needed," she said. "And they can search street traffic camera footage with facial recognition in most any city."

"Okay," he said. "Except there aren't many street cameras in Abaddon, and even fewer on the south side. And it appears that the conditions surrounding this case may have been active in Abaddon for at least a couple of weeks; maybe even a month, if not more. Given that, why wouldn't you leverage local resources?"

"Maybe they suspect a leak?"

"Hm," he said. "I'll grant you that."

"Of course, if you had something to hide, you'd also want to keep the circle of knowledge to a minimum," she said.

"Also, true," he said.

He strummed the arms of his chair with his fingertips. "Jenny Vance," he said. "This whole case revolves around her."

"Maybe that's because she might be the only person who walked away from that bloodbath," she said.

"Maybe," he said. "But do you remember the pattern of shell casings lying around the warehouse?"

She shrugged. "Sure. Looked a lot like a gunfight gone bad to me."

"Yeah, sure did," he said. "The operative word being *looked*."

"Well, I doubt someone took the time to stage it that way," she said.

He shook his head. "No, that's not what I mean."

"Well," she said, strumming her fingertips against the desk. "Tell me what you mean, then."

"So, I suspect you weren't wrong about a gunfight going bad," he said. "However, the reason for it going wrong feels like more than just a case of greed. Each of the dead bodies represented someone with a reasonable expectation to be there. I can't help wondering who else we're missing. And why."

"Why do I get the feeling that you're a guy who likes conspiracy theories?" she asked.

He leaned back in his chair and began scanning through a handful of case files.

She looked up and frowned. "I've got the Karatopia files here. What are you reading?"

"Ever hear of Sonny Blevins, Jose Ramos, or Wilky Jean-Lunet?" he asked.

She started to shake her head, but then looked at him with disdain. "What sort of question is that for someone to ask me? You know I just started here a few days ago," she said. "So, more to the point, why would I be interested?"

"All three are known associates of the very recently

deceased Decebal 'The Lion' Lungu," he said.

"Oh, no," she said. "Here we go again with the crazy nicknames."

"Street names," he said.

"Okay," she said. "By any chance, are any of them jewel thieves?"

"Nope," he replied. "But all three numbered among the dead at the warehouse."

"Naughware, you and that warehouse."

He paused and watched as Vigoda walked slowly past their desk and then stopped. The Detective Sergeant turned and looked at them.

"So, Naughware," he said. "Heard you had a busy weekend."

"Pretty busy, Sarge," Naughware said.

"In fact, I heard that you're lucky not to be filled full of lead this morning," Vigoda said.

"That about sums it up," Naughware said.

"Now you two have a new robbery case. Jewelry thieves?" Vigoda asked.

"Yep," Naughware said.

"Any leads yet?"

"Working them now," Naughware said.

"You wouldn't, you know, also be working any other cases, would you?" Vigoda asked.

"Me? Nah," he said.

Vigoda looked at Keane.

"I am fully committed to this Karatopia case," she said.

Vigoda nodded. "Good. Keep it that way. And Naughware, try to limit the shootings for now. At least until the brass and Internal Affairs clears you from this latest one."

As the sergeant walked away, Naughware discreetly gave him the middle finger.

"Thanks, Keane," he said.

"Hey, I didn't lie," she said. "I'm solidly focused on the Karatopia case. You should be, too."

He grunted and took a swig of coffee.

She stopped and looked at him. "Naughware, give me one—just one—good reason why I shouldn't march right into the lieutenant's office and tell him you're working a case behind the department's back?"

"C'mon, you wouldn't," he said.

She arched one brow. "I've only known you a couple of days, so I'm not that committed. For that matter, I don't even think I *like* you yet."

He gave her a flat look. "You said one reason. How about if I give you three?"

She stared back at him and waited.

He removed a folded piece of paper from his pocket and read from it.

"Packages of 25C-NBOMe laced with human bone powder, serpent bone powder, and ground rose thorn," he said.

She held up one index finger.

"Mosqos 'Skeeter' Rowe and a connection with Midas Hyde," he said. "That's a two-fer right there."

"That's only a one-fer," she said. She lifted her middle finger beside her index.

"Okay, after you bolted out of Prescott's office yesterday morning, he told me something ominous," he said. "He said that a storm's coming to Abaddon."

"Sorry, I'm not counting that one," she said. "Even if I thought it meant anything, which I don't, there's no reason to believe it might have a thing to do with the Bouquet Corral killings."

He gave her a hopeful look.

"You're still at two, mister," she said, wriggling her two fingers.

He frowned. There was no way he could confide in her about the vague clues from his digital music player.

Not that she'd believe him to be anything other than schizophrenic.

Then his features brightened.

"Maybe you don't have any regard for Prescott's

visions," he said. "But you can't deny that the guy really paid off when he told me that Vance was seen at The Velvet Taco."

"But you didn't find Jenny Vance there," she said. "And please don't say Velvet Taco again. You make it sound creepy."

He silently mouthed her last statement in mocking fashion.

She gave him a hard look.

"No, instead of Vance I found an FBI SAIC who shouldn't have been there," he said. "And if she was waiting for Jenny, there's something fishy going on with this case … and it's all happening right here in Abaddon. And this is *my* city."

She stared back at him, and from the expression on her face, he could practically see her neurons rapidly firing.

Finally, her ring finger rose alongside the other two.

"Yes!" he said, pumping his fist in the air.

She dropped her hand to her side. "All right, calm down, sport."

He watched her expectantly.

"One condition," she said.

"Name it."

"You work the jewelry case with me during regular work hours," she said. "And the Bouquet Corral is on your own time."

He smiled.

Lieutenant Dakwins exited his office and motioned at them with his hand.

"Naughware," he said. "Captain wants to see us in her office, right now."

* * *

Dawkins and Naughware entered the captain's office to see she wasn't alone.

"Naughware," Gunderson said. "Take a seat, please."

As he took one of the two empty chairs before the captain's desk, Lieutenant Dawkins walked over to stand beside District Attorney Jorge Abasolo and Deputy Police Commissioner Charlie Schmidt, who loomed off to one side of the office, observing.

"Naughware, what the hell was last night about?" Gunderson asked.

"Captain, I was pursuing a lead on the stolen jewelry case," Naughware said. "Among other things."

"Like hell you were," Dawkins said.

Gunderson gave the lieutenant a sharp look before returning her attention to Naughware.

"I showed Lungu photos of the stolen merchandise and asked if he knew anything about it," Naughware said. "Unfortunately, he didn't. And soon after that, his head exploded."

The Deputy Commissioner moved to stand beside the captain's chair.

"Speaking of which," Schmidt said. "Detective, would you mind explaining to us how seven people ended up being gunned down—"

The door to the captain's office burst open, and Taylor walked in, closing the door behind him.

"Captain," he said.

Gunderson frowned. "Taylor, you're retired. This is an official inquiry."

"Once a cop, always a cop," Taylor said, taking the empty chair beside Naughware. "Besides, I'm a material witness."

"Or a potential perpetrator," Schmidt said.

"Kiss my ass, Mister Deputy Commissioner," Taylor said, to which Naughware barely contained a smile. "I was aiding an officer in distress, and that's never a crime."

Even Gunderson fought to maintain a straight face. "And I'm sure the city appreciates your efforts."

"Captain, this is a blatant attempt—" Dawkins said, but the captain raised her hand.

"Taylor, I couldn't help but notice you've already jointly filed a report with Naughware on the events that took place," Gunderson said.

"Old habits. Consider it witness testimony," he said before turning his attention to Schmidt. "Besides, it's never too early to cut off the bullshit before it gets started."

"Captain, if I may," Dawkins said.

The captain looked over at him and nodded.

"Naughware, I have reason to believe that you're pursuing a case in clear violation of orders to cease and desist," Dawkins said. "As well as interfering with a federal investigation."

"Really?" Naughware asked. "Because if you'll check the outstanding cases, you'll find there's an unsolved robbery involving a stolen handgun."

The lieutenant frowned.

"What case?" Schmidt asked.

"Less than a year ago, a thirty-eight caliber, pearl-handled revolver was taken during the robbery of Ms. Marilyn Beatrix," Naughware said.

"Wait a minute," Absolo said. "I think I remember that one. It raised a stir in the local news because she's a wealthy widow, as well as a former model and local socialite. That wasn't a robbery. It was theft."

"Naughware, you're assigned to Robbery-Homicide, which means you've just admitted to pursuing cases outside your assigned jurisdiction," Dawkins said, his features veritably beaming. "That's dereliction of duty—"

"Now wait just a damned minute," Naughware said, raising his index finger. "You look at the report as filed. Ms. Beatrix was behind the wheel of her car when someone illegally entered her vehicle."

"But she was unconscious," Absolo said. "Intoxicated, as I recall."

Naughware wagged his finger to and fro. "Oh, but cash was taken, as well as the firearm. And forcibly taking personal possessions and/or money while in the presence of a victim is technically robbery."

Taylor chuckled while nodding. "Couldn't have said it better myself."

Dawkins shook his head, clearly flummoxed. "You're both incorrigible pieces of work."

The captain rubbed her chin and Naughware thought he saw the beginnings of a smile on her face.

"It's weak," the captain said. "But Naughware has a point. Let's not force that issue for now."

"But Captain—" the lieutenant protested.

"All right, I've heard enough," Schmidt said, glaring at Naughware. "For now, anyway."

The Deputy Commissioner headed for the office door. "We'll discuss this further in the near future, Gunderson, after you issue a recommendation for discipline."

"Yes, sir," Gunderson said before glancing over at the other two men left standing in her office. "Thank you both for your time, Mr. Absolo and Lieutenant Dawkins," she said. "I'll be in touch soon, pending my recommendation to the Deputy Commissioner on any disciplinary actions. Is there anything else we need to discuss?"

"I suppose we're done, but I'll call you later, Gunderson," Absolo said. "Now, if you'll excuse me, I'm late for another meeting."

"Of course," Gunderson said. "Naughware and Taylor, you stay."

Absolo gave Naughware a cautionary look as he left the office, followed closely behind by Dawkins, who sneered at both of them.

When the door shut behind them, Gunderson took a deep breath and then slowly exhaled.

"You two are a frequent pain my ass," she said. "Even when one of you is retired. Taylor, what were you thinking?"

"That boredom is the shits," Taylor said. "And that once a partner, always a partner."

Naughware beamed with pride as he looked sidelong at Taylor.

"Hard to argue against either point, really," she said. "Officially, and on the record, stay out of active departmental cases unless invited.

"But, off the record, thanks for backing up Naughware," she said. "We're finished for now, Taylor."

"Good enough," Taylor said, winking at Naughware as both of them stood to leave.

"However, Naughware," Captain said. "I'm not done with you yet."

"Yes, ma'am," he said, sitting back down.

"Taylor, go fishing or collect stamps," she said. "I don't want to see you back in here anytime soon."

"I'll consider it," Taylor said with a nod. "Always nice to see you, Cap."

After Taylor left, Gunderson focused her attention on Naughware.

"You do realize that Keane should've been the one sitting there, and not Taylor, don't you?" she asked.

He took a deep breath and let it out slowly. "Yes, ma'am."

"Dawkins did have a valid point," she said. "You were pursuing an unassigned case."

"But only on my own time, Captain."

She leaned back in her chair. "Let me give you some important advice, Peter," she said. "Everything you do could potentially be on the record because anything you do in your off time could affect your duties and responsibilities as a detective."

"I understand," he said. "Strictly speaking, is that advice on or off the record?"

She gave him a stern look and raised her forefinger in warning.

"Yes, ma'am," he said.

"Look, I don't like the fact that the Bouquet Corral case was taken from us by the feds either," she said. "But you're treading heavily into obstruction territory."

"Theft of a firearm is a separate local matter not directly

in conflict with the federal investigation," he said. "Besides, there's more to this than meets the eye."

The captain leaned forward in her chair. "Oh?"

CHAPTER 13

Naughware confided in the captain with as much information as he dared, including his impromptu meeting with Skeeter Rowe on the evening of his birthday dinner. However, he pointedly left out The Monk's metaphysical-sounding warnings.

He ended with the sighting of Agent Denise Warwick at The Velvet Taco.

Gunderson gave him a sardonic look over that.

He paused to clear his throat. "It was from a tip, Captain. Completely above-board."

"Mm-hm," she said.

He continued, and when he was finished, Gunderson leaned back in her chair again and steepled her fingers before her in quiet contemplation.

"So, you think there's more to Jenny Vance than merely a felon on the run?" Gunderson asked.

"After all I've said, don't you?" he asked.

The captain nodded. "Your Skeeter Rowe and Midas Hyde angle is also interesting," she said with a frown. "I don't like the idea of one of the city's most wealthy and influential founding families having ties to a mobster like Rowe."

"No argument there," he said.

"The more I think about it, the more the details of this case strike me as odd," she said.

"Like something's missing?" he asked.

"Something or many things," she said. "Nothing fits together well enough for my satisfaction."

"So, you don't think I'm spinning my wheels on this?" he asked.

"Maybe," she said. "But I'm far more concerned with why Lungu was assassinated last night. Given his ties to the warehouse shootout, that can't be mere coincidence."

"The question is, where to start?" he asked. "I mean, someone in Lungu's business eventually attracts enemies. Likely, quite a few."

"True," she said. "And it's possible that all of these events aren't associated to each other."

"Maybe," he said. "But what if they are? Consider that Lungu's assassin chose that night to shoot him, and no less during a meeting with me, which was impromptu; unplanned."

Gunderson considered him at length and nodded.

"Peter, I'm suspending you with pay for the next seventy-two hours," she said.

"What?" he asked. "Why?"

"Because that's all the time I can give you to dig around before I'll have to forward our department's final reports to the feds on the Corral case and other recent developments," she said.

He nodded. "Fair enough. Anything else?"

"Officially, on the record, I'm advising you to take the time to cool down and reflect on recent events," she said. "Unofficially, I suggest that you and Taylor take the time to go fishing together."

He blinked, dumbfounded, at her.

Then he grinned. "*Fishing.*"

He rose to leave.

"And Peter," she said.

He looked back over his shoulder at her.

"Be careful," she said. "And *only* seventy-two hours … tick-tock."

He nodded and hurried downstairs.

* * *

Keane looked up when Naughware returned to his desk.

"Hey, you okay?" she asked.

"Me? I'm golden," he said.

"Uh-huh. How'd the meeting with Captain Gunderson go?" she asked. "It was hard to read Dawkins when he walked in, other than to say he looked royally pissed."

"Good," he said, clearing his desk.

"Good that Dawkins was pissed?" she asked. "Or, that your meeting went good?"

"Both," he said. "Oh, and I'm suspended for the next seventy-two hours."

Her eyes widened. "Woah. Hey, I'm sorry to hear that. But it could've been worse, right?"

He winked at her. "No worries."

She frowned. "Naughware, you've got the look of a man who's getting ready to get his ass back in trouble again."

He grabbed his jacket from over the back of his chair.

"Listen, Keane," he said, slipping his jacket on. "If there's one thing you need to learn about me, it's that when things come crashing down, I don't go down easily with them."

She considered him for a moment. "Well, good luck to you then," she said. "I mean that."

He nodded. "Don't go solving that stolen jewelry case all on your own before I get back."

He left the office and called Taylor's mobile on the way out to the parking lot.

"Hey, partner," he said. "You wanna go fishing?"

* * *

By the time Naughware arrived at Taylor's residence, his ex-partner was loading fishing gear into the trunk of his car.

"Hey, when I said fishing, I didn't mean the tackle and

poles kind," Naughware said.

"Shut up, you cocky little bastard," he said. "It's a cover."

Naughware shook his head and watched Taylor walk back into his garage to retrieve a combat shotgun and automatic rifle, along with a metal, military-grade ammunition canister.

"And what about that?" Naughware asked.

Taylor slammed the trunk shut. "In case we decide to do some hunting."

"You know, I'd planned on doing the driving," Naughware said.

"I always did the driving," Taylor said. "In fact, I'm going to drive your happy ass back to your apartment, and then we'll be on our way."

"No need," Naughware said. "I've got everything I need."

Taylor shook his head. "Nope. You're not ready quite yet. First, you need to change into something a little less official-looking."

The old man walked over to part Naughware's sports jacket and thumped on the handle of his revolver with his finger. "And you're one wheel gun too light, partner," he said. "At least, you'd better still have that Ruger's counterpart stored away at home."

"You're figuring I'll need it?"

"After last night, you have to ask me that?" Taylor asked. "As a matter of fact, I have a bad feeling you just might."

Naughware hoped he was wrong about that.

***

Once Naughware had a Ruger Super Redhawk nestled under each arm, the first item on his and Taylor's list was to seek out Skeeter Rowe.

After stopping by two restaurants and Skeeter's favorite gambling haunt, they finally found Rowe at a south side auto shop, standing beside a shiny red Corvette convertible, surrounded by bodyguards who looked like cage match wrestling types. They faced off against Naughware and Taylor as soon as the two entered the garage.

"Do I want to know why you're looking for me, Naughware?" Rowe asked. "Or, are we just hanging out with old friends today?"

Taylor pointed his finger at Naughware. "I'm *his* friend, not yours."

Two of the bodyguards each cracked their knuckles. One guy looked like he belonged on the cover of *Muscle Magazine*, and the other sported a big gut, crew haircut, and angular features that reminded Naughware of a *Dick Tracy* comic character.

Taylor walked right up to them. "Look, shitheads," he said. "We came for a conversation, but I'll be happy to throw down on your asses, if you'd prefer."

"Big talker. Don't make us hurt you, old man," one of the men said.

"There's not enough 'roid rage in you two limp-dicks combined," Taylor said.

Naughware tried not to grin.

Rowe snapped his fingers and waved the two men away, to which they reluctantly stepped back a few paces. Then he focused his attention on Naughware. "You have the look of men on a mission today."

"We need to chat somewhere private, Skeeter," Naughware said.

Rowe nodded to his men and led Naughware and Taylor to a small office at the back of the shop.

"This will have to do in a pinch," he said. "I must admit; I came away cool from our little chat the other night, so I'm a little surprised to hear from you. What can Skeeter do for you today?"

"Yeah, I've done some thinking since our visit," Naughware said. "What was it exactly you said Midas Hyde's interest was in that warehouse case?"

"That Mr. Hyde is a private citizen concerned about violence in the city," Rowe said.

"Yeah, but I've got to wonder why he came to you

instead of the police to voice his concerns," Naughware said. "Of course, I recall you mentioning an interest in anyone who might have left the scene that night, as well.

"That suggests maybe there's an interest that Hyde can't, or believes he shouldn't, mention to the authorities," he continued. "He wouldn't have interests in the N-bomb that was found there, would he?"

Rowe's features remained impassive. "He never mentioned any of that to me."

"Did he mention anything at all other than his beneficent concern for the public welfare?" Naughware asked.

Rowe tilted his head to one side slightly. "No, he was all about the community, as I recall."

"Hm," Naughware said. "Hey, did you hear about Decebal Lungu yet?"

Rowe gave a rather half-hearted sigh. "Ah, The Lion sleeps tonight. Such a shame, if you ask me. He was a good businessman."

"Yeah, Lungu did a lot of good business in this town," Naughware said. "Including some business that may be associated with victims in the Bouquet Corral shootout."

Rowe's responding smile didn't reach his eyes. "Oh, I wouldn't know anything about that."

Naughware stared at him. "The Lion had built quite a history from his time in Eastern Europe, including with the Volkov Domen. Of course, as you're a man of many connections, I'd be wholly surprised if you didn't know that already."

Skeeter Rowe nodded and thoughtfully rubbed his chin. "No secret there. At least, not in my circles."

"And I've only recently learned that a lot of drugs, like N-bomb, for example, flow out of Eastern European sourcing," Naughware said.

Rowe's expression remained impassive as he slowly stroked the stubble on his chin. "I may have heard that in passing, myself."

"That being said, you want to elaborate with me on what

you know about Midas Hyde's interests in all of this?" Naughware asked. "It seems like a lot of dark subjects for someone who walks in the limelight of our city."

Rowe's expression darkened. "I'm afraid I can't tell you a thing, Detective."

"Can't or won't?" Taylor asked.

Rowe looked at Taylor and then back at Naughware before glancing down at his gold Rolex. "Oh, man, will you look at the time. I've got another engagement that I'm nearly late for. Being late's never good for business, you see. But it's been a real pleasure catching up with you two."

Taylor and Naughware traded suspicious looks before turning to leave.

As they walked back to Taylor's car, Naughware felt disappointed that they were leaving with few insights more than when they had arrived.

"Well, that wasn't as helpful as I'd have liked," Naughware said.

"Actually, it was," Taylor said while starting the car. "Once you think about it."

"How so?"

"When Skeeter met with you the other night at Stringfellow's, you told me he was interested in making deals and sharing information," Taylor said. "And now, less than forty-eight hours later, he doesn't give two shits about you."

"Yep," Naughware said. "That much seems true."

"Which suggests to me that he's already got what he was looking for," Taylor said. "Maybe even what Midas Hyde was seeking. And that's if their business together has even ended yet."

"Fair points," Naughware said. "Only I'm suspended, and I don't have either authorization or authority to request surveillance on either Skeeter or Hyde now."

"True," Taylor said, pulling out into traffic. "And we don't have the luxury of time to do it ourselves, if it even panned out to anything useful."

"Nearly noon and we're fighting the clock," Naughware

said. "Any ideas?"

"Yeah," Taylor said. "But it's a long shot."

* * *

Naughware and Taylor parked outside a bar called Mackie's, located on the outskirts of the south side of town.

"What a dump," Naughware said as he exited the car.

"Well, maybe it ain't like your friend Bacardi's craft beer palace that you're used to," Taylor said. "Just a good old American bar where real men can get a decent drink at a fair price. I discovered it soon after I retired."

"Great, we're going back to the 1970s," Naughware said.

"Shut your hole," Taylor said, leading the way inside.

"Hey, Taylor," greeted a bearded, middle-aged man behind the worn-looking bar.

"Mackie," Taylor said. "This is my partner Peter Naughware. At least, he was until I retired."

Mackie reached across the bar to shake Naughware's hand. "Any friend of Taylor's is welcome here."

Taylor and Naughware took seats at the bar.

"What'll you have?" Mackie said.

"Bud," Taylor said.

"Same," Naughware said.

"Two Buds for two old buds, coming right up."

Taylor shook his head, placing a twenty-dollar bill on the bar before him. "Mackie, you're always turning a phrase. Here, keep the change."

"Thanks," Mackie said. "Sort of early for you to be showin' up, Taylor. You're normally part of the after-seven crowd."

Taylor took a swig of beer. "Yeah, sort of doing some legwork on the side and thought I'd see if Tinian's around."

Mackie nodded and gestured upward with his finger. "Yep, he's using one of the upstairs booths to do some paperwork."

"C'mon," Taylor said, nudging Naughware with his

elbow.

They carried their drinks up a time-worn flight of wooden plank stairs leading to the second floor. A series of booths and tables were unused, except for one where a white-haired man sat with a calculator and pile of paperwork.

"Let me do the talking," Taylor said.

"After you," Naughware said.

"Hey, Greg," Taylor said, to which the man looked up and grinned.

"Well, fancy seeing you here this early, Taylor," the man said as he slowly rose to shake hands with Taylor and then looked at Naughware. "Who's your friend?"

"Detective Peter Naughware. He was my partner up until I retired," Taylor said. "Peter, Captain Greg Tinian is, among other things, a Marine who served as my platoon commander for a time."

Naughware and Tinian shook hands.

"That was a long time, and a couple of careers, ago," the man said. "Now, I'm just Greg Tinian. Pleased to meet you, Detective."

"The pleasure's all mine, sir," Naughware said.

"Sit down. Take a load off," Tinian said. "What brings you around, Taylor?"

Taylor and Naughware slid into the same booth seat directly across from Tinian.

"Just running down information," Taylor said. "And, as you might expect, with too little time and too little to go on."

Tinian nodded. "What's the topic, and what can you tell me about it?"

"Topics, really," Taylor said while removing a small notepad and pen from his interior jacket pocket. He proceeded to write down some information.

"Let's see," Taylor said. "Midas Hyde, Decebal 'The Lion' Lungu, Mosqos 'Skeeter' Rowe, Jenny Vance, and 25C-NBOMe."

"Wow, that's a mouthful, for sure," Tinian said, looking down at the slip of paper once Taylor pushed it toward him.

"Anything else?" Tinian asked.

"Ties to FBI and DEA on those, too," Taylor added. "Associated with the Bouquet Corral shootout."

Tinian whistled. "Nasty business. What's your timeline?"

"Less than forty-eight hours," Taylor said. "But faster is better."

"I'll get right on it," he said. "Budget?"

"Calling in a marker," Taylor said. "And I'm good for an additional gratuity, on top of that."

Naughware's eyes widened, but he remained silent.

"Done," Tinian said, reaching across the table to shake Taylor's hand. "I'll contact you as soon as I have something."

"Let's go," Taylor said, nudging Naughware in the arm with his elbow. "Bring your glass with you."

They left their largely undrunk beers on the bar downstairs and went out to the car.

"Evan, what marker?" Naughware asked.

Taylor stopped and looked at him. "Just like with you and The Monk, I took one or two for the team and earned a marker here and there."

After they got back into the vehicle, Naughware looked sidelong at Taylor. "You want to tell me about it?"

Taylor turned to look at him. "Kid, I'll tell you what. One day, when we've had one too many beers, and you catch me in just the right mood, I might."

Naughware let it drop.

During their return drive into town, Naughware received a text message.

"What is it?" Taylor asked. "Anything good?"

Naughware frowned. "It's Patti Drew."

"CSI Drew?" Taylor asked. "What the hell does she want?"

Naughware's eyebrows rose. "To have lunch. Right now."

CHAPTER 14

Taylor and Naughware turned onto Bell Avenue and pulled into the parking lot of a restaurant called Wuthering Bites.

Inside, they spotted Patti Drew sitting in a booth at the very back of the restaurant. She waved at them, and Naughware gave a small wave in acknowledgment.

"She acts as if we couldn't pick her out of a crowd," Taylor muttered. "We're detectives, for God's sake."

"Be nice," Naughware said.

Naughware sat next to Patti while Taylor scooted onto the bench seat across from them.

Taylor stared down with disgust at the plate of salad before her. "What the hell sort of monstrosity is that?"

"Uh, it's a salad," she said. "It's their vegan special called The Bronte."

Taylor made a face. "Vegan, my ass. Do they serve anything with meat here?"

"Never mind that," Naughware said.

"Screw you, I'm hungry," Taylor said.

Naughware gave him a wan look and turned to Drew. "What have you got for us?"

She discreetly handed a manila folder to him below the table. Taylor frowned and leaned forward as Naughware opened it.

"The captain said to get this to you immediately," she said.

"Well, actually, she handed the folder to me and pointedly said for me to take it to Records *after* I went to have lunch with you."

"Good old Gunderson," Taylor said. "What is it?"

"Preliminary ballistics report on Lungu's murder," Drew said.

"You read it, right?" Naughware asked, scanning the paperwork. "Anything big?"

"Yep," she said. "Lungu was shot from close to a thousand yards away. We found a spot at the top of a tower nearly a block away with a clear line of sight to where Lungu was standing."

"Shit. That's half a mile," Taylor said. "That's a serious pro's hit. Or better."

"Yeah, but there's more," Drew said. "On the very spot where the shot was fired, there was an odd sulfur-based powder residue."

"What the hell was that from?" Taylor asked.

"Nobody has a clue, but I did some quick research," Drew said. "It has no purpose directly related to either weaponry or ammunition, or even anything used to treat a medical condition of any kind. At least, not one we know about yet."

Naughware and Taylor exchanged odd looks.

* * *

Following lunch with Patti Drew, Naughware and Taylor returned to the parking lot where both of them leaned against the side of Taylor's car and crossed their arms before them.

After a moment, exchanged matching perplexed expressions.

"What are you thinking?" Taylor asked.

"I've got shit," Naughware said. "You?"

"Yeah, ditto," Taylor said. "And it's shitty in a way that makes me feel like I should retire … again."

Naughware nodded. "Wish I could, too."

Minutes passed as neither said anything.

"Let's review what we've got," Taylor said. "Rattle it off for me."

Naughware collected his thoughts and took a deep breath and let it out slowly. "Okay, here we go …"

"We start with a crime scene and eleven victims from established crime families representing Boston, Chicago, and Abaddon," he said. "Victims Wilky Jean-Lunet, Jose Ramos, and Sonny Blevins have direct ties to 'The Lion'."

"We've got a tote bag filled with newly minted currency and a white powdery substance found at the scene," he continued.

"Yeah, what was that stuff called again?" Taylor asked.

"Technically, 25C-NBOMe, but on the street, they call it N-bomb," Naughware said. "Though it was combined with human bone powder, serpent bone powder, and ground rose thorn."

"Damned crazy shit," Taylor said, arching his brows. "I don't even know what to make of that. Keep going down your list."

"We found a revolver at the scene with fingerprints from a twenty-four-year-old woman named Jenny Vance from Sioux City, Iowa," Naughware said. "And there's reason to believe she's been hanging around Abaddon for up to a month prior to the shootout. Maybe longer."

"Add to that, there's interest in the case from Skeeter Rowe, who's allegedly representing Midas Hyde," Naughware said.

"And Hyde is just who we need to complicate matters further," Taylor said. "A town-founding family powerbroker, and God only knows what the hell he's got invested in this."

"Then we have the FBI and DEA swooping in here on day two to order us to stand down," Naughware said with a frown. "Only, that's where things get interesting."

"Yeah? How so?"

"I got a tip from The Monk on the location of Jenny Vance at The Velvet Taco," Naughware said.

"The what Taco?" Taylor asked. "Where the hell's that

place at?"

"North side. But never mind that," Naughware said. "Instead, guess who shows up? FBI SAIC Denise Warwick."

Taylor thoughtfully rubbed his chin. "Yeah, that's interesting, to say the least. But what's so special about that Taco place?"

"It's just a restaurant and cantina. Though I discovered it's also a popular place where same-sex couples hang out," Naughware said. "Mostly lesbians, I noticed."

"Warkwick and Vance are lesbians?" Taylor said, squinting.

"What? I never said that," Naughware said, wincing. "Even if they were, that's not the point."

"All right, I'll let that slide for now," Taylor said. "What's your angle again?"

"It gets me to wondering," Naughware said. "Is Jenny Vance merely a surviving perpetrator, or is she a federal informant?"

"Odds either way at this point," Taylor said.

"And then I try to pressure The Lion for information, and he gets knocked off during the effort," Naughware said.

Taylor whistled. "Yep, and by a thousand-yard shot. That's one pro hit."

"And sulfuric powder residue is found at the shooter's site," Naughware said.

"Yet more crazy mumbo jumbo to convolute things," Taylor said.

"Hm," Naughware said. "I don't know."

Taylor looked at him. "Don't go there, Peter."

"What do you mean?"

"Put the weird shit aside," Taylor said. "Just stick to the hard facts. Work the evidence. Anything else?"

Naughware thought about pressing the matter further, but decided to let it go.

Trusted mentor and friend aside, it wasn't as if he could easily confide in Taylor about any of the actual "weird shit" in his life.

What sane person would believe him, anyway?

At least he could talk to Glenn about his audio player.

Naughware shook his head. "Oh, and one more thing," he said. "We're quickly running out of time."

"Uh-huh," Taylor said. "Well, that just about does it then. Who knows if Tinian will come up with anything helpful, especially within the window of time available to us. I guess we'll have to resort to additional seat-of-our-pants desperate measures."

"Like what?" Naughware asked.

"It's a long shot, but maybe I can squeeze a Hail Mary outta this for us," Taylor said. "But it's something I have to do alone."

"Dangerous?"

"For me, very," Taylor said. "It involves a woman and gossip."

Naughware gave him an odd look as the old man removed his mobile phone from his pocket.

"Worse still," Taylor said, shaking his head as he scrolled through his phone's contacts list. "I think I'm going to need to shave and put on a tie."

* * *

After Taylor and Naughware returned to Taylor's home, Naughware drove back to his apartment while his friend prepared for his mysterious rendezvous with a woman he refused to name.

In truth, Naughware needed the break, if only to contemplate the more outrageous aspects of the case. In the absence of a reliable confidant, it was all on him to contemplate all things strange and mysterious.

He lay atop his bed listening to his music player with his arms folded before him. He closed his eyes after queuing up "Long Cool Woman".

Despite it being only midday, he already felt drained from his and Taylor's efforts. He was desperate; like a drowning man clawing wildly for anything to grab onto.

"Damned deadline," he said.

The captain's extension of time felt like both a blessing and a curse wrapped into one.

He tried to relax, and struggled to clear his mind via some deep breathing exercises.

When that failed, he relented.

"Nowhere," he said, squeezing his eyes shut.

After a few seconds, his body experienced the sensation of momentarily floating, then dropping in mid-air. Seconds later, he came to a full stop.

When he opened his eyes, he was lying in the dark on the cool surface in the Nowhere Zone.

The sense of nothingness around him felt strangely soothing.

"This is better," he said, queuing up The Hollies' song again.

Next, he mentally reviewed all the aspects of the case that he and Taylor had discussed that afternoon. When his reflections turned to the topic of Jenny Vance, something about the song's lyrics struck him.

He replayed the tune from the beginning and closed his eyes as he began to deconstruct the lyrics.

Essentially, the narrator was with the FBI, and he was smitten by some woman wearing a black dress. During the song, there was a shootout.

That much seemed to fit with the nature of his case.

Yet, he kept thinking about how the mysterious woman in the song was a distraction for the narrator.

Was that Jenny Vance? If so, who was the song's narrator relative to the Bouquet Corral crime scene?

Or, was Jenny the FBI agent who got distracted by a man?

"Wait," he said, opening his eyes to stare into the blackness around him. "Moreover, was Jenny distracted by another woman?"

Why else would Agent Warwick be looking for her at The Velvet Taco?

He let that idea go, but something about the basic concepts in the lyrics felt more right than wrong to him. He just wasn't quite how they might pan out to what actually occurred.

Smiling, he recalled how many times over the years Taylor had frequently urged him to trust his instincts, as any good investigator should.

Fleetingly, he wondered who the mysterious woman was that Taylor was going to meet with.

"Back to the case," he said.

He considered the remaining facts, and then moved on to the stranger aspects surrounding the case.

He recalled his visit with The Monk, warning him about a storm coming to Abaddon. Add to that, the odd ingredients in the 25C-NBOMe powder, and the sulfuric powder residue found at the sniper's site.

Opening his eyes, he held his digital player out before him as its dim light illuminated the small screen.

The player had pointed him in helpful directions many times over the years.

"I'm stuck, buddy," he said. "Play me something helpful, won't you?"

He selected random and waited.

Jefferson Airplane's "White Rabbit" began to play.

"This is new," he said. "Or rather, very old."

He listened to the song all the way through and then played it again.

"Trippy," he said.

Then he started to pick out things from the lyrics that he might make sense of.

He suspected the lyrics were about drugs, which might refer to the 25C-NBOMe powder. Or, perhaps the sulfuric powder?

Naughware certainly felt as if he was chasing rabbits, given his struggles on this case and running down both clues and suspects.

He replayed the tune and closely listened to the lyrics.

It was easy to consider that the chessboard men could be the FBI and DEA, and perhaps even the department's leadership. They all definitely were ordering him to stay away from the case, except of course for the grace period granted him by the captain.

He needed someone, or something, that could help break open the case.

And if the song was of any help at all, one key question remained: Who was his version of the song's central character, Alice?

He pressed stop on his player and stared at the device's small screen.

"You're all about the riddles, aren't you?"

The device grew warmer in his hand.

He frowned.

Within seconds, it felt white hot, and he abruptly dropped it, whereby it landed atop his chest.

He clamored to sit up while knocking the device away from him.

However, given the attached earbud cord, it simply bounced back toward him and popped down into his shirt pocket.

His hand darted to remove the player before it burned him, but strangely, the device had already cooled by the time he touched it.

It had never done anything like that before.

"What the fuck is up with you today?" he asked while removing the player from his pocket. As he did so, he caught a brief glimpse of something as it dropped to the floor.

He frowned and reached down to pick up a plain white business card.

Using the player's lit screen for illumination, he read the card.

Eva Shyne
The Spooky Word
"Your Occult and More Store"

1122 Hyde Street
Abbadon, Iowa

His thoughts reeled. Given everything that had happened recently, he had nearly forgotten about even meeting Ms. Shyne.

"But—how did that get in—?"

He realized he wasn't even wearing the same shirt he had worn the night of his birthday dinner.

Abruptly, his audio device started playing "White Rabbit" again.

* * *

Evan Taylor straightened his tie as he entered what was likely Abbadon's most upscale coffee shop, Josephine's Cupper.

"Damned ties," he mumbled.

A smartly dressed young woman stood behind an ornate podium.

"Good afternoon, sir, and welcome to Josephine's Cupper," she said with a practiced smile. "Reservation, first seating, or to-go?"

"Reservation for—"

"Yoo-hoo, Evan!" came the near-shrill voice of a woman from inside the nearby dining room.

"Er, I'm with her," he said, gesturing with his thumb toward the dining room.

The young woman nodded. "Of course. This way, please."

Taylor set eyes upon Imogene Prattler, a woman around his age who was seated at one of the small posh tables interspersed throughout the room.

She rose from her seat as he approached.

"Imogene, how are you?" he said, awkwardly returning her proffered hug.

"Oh, Evan, so formal," she said. "I've told you before to call me Ima. Just plain, ordinary Ima."

Ima Prattler.

Evan tried to maintain a straight face. "There's nothing plain about you … Ima."

Taylor started to take the chair opposite Ima, then thought better of it and took the seat immediately to her right. The gesture brought a smile to Ima's face.

As they perused the menus, he struggled to make sense of the complicated and exotic tea and coffee options, wishing he could decipher what even half of it meant.

Meanwhile, Imogene appeared nearly giddy as she perused her menu.

"Oh, so many excellent choices," she said.

"Hm," he said. "I've always been a plain black cup of joe sort of guy, myself."

She looked up with amusement. "Oh, Evan, you delight me. Please let me order for you. I have something wonderful in mind that I think you'll like."

"Erm, sure," he said.

"Now, now," she said. "Such a brave man shouldn't be intimidated by something rich and exotic once in a while."

He arched one brow. "Coffee, you mean?"

She giggled and wagged her finger at him. "Oh, Evan, you ribald man."

When the waiter arrived at their table, Ima ordered something foreign-sounding with the word cappuccino in it and then added, "Indian Malabar Monsooned AA for my gentleman friend. Oh, and some lemon cranberry scones with lemon glaze, if you please."

"Certainly, ma'am," the waiter said and hastened away.

"Now, Evan," she said. "It's been months since we last spoke, and that was merely in passing while I was out and about, as I recall."

He forced a pleasant smile. "Well, you know how time passes faster and faster, they say."

She reached over to lightly pat the top of his hand. "Oh, how I know, dear.

"You're looking lovely as ever, Ima," he said.

"And you as handsome as ever," she said. "You can't

imagine how happy I was that you called."

"Well, thank you for meeting me on such short notice," he said.

He felt like a fish out of water, and nervously reached up to adjust his tie for what felt like the twelfth time since he had arrived.

"How have you been?" she asked. "Keeping busy in retirement?"

"Oh, yes, very busy," he said, searching for small talk topics. "There's the occasional fishing trips, and I went to see my sister, Janice, and her husband, Bruce, in Des Moines recently. Of course, Bruce and I did some fishing while I was there, as well. He even mentioned us going out hunting together during early deer season."

"Mm, and how is the family doing?"

"Very well, thanks," he said. "Everyone's just fine, including my niece, Tina."

"That's lovely," she said.

"Well, Ima, how are your children?" he asked.

"My son, Solomon, I rarely see, what with him running the *Abbadon Daily* since my dear Guy passed, barely five years ago now," she said, momentarily adopting a sober expression. "I dare say it suits him. But my eldest daughter, Tildy, confirmed recently she's expecting her first child. Oh, I'm finally going to be a grand-mama!"

"Well, that's fine news, for sure," he said. "Congratulations."

"And young Christine is as active as ever," she continued. "Always jet-setting around the globe, much like her father. Of course, she's twenty-seven now …"

Evan tried to pay attention, but quickly lost track of the ensuing stream of information, all the while working toward any polite angle to guide the conversation in the direction he needed.

Their beverages arrived in elegant-looking porcelain cups with scones stacked atop a serving plate. Evan awkwardly picked up his cup by its ornate handle with disdain. He did, however, eye the pastries with interest.

"Cheers, Ima," he said.

"Cheers, my dear," she said. "How fun this is."

She served a scone onto a small plate before him and urged him to try it. He found it quite tasty.

"Oh, I love these little darlings," she said, eagerly serving two onto her plate.

"With all my recent traveling, I feel as if I've lost touch with Abaddon," he said.

"Indeed?" she asked. "Well, surely you've heard about the mayor? They say he may not run again when his term is up."

"Hadn't heard that," he said. "Interesting, for sure."

"And then there's that dreadful business at the Bouquet Corral. Grisly scene, by all account. So many people killed in one fell swoop."

"Yes, I'd heard about that, too," he said.

"I'll wager you're wishing you were on the case yourself," she said.

He smiled. "Oh, you might well imagine."

"Word is that Peter Naughware is one of the investigators," she said. "He was your young protégé, wasn't he?"

"Yes, indeed he was," he said. "He's a good man."

The edges of her eyes crinkled. "Oh, I think I see a proud father figure before me."

"Aw, Ima," he said, though he felt the heat rise to his cheeks. "I can hardly claim him, though I suppose I'd proudly do so, if I could."

"Cherished mentor, at the very least," she said.

"Yes. At least that, I'd hope," he said.

Her expression turned sober once more. "But as I said, horrid business all around. One wonders if they'll put all the pieces together in the end. Strange times in Abaddon, it seems."

"Oh?" he asked.

She leaned closer to him, as if conveying something intimate. He found himself leaning in toward her, as well.

"The local news leads with it every evening. It's as if everyone's preoccupied with that dreadful event," she said. "As a matter of fact, Delores Hyde was just telling me no more than a day ago that her husband, Midas, is completely obsessed with the Bouquet Corral."

"You don't say," he said.

"Indeed. Delores went so far to say it's as if he's possessed or something," she said. "She simply can't distract him to save her life. Well, I told her I wasn't about to abandon her in her time of need. As such, we're going shopping in Ames this weekend for some retail therapy. My treat."

His eyes narrowed as he thoughtfully scratched his chin. "And quite a treat it will be, I'm sure. But why would Midas be so troubled with the Corral shootout?"

"One can only wonder," she said. "Though the Hydes aren't the only founding family with troubles these days, it seems."

He looked up sharply at her. "Really?"

"I was visiting with Constance Spight the other day," she said. "She told me that she hasn't heard from her eldest son, Lev, ever since that night."

"That night?"

"Of the Bouquet Corral carnage, of course," she said. "Now, I'm not saying that Lev had anything to do with such base people as were found in that warehouse. But one must wonder over the coincidence. After all, I've heard often enough that Constance's husband, Viktor, isn't exactly an angel, if you catch my meaning. Frankly, those international corporate types rarely are, in my experience. Perhaps the apple doesn't fall far from the tree with Lev, though it's such a shame, if true."

Evan nodded. "Constance Spight told you all that?"

"Well, of course, Constance and I go back many years together," she said. "However, I've known her long enough to sense when something's genuinely wrong. Poor dear."

"She told you that Lev disappeared the night of the Bouquet Corral?" he asked.

She gave him a shocked look. "Why, Evan, are you interrogating me?"

His eyes widened. "What? No, not at all. Just interested."

She patted his hand and gave him a sly look. "Oh, I had you there, dear man. But what's not to find compelling?"

Evan tried not to let out a relieved sigh. "Yes, just like any good whodunit come alive in our own city."

She adopted a sly expression. "I know. Exciting, and yet, so scandalous, isn't it?"

"Mm-hm," he said.

He paused to sip his coffee, which he thought tasted very good.

"You like the blend?" she asked.

"Oh, yes," he said. "Very much. Never had anything like it before."

He deliberately took another sip and gave an approving look, to which she beamed.

"Somehow I knew you would," she said. "I have a knack for these things."

"Mm," he said. "Ima, I feel as though I interrupted you. What more were you just saying about Constance and Lev a moment ago?"

"I'll get back to that in a moment," she said, leaning over toward him again. "But first, a question."

He arched his brows. "Oh?"

"And one that you should answer most honestly," she said in a mock-conspiratorial tone.

He shifted in his seat. "I'll do my best."

She gently pushed the plate of scones in his direction. "Will you have another scone with me?"

His eyes darted from her to the scones and then back to her again.

"Sure."

CHAPTER 15

Naughware quickly left the Nowhere Zone and returned to his apartment only long enough to grab his light jacket before rushing downstairs to the nearby parking garage to retrieve his car.

He didn't know precisely why, but as he drew closer to Ms. Shyne's shop, his pulse increased noticeably, as well as his sense of anticipation.

Despite a street address that referenced one of the town's founders, The Spooky Word was located in a particularly run-down and progressively dangerous side of town.

He parked before an empty meter in front of the shop where he could more easily keep an eye on his car.

The shop was quaint-looking in a dated style that reminded him of city archives photographs from times long past, well before he was born. Only more modern were the retractable security shutters for the windows and entrance, which broke the nostalgia and further reinforced how that side of town had declined over the years.

Inside, he was greeted with a variety of both acrylic and glass display cases containing odd-looking items, and a few rows of faux-wood bookshelves, giving the place a part-museum, part-used bookstore sort of appearance. The faint scent of spiced incense permeated the air around him. Classic rock music played softly in the background, and the sound of two women's voices drifted from the back of the shop.

As he looked in that direction, he saw Eva Shyne talking to another young woman, and they both glanced over at him.

Eva smiled at him in a manner that sent a warm feeling flowing through him.

"Detective, how nice to see you," she said.

He walked over to the counter. "Ms. Shyne."

"If you can spare a few minutes, I'll finish here and be right over," she said.

He raised his hand. "Please, take all the time you need."

"Thanks," she said. "In the meantime, feel free to peruse the shop. Hopefully, it won't scare you too much."

Given that her business was located in a city that's squarely in the nation's Bible Belt, she'd seen many a curious patron leaving her shop visibly bristling over its contents. She wondered how much less a law enforcement official might, as well.

He grinned. "Why, Ms. Shyne, I don't scare easily."

He found the responding playful gleam in her eyes striking, and forcibly broke his gaze with her to browse the shelves and display cases.

Naughware walked down one short row of bookcases to conceal his line of sight to Eva before slipping his earbuds into place and selecting random on his player.

Jefferson Airplane's "White Rabbit" immediately played, nearly startling him.

"And here we are," he said with satisfaction.

He paused the song and removed his earbuds, only to hear the same tune in the background.

"What?"

Frowning, he peered around the end of the bookshelf to stare at the set of speakers setting atop the main counter. He pulled his device from his pocket only to find the song still paused.

"Thanks for your help, Alice," the young woman talking to Eva said.

Naughware's eyes widened.

"Anytime, Grace," Eva said. "Call me when you're ready for another get-together."

Naughware walked over to where Eva stood. He was immediately struck by how appealing the scent of her perfume was, unlike anything he had recalled before.

As her attention turned to him, her warm smile deepened.

"It's a welcome surprise seeing you again, Detective," she said.

"You, as well," he said. "The young lady that just left. She called you Alice?"

She blinked. "Yeah. Why?"

"Just curious," he said. "I noticed that your business card says Eva."

"Correct, but my middle name's Alice," she said. "My friend Grace has called me Alice ever since we met because has already has a sister named Eva, who she's always talking about."

"Oh," he said, nodding. "Avoids confusion then."

"Exactly. And I don't mind it, really," she said. "But, now that I notice, you look a little puzzled."

He cocked his head to one side and still heard the Jefferson Airplane song in the background.

"That song playing … does it mean anything to you?" he asked.

She paused to listen.

"Huh, weird," she said. "I haven't heard that in years. My mom used to play it all the time when I was growing up. She always said it was my personal theme song."

Despite the subsequent reeling sensation in his brain, he merely nodded. "Ah."

"Are you a classic rock music fan, Detective?"

The corners of his mouth upturned. "Well, not necessarily, but I find that I'm inadvertently discovering vintage tunes all the time, nonetheless."

A curious expression crossed her face. "What brings you

to my little shop?" she asked. "Can I help you with something specific?"

"There's a—" he said, then paused to reconsider his approach. "That is, I ran into some strange substances at some crime scenes and don't know quite what to make of them. It's only a hunch, but something made me think your shop might have reference materials that could be helpful."

"Oh, that sounds perfectly mysterious," she said. "What sort of substances?"

"White powders," he said.

"Okay," she said. "Can you be more specific? Besides, don't you guys have access to advanced labs and stuff?"

"We do. How about substances such as human bone powder, serpent bone powder, and ground rose thorn?" he asked.

Her eyes widened. "Wow, that's really specific."

"I tried researching these on the internet, but didn't get much help," he said.

"Well, I'm not surprised by that," she said. "The stuff that's out there is typically from amateurs and hobbyists. Most of it is just plain wrong, and even the remotely accurate references are usually incomplete."

"Do you have any books or reference materials that might mention those powders?" he asked, glancing in the direction of the bookshelves. "Your collection looks fairly impressive."

"It's probably not going to help you much," she said. "It looks impressive, but it's mainly for the—"

"Amateurs and hobbyists?" he asked.

She gave him a sheepish grin. "Yeah, mostly. People in my line of work tend to refer to them as the paranormal tourists."

"Well, these are some serious roadblocks in the investigation, and I was hoping you could help me," he said. "Is there anything useful at all you could provide?"

"Wow, this is definitely a first," she said.

He frowned.

"I mean, helping in a police investigation," she said. "I don't get many people like you in here very often, you see."

"Like me?" he asked.

She shrugged. "Sorry, I meant police … or any government types, really. It's not as if most people take a business like mine very seriously."

"Hey, at this point, I'd welcome help from any corner."

Her expression turned wistful. "Compared to what you probably run into on a daily basis, this must seem like a pretty trippy corner."

"So, about those powders, let's pretend that I'm like the village idiot or something," he said. "Which, depending on who you talk to back at the precinct, may or may not be a stretch."

She chuckled. "All right. As for the powders and rose thorn you mentioned, those are commonly used in varying portions by someone trying to perform a summoning or channeling. Most attempts I've heard of failed. It's difficult even for skilled conjurers."

"Summoning?" he asked. "Like spirits?"

"No, for Powers and Principalities," she said. "Or maybe worse."

He paused, recalling something similar that The Monk had said to him in the past couple of days. "Go on."

"Well, those components are ancient in their use," she said. "Depending upon which cultures we're talking about, there's any number of entities or Powers that might be the focal point."

"Ah," he said. "So, whoever used these, actually believes they were summoning something, then?"

"Well, at least they're trying to," she said. "Or maybe they're just amateurs who think they are channeling something useful."

"But it's not like those powders actually work, right?" he asked. "Like *really* work?"

"Okay, so I've never seen it done in person myself," she said. "Though I have it on pretty good authority it's possible."

"There's an authority for that sort of thing?" he asked.

"Coven leaders typical serve in the role of local authority," she said, tilting her head slightly.

"Covens. Interesting," he said, making a mental note for future elaboration. "How about, let's say, channeling with sulfur powder."

"Sulfur?" she asked. "How was it used?"

"A small amount was found on the ground where someone was standing."

"Yeah, but like in a circle or just piled up?" she asked.

He frowned. "Not sure. I'll have to check on that. Why would it matter?"

"Okay, so if it was a circle, it may have been trying to contain something being summoned," she said. "Though if stacked or sprinkled over an area, it might simply augment a Power or conduit to it."

He paused to consider what she had said.

"Yep, definitely trippy," he said, struggling to formulate a structured understanding in his mind.

"Anything else?"

"Not for now," he said. "But thanks so much for your help. However, I may want to follow up with you sometime soon."

"Sure, anytime," she said. "Thanks for stopping by."

He nodded. "Enjoy the rest of your day, Ms. Shyne."

Naughware walked toward the front of the shop, not really wanting to leave, but having no further reason to stay. He felt as if he was back at square one again, and time definitely wasn't his friend.

"Detective."

He stopped and turned back toward her.

"You know, I could do some research and try to find out some more about those powders, if you'd like," she said.

"That would be great. Thanks," he said.

He glanced down at his watch with dismay. "Only, under my current circumstances, sooner would be better than later."

* * *

Given what he'd learned at The Spooky Word, Naughware drove to the scene of the crime to revisit "The Lion" Lungu's assassination. Only, instead of the garage, he went to the shooter's location; a multistory warehouse that was conveniently abandoned. Yet another example of a side of town whose economic outlook was teetering toward a nadir.

While he had reviewed the crime scene photos, he had yet to look over the site firsthand. Though he wasn't sure what he expected to find, given that the CSI team and other fellow detectives had undoubtedly already canvassed the crime scene.

Unfortunately, each of the building's prospective access points was either locked or secured with chains.

He returned to his car to retrieve a set of bolt cutters from the trunk. Yet another of Evan Taylor's essential tools of the investigator's trade.

Once inside, Naughware made his way up to the third, and topmost, floor of the warehouse.

The eastern side of the building was darkening as the late afternoon sun progressed westward.

A moment later, the faint scent of sulfur tainted the stale air.

He frowned, but proceeded onward, the scent increasing as he progressed.

Perhaps it was the eerie setting, or the nature of the crime, but it made his skin crawl.

As soon as he entered the room that was the shooter's vantage point, a strange tremor resonated through his body.

"What the hell?"

He braced himself with one hand against the nearby door jamb to steady himself. The scent of sulfur was strong there.

After a moment, the tremor passed, though he still felt a

nearly electric feeling flow through him. It was unlike anything he had ever felt before.

Strangely, as he made his way closer to the window where the shooter had stood, the electric sensation increased noticeably, nearly feeling like ants crawling across his skin.

He rubbed his forehead. "What's wrong with me?"

Looking down, he saw a circle of faint whitish residue, mixed with a hint of yellow throughout, where the sulfuric powder had been found. A pungent smell practically threatened to choke him.

It was standing there that Naughware also felt the strongest emanations of tremors inside him.

He withdrew his mobile phone and dialed Eva Shyne.

"The Spooky Word," she said. "How can I help you?"

"Ms. Shyne," he said. "It's Detective Naughware. You remember asking about the sulfur, whether it was in a circle or not?"

"Yeah."

"Circle," he said. "About a foot and a half width. And it looks like there's a yellowish tint to the powder in places."

"I see," she said. "I'll make note of that and let you know when I learn more."

"Thank you," he said.

He snapped a quick photo for himself. As he slipped his phone into one of his pockets, he stared out through the window.

The killing shot was impressively taken more than a half a mile away from the spot where Lungu fell, not to mention through a closed glass window on the garage itself.

"Damned impossible shot," he said, rubbing up and down his arms with his hands as the strange sensations buzzed through them. "And what the fuck is wrong with me?"

Maybe it was partly just the lingering unnerving effects of what he'd felt at the scene, but the entire setting felt eerie to him.

The sound and vibration of his phone ringing caused

him to jolt.

"Fuck," he said, fumbling for his phone. "What?" he demanded.

"It's Taylor," Evan said. "What the hell's your problem?"

"Nothing," Naughware said. "What have you got—wait, is that classical music I hear in the background? Where are you?"

"I'm in a bathroom at Josephine's Cupper, and I've only got a couple of minutes before I have to get back to someone," Taylor said.

Naughware frowned. "Josephine's Cupper?" he asked. "Who are you meeting there?"

"Never mind who, Curious George," he said. "It's going to take me longer than I thought to leave here, so you need to get your ass over to visit Constance Spight about her missing son, Lev."

"Missing son? What's that have to do with—"

"Stop flappin' your gums and listen to me for a minute, junior," Taylor said. "Lev Spight's disappearance mysteriously coincides with the Corral shootout."

"That doesn't make any sense," Naughware said. "Lev hasn't been reported missing that I know of."

"Which is awfully damned strange given that he's heir to one of the most powerful companies in the country, and the son of a key Abaddon founding family, don't you think?"

"True enough," Naughware conceded.

"Oh, and as soon as I get away from here, I'm going to look further into Midas Hyde," Taylor said.

"Really?" Naughware asked. "What did you learn about him?"

"Word has it that he's now remarkably focused on the Corral crime, which suggests he may be involved," Taylor said. "Or perhaps a vested interest in some aspect of it."

"Yeah, I had that feeling when Skeeter Rowe met with me that night at Stringfellow's," Naughware said. "But it was just a vibe I picked up, and I didn't have much more to go on at the time."

"Well, we do now," Taylor said.

"All right, I'll look into Lev Spight," Naughware said.

"Hey, kid?"

"Yeah?"

"Watch your back. There's an angle around every corner with the Spights," Taylor said. "I'll meet you at Beers to You to take stock of things."

"Got it," Naughware said. "You be careful, too, old man."

* * *

The Spight family mansion was more than an oversized house, it qualified as a sprawling estate that would rival even the finest across either the United Kingdom or Europe.

Though he had grown up in Abaddon, it was Naughware's first visit to the place. It was nearly revered by locals but typically visited in person by exclusive invitation only. For all their popularity, the Spights were surprisingly private people.

For that matter, he had never met Viktor Spight, the CEO of Spight Industries, in person either. The man was a household name around the globe.

The estate was famous as a local spectacle—a veritable monument that spoke of power, prestige, and substance. Numerous governors, legislators, and heads of state had dined there over the decades. Decisions of national, state, and local importance had been decided within those walls.

In no small way, it was one of the key reasons Abbadon was prominently placed on any contemporary Iowa map.

Despite all that, Naughware didn't feel the least bit intimidated.

He pulled up to a gate serving as the estate's public entry point and pressed a red button on the kiosk to call for assistance. The face of an older man with drawn features appeared on the screen.

"Spight estate," he said. "May I help you?"

"My name is Detective Peter Naughware. I need to meet with Viktor and Constance Spight, if they're home."

"Your credentials, if you please."

Naughware held up his badge and department identification card.

"Do you have an appointment, Detective?"

"No, but I know they'll want to meet with me."

"Wait a moment, please."

The screen went blank, and Naughware waited for a few minutes before the man's face reappeared on the screen.

"I'm afraid the Spights are not currently available for an audience. Good day—"

"Tell them that I'm here about Lev," he said.

The man frowned, and the display darkened again.

Naughware thrummed his fingers against the dash and reflected on how, over the years, Taylor had schooled him on the art of fishing.

You have to use the correct bait for the desired catch.

Within moments, the screen came alive again.

"Mr. Spight will see you," he said. "You may proceed to the front of the estate."

"Thank—" Naughware began, but the screen went blank again.

The gate slowly opened as he connected his digital player to his car stereo.

"Tell me what to expect in here," he said, selecting random play on the device. "Give me something helpful."

There was a pause before Gram Rabbit's "Devil's Playground" started to play.

His eyes narrowed. "Well, this is another new one."

He listened closely to the song's lyrics as he slowly proceeded up the lengthy two-lane concrete path, which reminded him more of a tree-lined country road than a driveway. At irregular intervals, he noticed discreetly placed video surveillance cameras among the trees.

As the song continued, he looked down at the player with surprise.

"Oh, hell. This doesn't sound good at all," he said. "Am I getting ready to meet the devil himself … or something worse?"

For some reason, an odd chill still ran down his spine as he contemplated the implications of that.

The estate loomed ahead, and just kept getting bigger and wider the closer he proceeded toward it. It quickly appeared larger than life as he drove past the open stretch of lawn leading up to the front-facing side.

"Damn."

He pulled up before the house and guided his vehicle off to one side so as not to obstruct other traffic flow.

A man wearing a blue suit emblazoned with the Spight family crest on his jacket quickly walked over to his driver's side window, which he rolled down.

"I'll park your vehicle for you, sir," the man said. "It will be brought back around for you when you're ready to depart."

Naughware nodded, and left the engine running, though he unplugged his digital player and slipped it into his interior jacket pocket before exiting the vehicle.

"It's all yours," he said.

"Someone will meet you at the front door," the man said before slipping into the driver's seat.

Naughware walked up the magnificent series of marble steps leading up to the grand front porch. He stopped before two twelve-foot-tall ornate wooden doors. Each door had a large gold knocker held by an ugly gargoyle-looking face.

"Ugh."

One door opened to reveal stern-looking men wearing business suits that screamed of private security. Their jackets sported the Spight corporate logo, a gold lion's head representing the family crest surrounded by three symbols; a beaker, a coin, and a missile.

"Good afternoon," one man said. "Would you mind showing us your identification?"

Naughware shrugged and withdrew his badge and ID

card, which both men took a moment to examine before looking back at him.

"Is this official police business?" the man asked.

"That's between me and Mr. Spight," Naughware said, resulting in a hard look from the fellow.

"You're sanctioned for now," the other man said. "Follow me, please."

Naughware gave the first man a cold stare as he walked past.

What an asshole.

He was led down posh hallways and past a variety of different rooms from sitting room to dining room to some that served any who-knew-what functions.

Finally, he arrived at what had to be a living room by any standard he was familiar with. It easily encompassed the total square footage of any number of small homes around town.

"Wait here," one of his corporate escorts said.

The two men turned and shut the door behind them as they left.

From there, Naughware began a progressive scan around the room, taking in the opulence of the place. It felt coolly formal and had the look of somewhere that was meant to be seen but not actually lived in.

He went to one of the large picture windows in the room and gazed out upon the sprawling grounds.

It was vast.

He wondered if its owners had personally seen all of their own estate in the decades they had resided there.

Turning at the sound of the door opening behind him, he set eyes upon the renowned Viktor Spight, who appeared taller than he expected compared to the occasions he had seen him on television or in photos. The man was in a league all his own compared to even the wealthiest corporate moguls.

"Detective Naughware," Spight said, walking toward him to shake hands.

Naughware thought the man had an unusually firm grip.

"To what do I owe this highly unusual visit?" Spight asked. "My butler tells me you mentioned my son, Lev?"

"Just following up on a lead," Naughware said. "I have reason to believe that your son may be in danger."

"Oh?"

"Naturally, given how important the Spight family is here in Abaddon, I felt it my duty to follow up," Naughware said. "Have you seen or spoken with Lev recently?"

Spight stared at him for a moment; his face devoid of emotion.

"Like me, both of my sons lead busy lives, Detective. My youngest, Erik, is away at college, for example," Spight said. "My family and I may go days without speaking, much less seeing one another. You only barely caught me at home, in fact, as I'm leaving tomorrow for Germany for an important meeting."

"I see," Naughware said. "When do you last recall having contact with Lev?"

"A few days ago, perhaps," Spight replied. "If I recall correctly."

Naughware doubted that someone of Spight's intelligence or accomplishments let very much get past him, much less lose grasp of when he last saw his own son.

"And what about Mrs. Spight?" Naughware asked. "By any chance, is she available?"

"I'm afraid Constance isn't available at the moment," Spight said. "You mentioned that you were following up on a lead a moment ago. Is there any specific reason that you suspect Lev may be in danger?"

"Indeed," Naughware said. "Why else would I trouble you?"

"And what case did you say you're working on?"

Naughware met Spight's level gaze. "I didn't, actually."

Spight's eyes narrowed, and he stared back at Naughware, which felt to Naughware like an uncomfortable contest to see who would blink first.

"I see," Spight said. "Well, there's nothing I'm aware of

that suggests Lev is in danger, so I'm afraid you've made a trip for nothing. I don't know that I can help you further, Detective,"

"Well, I certainly hope Lev is well," Naughware said. "Thank you for your time, sir."

He reached into his inner jacket pocket to retrieve a ballpoint pen and well-used notepad. He glanced down and casually flipped through the various pages of scratch notes he had taken, finally stopping on a blank page.

"Oh, before I go, is there any chance you could provide me with some contact information so that I might reach out to Lev?"

Spight looked at Naughware in a manner that suggested the man's patience was running thin.

"You're a very persistent person, Detective Naughware."

Naughware shrugged. "What can I say? I take protecting my city very seriously."

"How dedicated of you," Spight said. "However, you'll understand that, in this day and age, family contact information is especially sensitive, and I'll require further documentation in order to release that to anyone."

"Such as a warrant?"

Spight's cool expression spoke volumes. "Well, I'll leave that for my legal counsel to sort out with you. And I'm afraid our conversation has come to an end."

"Very well," Naughware said, practically feeling the temperature lower in the room. "Thank you for your time, Mr. Spight."

"Goodbye, Detective."

As if on cue, the door to the room opened, and the two men who had escorted him stood outside, waiting for him.

Naughware nodded back at Spight and walked between the bodyguards as he retraced his steps back through the house.

He heard rapid footfalls as the men strode to catch up with him.

They said nothing to Naughware as he was shepherded

back to the front entrance, where a butler was waiting with his hand gripping the door.

It was painfully obvious to Naughware that they were eager for him to leave.

"A moment, if you please," a woman's voice echoed through the cavernous entryway.

Naughware paused and turned to see a lady wearing a regal-looking dress walking toward them. He immediately recognized Constance Spight from photos; a woman famous as one of the premiere ladies representing Abbadon's high society.

"Mrs. Spight," the butler said. "This man was just leaving."

Naughware ignored the butler and instead stepped toward her. "Detective Peter Naughware, Mrs. Spight," he said. "Robbery-Homicide division."

Surprise momentarily crossed her face before she collected herself.

"If you please, Detective—" the butler said.

A glare from Mrs. Spight stopped him cold.

"What brings you to our doorstep, Detective?" she asked.

"I'm here about your son, Lev," he said.

"Why? What's happened?" she asked, clasping her hands before her.

"Is there somewhere we can talk privately?"

"Certainly—"

"Detective Naughware," interrupted the booming voice of Viktor Spight. "Are you still here?"

"I was just going to speak with—"

"No, you're not," he said. "I believe I referred you to my legal counsel."

Mrs. Spight's features hardened, even while she was quietly stepping aside as her husband moved into her personal space to face Naughware.

"We're done here, Detective," Mr. Spight said.

Naughware nodded, and his eyes briefly met Constance's

before turning to leave through the opened doorway.

The door shut almost immediately behind him, and his vehicle was already waiting for him outside as he descended the steps of the house.

The valet stood patiently until he approached the vehicle before briskly walking away.

"Helluva first visit," Naughware said, getting into his car.

He started the engine.

"And I suspect, my last."

CHAPTER 16

Naughware was surprised to find Evan Taylor already sitting at the bar when he arrived at Beers to You.

As Chris Isaak's "Heart Full of Soul" played over the speakers, he walked up and clasped his former partner on the shoulder.

"You're here already?" Naughware asked, taking a seat on the unoccupied stool to Taylor's left.

"Not fast enough," Taylor said, having a swig from his beer bottle.

Glenn leaned against the serving side of the bar with an amused look. "Taylor only bested you by about fifteen minutes," he said.

"So, Taylor, how did the rest of your meeting with your mystery lady go?" Naughware asked.

Taylor shook his head. "It went fine."

"You gonna tell me who you were meeting?"

"Imogene Prattler," Taylor said. "If you must know."

Naughware grinned. "You two hit it off then?"

Taylor gave him a flat look. "She's a kind enough sort of lady," he said. "But you do what you have to do for the case. Now, drop it."

"Oh, yeah, it's just the case," Naughware said, nodding. "Yep, of course."

"Shut up. It's been a busy day," Taylor said. "Glad I'm

retired, unlike you two hardly working sad sacks."

"Retirement suits you, Evan," Naughware said before turning his attention to his bartender friend.

"And what a better way to end a day than a cold brew with friends at your favorite bar," Glenn said.

"In truth, Glenn, this is our second bar stop today," Naughware said.

"Second bar?" Glenn asked with a mock-shocked expression. "Pete, are you cheating on Beers to You?"

"Hey, it was only a one-time stand," Naughware said. "It didn't mean anything."

"Ready for a makeup beer? Midnight's Call?" Glenn asked, reaching down into the below-bar refrigerator case. "I'll bet that *other* place didn't have anything this good, did it?"

"Good God Almighty," Taylor said, casting them a sour look. "You pair of craft beer pussies. Get a room already, why don't you?"

Naughware exchanged grins with Glenn as he uncapped the beer for him.

"Hey, nice job on the solid tunes this time," Naughware said, pointing overhead at the nearest speaker.

"Yeah, even Taylor likes everything so far," Glenn said.

"You just got lucky, that's all," Taylor said. "Ultimately, your taste in music sucks, Bacardi, and the night is still young. Mark my words, people will be flying outta here to go down the street to Thunder Joe's before nine o'clock."

Glenn shook his head. "You're nothing but old and angry all the way to the core, Taylor."

Naughware chuckled and held up his bottle of beer. "Here's to being old and angry. Cheers, guys."

Taylor took a swig of his beer and then waited for Naughware to do the same. "All right," he said. "We're outta time for chit-chat. Any leads with the Spights?"

Naughware nodded. "Yep. Viktor's hiding something about Lev, though how much he knows is still a mystery. There may be a tie-in to the Bouquet Corral, or it might be something totally unrelated."

"Yeah, but if true, the timing's a little suspicious," Taylor said. "Say what you will about Ima Prattler, she passes along clean information."

"Oh, so it's Ima now?" Glenn asked.

"Stow it, sarsaparilla salesman," Taylor said, pointing his forefinger at him.

"All I know is, Lev must be involved somehow," Naughware said. "The question is, does his father's behaviors extend to his son?"

"Hey, should I actually be overhearing this?" Glenn asked, exchanging curious looks between them.

"Can you keep your trap shut?" Taylor asked.

"Absolutely. Loose lips and ships and all that good shit," Glenn said, miming zipping his lips shut.

"Yeah, right," Taylor said.

"He's cool," Naughware said. "Besides, he'll never talk, even if those goons torture him."

"Those goons? *Torture?*" Glenn's eyes widened. "Actually, I'll just be down at the other end of the bar if you need me."

Taylor grunted and took a swig of beer.

"Anything else?" the retired detective asked.

"I think Constance Spight wanted to talk to me, but Viktor shut her down and tossed me out before she could say anything," Naughware said.

Then he paused, remembering something else.

"By the way, I've got someone researching some of the substances found at both the Bouquet Corral and the shooter's vantage point from Decebal Lungu's murder."

"I wouldn't waste my time on those substances. And, for the record, Lungu was killed, not murdered," Taylor said.

"There's a difference?" Naughware asked.

"Innocents are murdered, but scumbags get killed."

"What?" Naughware asked. "Where did you ever hear shit like that?"

"That's a Taylor special, my friend," Taylor said. "No

charge for that one."

"Yeah, and no tip either," Naughware said, to which Taylor nudged him hard with his shoulder as Naughware tried to drink from his beer.

Naughware barely recovered in time to keep from spilling his beer all over himself. "You asshole."

"Takes one to know one," Taylor said. "Speaking of knowing, I know we've got less than twenty-four hours to crack this case, so what do you think our next move should be?"

Naughware started to say something, then stopped.

"That's right," Taylor said. "Think before speaking."

"If you know what I need to say, then why not just say it?"

"Hey, I'm the retired one here," Taylor said. He poked Naughware in the shoulder with his forefinger. "Youngster, you're the one the public is relying on to solve the case."

"Youngster? At thirty-three?" Naughware asked. "If only."

He took the time to drain his beer and thumped it down atop the counter. "All right, we do everything we can to find Lev Spight."

"You sure? There's also Midas Hyde to consider," Taylor said. "We've only got time for one effort, and that's where you want to stake your claim?"

"It's the better of the two leads so far, and something feels so wrong about Lev's disappearance that it's gotta be our best shot," Naughware said. "That meeting I had with Spight left me aching to dig into things further, and I have yet to shake that urge. Are we agreed?"

"Damn straight," Taylor said with a nod. "I knew you'd get it, kid. Now, pay the tab so we can get back out there."

* * *

The sun was just making its final appearance on the horizon when Naughware and Taylor left Beers to You.

As they walked out to their vehicles, they spotted Detective Keane leaning against the hood of her nearby car.

"What are you doing out here, Keane?" Naughware asked.

"Waiting on you two heroes to finish your beers," she said. "It's a quiet evening, and besides, I didn't want to break up the bromance you had going on in there."

"Bromance, my ass," Taylor said.

Naughware gave him a wan look. "Evan, you've really got to start listening to your internal voice before speaking."

Taylor grumbled and shrugged.

Naughware returned his attention to Keane. "I thought you shut me out when it comes to my working on the Bouquet Corral case?"

An amused look crossed her face. "Naughware, I'm beginning to learn that there's no shutting you out. And after your little Viktor Spight show today, I'd say you could use all the help you can get."

Naughware winced. "You heard about that, huh?"

Keane nodded. "Oh, yeah. Word spread like wildfire after Viktor's legal team descended on the DA's office. It didn't take long for Captain Gunderson to get a call from downtown, either."

Naughware considered Keane's remarks, including the risks of going after Spight. Even if future evidence generated a strong case, he realized he would have to choose his battles carefully.

However, for the time being, he had to confront the present political maelstrom.

"Aw, shit," Naughware said. "I'm sunk for sure now."

Keane walked over to stand before Naughware.

"Not before tomorrow, you're not," Keane said. "The captain offered me a day of discretionary leave for tomorrow and asked if I would mind checking in on you."

"That was a big ask," Taylor said. "What with you being new and all."

Keane nodded. "Maybe, but I figured that the worst I

can get is a reprimand, while Naughware might end up getting fired. It seemed like a fair trade."

Naughware smiled. "Fair trade? Why risk it at all? I thought you don't even like me."

"Like you? Not yet," she said. "But I respect what you're doing. And besides, for some strange-ass reason, Brooke really likes you."

Naughware grinned. "Brooke's got good taste."

"Not really," Keane said. "She's just got the world's biggest heart, and she stops for every stray puppy she runs across."

"You hear that, Taylor? I'm a stray puppy now," Naughware said.

"Yep, and you're going to get neutered, or worse, if we don't solve this case before tomorrow night," Keane said.

* * *

After Taylor and Keane exchanged mobile numbers, in order to cover territory more quickly, Taylor went off on his own to reach out to his old informants, seeking the whereabouts of Lev Spight.

Meanwhile, Keane accompanied Naughware, who drove them around town seeking out informants that he had previously relied upon, including Thaddeus Prescott.

At one point, a reminder went off on Naughware's phone.

"Oh, shit," he said, pulling the car over into the first available parking lot.

"What? What is it?" Keane asked.

"Forgot an appointment," he said. "Give me just a minute."

He quickly exited the car and walked a short distance away with his phone in hand. He spied Keane watching him as he dialed.

"Miss Millie's House of Perdition," said an alluring-sounding woman. "I'm Candy. How can I assist you?"

"Hi. This is Peter Naughware," he said. "I have an appointment tonight with Becki?"

"Oh, Mr. Naughware," she said. "Yes, of course, sir. She's looking forward to seeing you."

"Yeah, well, that's going to be a problem," he said. "You see, I'm going to have to work late and can't make the appointment. Could you possibly let her know it will be next week before I can reschedule?"

"Certainly, Mr. Naughware," she said. "Becki will be so disappointed. She looks forward to Thursday evenings with you."

"Uh, sorry about that," he said.

"No problem," she said. "I'll let her know, and we'll anticipate your arrival next week. Oh, and would you like for me to contact you if an opening is available this weekend?"

"Oh, no, but thanks. I'll likely be out of pocket until next week," he said.

"Certainly, Mr. Naughware," she said. "I'll convey the update to Becki. Until next week then."

When the call ended, he paused for a moment at how odd that call sounded to him. It was as if the receptionist was canceling dinner reservations at a restaurant.

He also felt disappointed. He, too, had looked forward to the escape that Thursday nights provided to him.

"Is everything all right?" Keane called from the passenger window.

"What? Oh, yeah, fine," he said, walking back to the car.

"Where to next?" she asked.

"There's still a couple of—" he said, only to be interrupted by his phone.

The caller ID indicated it was the precinct.

"Naughware."

"Detective, this is dispatch," said a man's voice. "I have a patch-in call for you."

"Okay."

"Hello?" asked a woman with a familiar voice, though she sounded distraught. "Have I been handed off to yet another operator again?"

Naughware frowned. "Mrs. Spight?"

"Yes," she said. "Is this Detective Naughware?"

"Yes, ma'am. How can I help you?"

"Detective, I need to speak to you about my son, Lev, immediately."

* * *

Within the hour, Naughware and Keane met Constance Spight at a neutral site, a coffee shop called Latte Ground.

"Please, Detectives, you must find Lev," Mrs. Spight said with a pleading tone. "I don't know if I could bear it if something ill-fated happened to him."

"I'll do everything in my power to secure his safety, Mrs. Spight," Naughware said.

"When was the last time you heard from him?" Keane asked.

"Four days ago," Spight said. "We spoke early in the evening."

"The night of the Bouquet Corral killings?" Naughware asked.

"Well, I suppose it could be," Spight said. "I don't really follow such sordid affairs."

"Do you have reason to believe that Lev was at the Bouquet Corral?" Keane asked.

Mrs. Spight's expression tensed for a moment, but the sadness in her eyes spoke volumes.

"I don't know," she said. "But I hope not."

Naughware and Keane exchanged surprised looks.

"Where was he when you spoke to him that evening?" Naughware asked.

"I-I think he was with some woman he's been seeing," she said.

"Do you have her name?" Keane asked.

Spight shook her head. "Oh, I don't recall. He's a young man sowing his oats. How am I supposed to keep up with every woman he goes out with?"

"Can you tell us anything about her?" Naughware asked.

Mrs. Spight sat quietly for a moment. "Lev has been seeing her for at least a month or so, as I recall. But he was reluctant to mention her name, as if he was afraid to reveal something. I don't know why. Perhaps he thought we wouldn't approve of her. Perhaps she was low born … I don't know, really."

Keane's expression hardened. "Low born?"

"Let's get back to Lev," Naughware interjected. "Mrs. Spight, can you share anything that might help guide us to where Lev was last? Perhaps anyone else he may have been in contact with that night?"

She thought for a moment and shook her head. "I'm not sure, actually. Perhaps my husband knows more, except—"

She fell silent.

"Do you know why your husband is reluctant to speak about it?" Naughware asked.

Her expression turned pensive. "I don't interfere in my husband's business matters, you understand."

"Business matters?" Keane asked. "You mean, Spight Industries, correct?"

Naughware watched Spight as she fidgeted slightly. He momentarily contemplated the notion that Lev's disappearance may have anything to do with outstanding Spight Industries interests. That was a rabbit hole that required further evidence before pursuing further. He was already trailing more than enough loose ends for the time being.

"Mrs. Spight," Naughware said. "In the interest of locating your son as quickly as possible, let's consider your information confidential and protected for the moment."

"You can do that?" she asked.

"I will," he said. "For now."

She nodded. "I fear Lev was representing some financial interests on behalf of my husband that night."

"Financial interests?" Keane asked. "Can you elaborate

further?"

Spight's expression remained impassive. "I'll make no comment regarding my husband's business interests. My realm of expertise is strictly charities and fundraisers, you see."

"But, if you think it might relate to Lev—" Naughware said.

"Stop! This is all so pointless," Mrs. Spight said. "We're wasting valuable time. Can't you form search teams to canvass the city or something?"

"Mrs. Spight," Keane said. "That's not how this works."

The woman's expression turned desperate. "Can't you do *anything*?"

"Believe it or not, we're trying," Naughware said.

Mrs. Spight stared back at him.

"One way or another, I'll find your son," Naughware said.

Keane gave him a warning look, but he pointedly ignored her.

"Promise me, Detective," Mrs. Spight said. "Promise me now that you'll bring Lev back to me."

Naughware nodded. "I will, Mrs. Spight. If it's the last thing I do."

CHAPTER 17

Outside the coffee shop, Naughware and Keane watched Mrs. Spight get into her luxury sedan and drive away.

"Naughware, where the *hell* do you get off making promises to that lady?" Keane asked.

"I'll find Lev Spight," Naughware said. "I don't have any choice. It's that, or I'm completely screwed."

"You're practically married to screwed," she said. "Tomorrow you'll finish tying the knot."

Something struck Naughware's memory, and he reached into his jacket to retrieve his digital player.

"Seriously?" Keane asked. "We don't have time for tunes, Naughware."

He scrolled down through the playlist. "I've found there's always time for tunes."

Keane hiked her hands atop her hips. "I don't believe this."

Naughware plugged his earbuds in and played The Hollies' "Long Cool Woman."

Keane appeared to be close to losing her patience when he jerked the earbuds from his ears.

"*Damn,*" he said. "I should've seen that. It makes more sense to me now."

"What are you talking about?" Keane asked. "How's about *you* start making some sense?"

"Get in the car," he said.

He fumbled with his phone to send a text message.

Frozen custard, anyone?

* * *

Fifteen minutes later, Naughware and Keane walked into Frenzied Frozen Custard.

"Helluva time for a sweet tooth, Naughware," she said.

The place was relatively dead with only a few patrons sitting throughout the dining room.

He stepped up to the ordering line with Keane trailing him.

"Two chocolate wonders in a cup," he said to the clerk.

"How do you know I like chocolate?" Keane asked.

"All women like chocolate, don't they?" he asked.

"Mm," she said. "What if I said I was lactose intolerant?"

He gave her a sheepish look. "Oh."

"Ha," she said. "Not really, but I made you wonder, didn't I?"

He paid for their custard and led the way to a booth well away from other patrons. He made sure to sit in a position that commanded a view of either entryway.

"Naughware, I can't say that I don't appreciate dessert and all," she said. "But why are we here wasting valuable time?"

"You'll see," he said.

"This night just keeps getting weirder," she said.

After a moment, she frowned. "You're not eating yours."

A faint smile crossed his lips.

A few minutes later, a rather haggard-looking Captain Gunderson entered and briefly scanned the dining room before walking directly to their table.

Naughware slid over in his booth seat until he was next to the window.

Keane looked up in time to see Gunderson sit down beside him.

"Oh—" she said.

Gunderson appeared amused. "Go ahead, Detective. Finish."

Keane swallowed. "*Shit.*"

"Much better," the captain said before turning to Naughware. "Why am I here?"

He slid the cup of frozen custard in front of her. "Your favorite, Captain."

"Mm-hm," she said. "And?"

"Big break," he said. "Need your help."

The captain looked down at the frozen treat. "Talk," she said while scooping up a spoonful of custard.

He quickly, and quietly, recounted everything that had happened that day, including his suspicious meeting with Viktor, and their meeting with Constance Spight.

At that, Gunderson looked at him with surprise. "That's unexpected. I see why you called me."

He nodded.

"What do you need?" she asked. "Bear in mind, by tomorrow evening, you'll likely be in even deeper shit with both the feds and city hall. And heaven knows, there's nothing I'll be able to do to help you then."

A wry expression crossed his face. "Frankly, heaven's never been of much use to me, Captain."

Gunderson gave him an odd look. "Just tell me what you need."

"I need every resource you can muster to immediately poll all local clubs, bars, and restaurants for video footage that might contain Lev Spight," he said. "And maybe put out a citywide bolo for him, while you're at it."

"Not an easy request," she said. "For one, it's going to attract a lot of attention, including the press. And second, how do I even begin to justify the overtime? Nevermind the trouble I'd expect from Viktor's legal team."

"Think of it as a high-visibility welfare check," he said. "After all, there's no clear line between Lev Spight's disappearance and the Bouquet Corral case, so it shouldn't alert the feds."

"Oh, I realize that, Peter," she said. "Yet, notice my concerned expression?"

"What I mean is, it shouldn't raise the ire of the feds if all we're doing is a welfare check on a son to one of the city's most influential families," he said. "Who wouldn't appreciate such a gesture of concern?"

"Internal auditors, perhaps?" she asked.

He stared back at her.

"Fine," she said. "I'll do it. Your argument makes sense, but just so you know, I'm taking a huge risk."

The captain paused and looked across at Keane. "Given everything, you've had very little to say thus far, Detective."

Keane shook her head. "I wouldn't dare. Besides, I'm just here for the custard."

"Smart answer," Gunderson said before picking up her cup of custard and rising to stand. "I'm beginning to wish I were, too."

She looked down at Naughware. "You'd better pray you're right."

"Nah, I gave that up years ago," he said. "It never really helped. But I might hope a little bit, if that's worth anything."

Gunderson arched her brow at him. "Thanks for the custard."

***

While driving in the car, Naughware called Taylor to catch him up on the latest developments.

After he finished, Keane stared at him.

"Naughware, you look surprisingly unrattled for someone who's close to ending his career in an epic way," she said.

He gave her a half-smile. "Thanks, but looks are deceiving," he said. "On the inside, I feel worried shitless enough that I'm pretty close to pissing myself."

She looked out the passenger window. "Good to know,"

she said. "And now I'm really glad we took your car."

He looked sidelong at her.

When he pulled up into the parking lot near Beers to You, she appeared surprised.

"What are we doing back here?" she asked.

"You need to go home and get at least a few hours' sleep," he said. "We'll start fresh in the morning."

"But—"

"We've gone as far as we can for now. Besides, I'll need you as sharp as possible from here on out," he said. "If anything comes up before morning, I'll call you."

"And just what are you going to do?" she asked.

"Go back to my apartment to take a shower," he said. "I could also stand a change of clothes, and it'll give me time to mull things over some more."

She shrugged. "Whatever. It's your funeral, partner."

* * *

Naughware opened his apartment door and knew immediately something was wrong when he saw the glow from interior lamps.

He had half-drawn one of his pistols when he spied one of his intruders.

"Detective Naughware," said SAIC Denise Warwick, sitting in a recliner beside a lamp in his postage-stamp-sized living room.

"Agent Warwick," Naughware said. "You're an unexpected house guest."

He looked to his right and saw an agent standing in his kitchen holding two steaming coffee mugs.

"First off, there's sugar in the cabinet beside the refrigerator, if you need it," he said, refocusing his attention on Warwick. "And second, do you want to tell me what the hell the FBI is doing in my apartment? Uninvited?"

"Just as soon as you tell me what the hell you're doing still working on the Bouquet Corral case," she said.

"Currently, I'm working both an open-books robbery and a missing persons case," he said. "On my own dime, I might add."

"Yes, we're well aware of your convenient leave of absence," she said. "As well as leveraging your ex-partner-turned-private-eye."

He frowned.

"Taylor didn't tell you?" she asked. "And I thought partners told each other everything. My, but how times change."

His mind raced, wondering why Taylor hadn't mentioned that.

"Taylor's retired," he said with a shrug. "He also fishes; in case you weren't aware. But let's get back to the FBI surveilling me."

"Just watching," she said.

"Fine, watching," he said. "Then let's talk about Lev Spight."

"Why?" she asked. "I didn't mention Lev Spight."

"You mentioned the Bouquet Corral case," he said. "And if we're talking about that, then we're talking about Jenny Vance."

Warwick appeared unimpressed. "I'm afraid I don't see the connections."

"Well, if we're talking about Jenny Vance," he said. "Then we're damned sure talking about Lev Spight, aren't we?"

Warwick's eyes narrowed. "Oh, Detective Naughware, you're really grasping at straws. What makes you think there's even a connection between Vance and Spight?"

Naughware shrugged. "Something I heard in a song."

Her eyebrows rose as she accepted one of the coffee mugs from the other agent, who stood beside her. She appeared intrigued.

"You're risking your career on a hunch that you gained from hearing a song?" she asked.

"It was a really good song," he said.

She frowned. "Given your highly unorthodox rationalizations, I'm surprised they actually made you a detective."

"Well, if you're sitting in my living room, I can't be too bad of one, now can I?"

"You're terribly impertinent," she said. "And cocky."

"Tell me something everyone else doesn't already know," he said.

She considered him for a moment. "Does everyone know that you're getting ready to be busted to patrolman, if not fired and imprisoned, for interfering in a federal investigation?"

"You're not going to let that happen," he said.

"Oh," she said. "And what makes you think that?"

"Because you're sitting here talking to me instead of arresting me," he said.

He felt as if he was gambling in one of the highest-stakes poker games of his life.

"Give me one reason I shouldn't arrest you here and now," she said.

Naughware walked into the living room but remained standing.

"Because you've been here in Abaddon for days," he said. "No, wait, likely weeks already. And yet, you're still no closer to bringing Vance into custody."

"Now, time's running out, and you need my help more than you'd care to admit," he continued. "You should let me take lead on your investigation."

"What could you possibly do for me that the might of the FBI can't bring to bear?"

"Local expertise," he said. "If you've been staking me out, then you know I have local contacts—resources on the ground—that the agency doesn't. And I suspect you're even aware of my recent breaks in the case, which means I'm making progress that you're not."

Her eyebrows rose. "Keep going."

"Finally, the Bureau must be desperate," he said. "Hell,

for all you know, both Spight and Vance may have already fled the city."

He caught a brief moment of surprise in her eyes before her expression hardened.

"You're associating the two of them again," she said.

He felt as if the ante were raised. And it was time for him to either thrown down or fold.

He recalled a key element from The Hollies' song.

"They're a couple," he said. "And Vance is either your primary field informer for the case, or—"

"Or?" she asked.

"Or," Naughware said. "Vance is also an agent, and the Bureau can't afford to have one of their own going rogue."

He noticed that, while Warwick appeared practiced in her emotional control, the agent beside her wasn't. The young man momentarily fumbled with the coffee mug he held.

Warwick gave the agent a sharp look and he returned an apologetic look.

At that point, Naughware became intrigued.

"So, Vance is also an agent, then?" he asked, pointing an accusing finger at the young agent beside her.

Warwick looked up at the agent with disdain. "Go stand by the door."

"Yes, ma'am," he said, carefully balancing his mug in hand as he walked past Naughware. "Sorry, ma'am."

"Don't look so smug, Naughware," she said, refocusing her attention. "One day, your seat of the pants approach to investigation will be your undoing."

"Maybe someday," he said. "But not tonight."

CHAPTER 18

In a relatively short span of time, Evan Taylor managed to track down a number for former contacts and informants who had aided him during his time as a police detective.

His last stop was one of the south side's best-known café's, Daisy's Diner.

He walked over to the old-fashioned main counter and sat on an unoccupied well-worn stool. While there were only a couple of patrons in the place, he didn't spot any staff.

Instinctively, he reached beneath his jacket to touch the hilt of his Smith & Wesson revolver.

"Well, if it ain't Detective Taylor," said the waitress who walked out of the kitchen with a plate of food in hand. "Long time no see, honey. I'll be right with you."

"Thanks, Susie," he said, relaxing a bit.

He glanced back over his shoulder to watch her deliver thc food to a single patron sitting in the far back booth.

She returned to behind the counter, grabbed an empty mug and full coffee carafe, and walked over to him. She smiled at him as she filled a mug of coffee before him.

"You still take your coffee black, right, Taylor?" she asked with a wink. "I thought you retired sort are usually in bed at this hour."

"Funny," he said. "Actually, I'm working a few leads."

"Oh, so you're a working man again, are you?"

"Nah, just helping a friend out," he said, picking up the coffee mug and taking a quick swig. "Mm. Good as I remember."

"Best brewed canned coffee in town," she said. "You hungry, dear?"

He eyed the plates turning inside a nearby old-fashioned dessert display kiosk behind the counter.

"How old's the pies in there?" he asked.

"Most of them were baked last night," she said. "But I'd stay away from the pecan. It's a store bought, and not a very good one, either."

He nodded. "One of those apples would be fine."

She retrieved the piece of pie and turned to place it before him.

"You doing okay, Susie?"

"I'm getting along all right," she said.

"How about the little ones?" he asked before taking a bite of pie.

"My youngest is battling the tail end of a cold, but he's on the mend," she said. "My eldest daughter just won a big regional spelling contest for her school. I'm really proud of her."

"Good to hear," he said. "Hey, this pie's better than I remember."

"Bettie still makes them for us, same as always," she said. "How about you? Getting tired of being retired yet?"

"Oh, I'm keeping busy," he said. "Doin' a little fishing now and again, for one."

She arched her brows at him.

"Yeah, a little bored, to be honest," he said. "Only, maybe a little less bored recently. Feels like old times, if you follow me."

She leaned on her elbows on the counter before him. "Oh?"

"Susie, you know what I like the most about Daisy's Diner?" he asked.

"It's me, isn't it?" she asked with a grin.

He chuckled. "Yes, Susie, you're priceless. However, it's also that it's one of the city's best intersections for buzz and rumor," he said, lowering his voice. "Every generation of cop quickly learns where the best conversations are held. And for the south side, it's definitely Daisy's."

"Sort of makes this place historic then, doesn't it?" she asked. "And it's true. We do get a little of everyone in here at one time or another, though mostly the working class."

"And, around here, you're the person I rely on for good tips," he said.

"You've always been good for a generous tip yourself," she said. "Any particular buzz you're especially interested in right now?"

He took another swig of his coffee. "Heard anything about the Spights? Lev, in particular."

She appeared surprised at first, but then frowned.

He noted her response and then looked down at his pie and casually broke away a small chunk of it with his fork. “Any chance you’d tell me more?”

“That’s not a family name that you hear talked about regularly around a blue-collar café like this,” she said. “And most everybody knows that talking about Spight business could be bad for a person’s future, especially a nobody like me.”

He reached into this pocket and withdrew a quarter-folded greenback, which he discreetly slid under the edge of her arm.

“Nobody?” he asked. “Susie, make no mistake, you’ve always been a real *somebody* to me.”

She looked down at the corner of the hundred-dollar bill and then back up at him with a wry smile.

“Thank you, Taylor,” she said, pausing to slip the bill into her apron pocket. “Well, the past few days, Trudy—you remember her? She’s the one who likes to work the split shifts.”

“Go on,” he said.

“She said that the Spights kept coming up in conversations she overheard recently,” Susie said. “It’s sort of a game for us here, just to break the monotony, you understand. Anyway, it seems the Spights are the popular family name, just behind Luna McDoom. So far, Trudy has the most points of all of us.”

Taylor took another bite of pie.

“And then, I added my own Spight point to the list ...” she said.

“Yeah?”

She paused and scanned the dining room before looking at him. “A couple of guys—they looked like west-siders to me—came in here last night, and I heard one of them whispering about Lev Spight, but only a few words before he hushed up."

"Go on."

"Something about Lev laying low," she said. "That struck me as a little odd. Absurd, really. I mean, the Spights don't have to lay low from anyone, do they?"

"True enough, I expect," he said. "You said west-siders? You know either of their names?"

"Only one guy by his nickname," she said. "Goes by Dozer. He shows up now and again when his construction jobs are on the south side. Odd to see him in so late, as he's normally one of the rise-and-shiners."

He considered that for a moment. "Hm. I've heard that nickname in passing."

"He's a regular. Word is, Dozer got outta prison a couple of years ago," she said. "Working construction and turning his life around, he says."

"Mm-hm," Taylor said. "Was he the one who mentioned Lev?"

"No, it was the other guy," she said. "I'd seen him in here a number of times before, but never got his name."

"He ever pay with credit card or check?"

"Nah," she said. "Like Dozer, he always pays with cash."

"Interesting," he said.

"Not much help to you, I'd imagine," she said. "You want your Ben Franklin back?"

"What? Heck, no," he said. "Plenty helpful."

She gave him a shy smile. "Glad I could help."

"You'll call me if you hear something new, right?" he asked, placing a business card down before her.

She nodded and picked up the card.

He placed a ten-dollar bill under the edge of his pie plate. "Good pie, Susie," he said. "Really good see you again, too."

"Good to see you, too, Taylor," she said as he walked toward the door. "You don't be a stranger now."

He looked over his shoulder to wink at her and made his way back into the night.

After calling in a favor with someone working nights in dispatch, he was able to get Dozer's full name and last known address.

A short time later, he stood outside the front door of a run-down apartment on the city's west side.

At first, he pressed the doorbell, which seemed to be out of order.

He scanned the nearby parking lot to make sure nobody else was around.

Taking up a position off to the side of the door frame with one hand gripping the hilt of his pistol, he banged three times on the door with his fist.

"Who is it?!" demanded an angry, gruff voice inside.

"Looking for Billy 'Dozer' Nelson."

"Oh?" he asked. "Who the fuck's asking?"

"Somebody who'll send your sorry ass back to the joint if you keep giving me shit, that's who," Taylor said. "Just open the damned door, Nelson. I've got a question for you."

There was a tense silence before Taylor heard a series of locks being clicked and the door opened.

A tall, broad-shouldered man wearing only sweatpants stood in the doorway.

"You a cop?"

"Who the fuck else would I be at this time of night?" Taylor asked.

"What do you want?" he asked. "I ain't done nothing wrong, and I'm stayin' in touch with my payroll officer."

"The name Lev Spight mean anything to you?" Taylor inquired.

"Man, I ain't got nothing to do with him," the man said, though his expression alone spoke volumes.

"Know anybody who might?" Taylor pressed.

The man's eyes darted to and fro before he bolted past Taylor at a dead run.

"Sonofabitch—Freeze!" Taylor yelled as he chased after him, but Nelson was far more athletic and younger, and had made it halfway across the parking lot before Taylor could catch up to him.

Taylor jumped into his car and whipped out onto the nearly deserted street to chase after him.

He chuckled as he saw Nelson running down the sidewalk alongside the street.

"What a numbnut," he said as he floored the accelerator and steered the car toward him.

The man looked over his shoulder as Taylor hit the brakes and skidded forward in a semicircle. The back quarter panel knocked the man about ten feet forward until Nelson rolled to a stop against a nearby curb.

Taylor exited his vehicle and rushed over to him. "I said freeze, dumbass!"

Nelson moaned. "You ran me over, motherfucker! You can't do that shit!"

"Kiss my ass," Taylor said. "Now, tell me who the hell you were talking about Lev Spight to, and I *might* consider calling it a night."

"You're crazy," Nelson said. "I could get your badge for this."

Taylor tapped the hilt of one of his pistols. "This is the only badge I need nowadays."

The man's eyes went wide with horror. "Man, you're fucking crazy."

"Time is not on my side, Nelson," Taylor said. "That means, time isn't on yours, either."

"Listen, I ain't got nothing to do with Lev Spight."

"Give me the name of who you were talking to," Taylor said. "Or you end up buried some place real special."

"Sh-shit," Nelson said. "M-Mudd Jenkins."

"Mudd?" Taylor asked.

"Mudsen," the man said. "Mudsen Jenkins."

"What's his angle with Spight?"

"Hell, I don't know."

Taylor punched him in the face.

"All right, all right," Nelson said. "Shit!"

Taylor reared back to punch him again, but Nelson blurted out, "Dammit, Mudd was just name-dropping about Lev. He said Lev needed a business reference, so I told him about Sham Koda, that's all."

"Why?" Taylor demanded. "Who's Sham Koda?"

"Fake IDs! Sham makes fake IDs," Nelson said.

For the first time that night, things were finally starting to click into place for Taylor.

"Tell me where I can find Koda," Taylor said.

CHAPTER 19

Naughware stared back at Agent Warwick before him.

"So, what do you say, Naughware," she said. "Will you collaborate with the FBI on this?"

"And I take lead on the investigation?" he asked.

"For the time being," she said.

He quickly assessed the prospect, as well as his outstanding options.

"Think of it as a partnership," she said.

"One condition," he said.

"Name it."

"Complete latitude to operate as I see fit."

"Only if you keep me informed of your every move," she said.

"Fair enough," he said. "Shake on it?"

He stepped forward with his hand outstretched as she rose from her seat.

As she stood, Warwick lurched forward and fell to the floor amidst breaking glass and the telltale whizzing sound of a bullet.

"Sniper!" Naughware yelled, dropping down for cover.

Another breaking of glass and whizzing sound followed, and he looked over his shoulder at the other agent just in time to see the bleeding hole in his forehead as he collapsed onto the tile. The wall and front door behind him were splashed with a mix of blood, hair, and brain matter.

"Shit, shit, shit," Naughware chanted as he crouched low beside Warwick using the chair as a visual barrier.

He felt a weak pulse and quickly assessed her injuries.

She was unconscious and bleeding profusely from a neck wound, which he pressed against with his handkerchief.

"Easy, Warwick," he said, though she was both limp and silent.

He ran into the nearby bathroom while speed-dialing dispatch. "This is Detective Naughware," he said. "Active shooter at 410 Empire Street and two FBI agents down in apartment 22."

He grabbed a large towel and ran back to Warwick's side to wrap her neck snugly.

Despite the lull in activity, he realized that the sniper was either waiting for another clear shot, or—

"Getting away," he said aloud while bolting for the front door with phone in hand.

He slipped on spilled coffee on the tile floor and dropped his phone as a bullet whizzed past his ear.

"Fuck!" he yelled, righting his balance.

He lurched forward, grasping at knob and jerking the door open, despite the dead weight of the agent leaning against it. He practically stumbled over the agent on his way into the public corridor.

Another round impacted the plaster wall of the apartment opposite him as he drew one of his pistols and crouched in the corridor. He hoped nobody in there was hit.

"Everybody stay down!" he yelled. "Active shooter! Police are on their way!"

Based upon the height of the latest round, he figured the shooter had to be directly across the street from them.

He ran to the end of the hallway and hurried down the flights of stairs to the street level.

As he burst through the fire exit door, alarms immediately sounded, which he realized were about to fill the street outside with new targets.

"Damn it!"

He peered around the front corner of his apartment building and looked across the street to the windows of the older-era office building opposite his apartment.

A second-story window was slightly open on one of the darkened offices.

If only he still had his phone, he could notify dispatch.

He ran forward, narrowly avoiding being struck by a passing vehicle that blared its horn.

"Watch out, asshole!" the driver yelled.

Naughware kept running until he reached the front entrance to the office building. He pulled on the front door and was surprised when it freely opened.

"Found your entrance," he said, raising his weapon before him as he entered the dimly lit lobby.

There was nobody visible, and he hurried to the nearest stairwell and raced up toward the second floor.

Halfway up, he heard muted footsteps above him, and he slowed.

The other footsteps abruptly stopped.

After a moment, the footsteps rapidly retreated back upstairs.

He raced up the concrete steps, heedless of the dangers that might await him.

* * *

Alicia Keane was nearly home when she received the call from the captain.

"Get over to Naughware's apartment ASAP," Gunderson ordered. "He called in that FBI agents were down and a sniper was nearby."

"On my way," Keane said.

She did a U-turn in the middle of the street and raced back down the road.

While driving, she fumbled with her phone to dial Taylor.

***

Evan Taylor made his way back to a seedier portion of the south side to the address that Dozer Nelson had given him.

The apartment building was something out of the 1970s with its plain, institutional architecture. Unfortunately for the residents, it looked like the proprietors hadn't put any money into the place since then, either.

The front entrance was unlocked, and one glance at the older-model security cameras suggested that they weren't in working order.

He started to press the call button for the elevator, then thought better of it and instead headed for the nearby stairwell.

"This place is the shits."

He made his way downstairs to the sublevel below, which opened into a musty-smelling, dimly lit hallway.

Quickly finding the apartment he wanted, he stood off to one side and reached over to knock using the rapid sequence that Dozer told him to use.

Two locks clicked, and then a chain sounded on the interior.

Slowly, the door opened a crack.

"Hello?" a tentative male voice asked.

Taylor burst into the apartment, knocking the man back onto the floor before him. He slammed the door shut behind him and looked down at the scruffy-looking man.

"Sham Koda?" Taylor asked.

"Uh-huh. W-who are you?" he asked fearfully. "Who sent you?"

"I sent me," Taylor said. "And now, you're going to tell me everything you know about Lev Spight."

"I don't—"

Taylor drew one of his revolvers and knelt to stick the barrel underneath the man's chin.

Koda's eyes practically bulged out of his head.

"Listen to me, fuckhead," he said. "I've got a handful of hours left before daybreak, and if you want to keep the contents of that ugly skull of yours, you'll tell me what I want to know."

"Listen, y-you don't know what you're asking," Koda said, clearly terrified. "I'm a dead man if I—"

"Pay attention, dipshit," Taylor said. "The way I see it, if you don't start talking, you're definitely a dead man. But if you talk, there may be a way for me to clean up a mess that won't show back up at your front door again. Got it?"

Koda stared up at him with a wild-eyed expression, and he swallowed hard.

"I see the wheels turning in your head," Taylor said. "But think faster, because my trigger finger's getting twitchy. And for God's sake, try not to piss yourself while you're doing it."

"A-all right," Koda said. "I'll tell you whatever you want to know."

Taylor nodded once and holstered his pistol. "See there? You're not as short-sighted as you look."

He watched closely as Koda slowly got to his feet. "I'll show you what I've got."

"Move slowly," Taylor said. "And if you try anything, I'll plug you here and now without a second thought."

Koda slowly made his way over toward the dining room table, which sported a variety of computer equipment.

"I never actually met Spight," Koda said. "I'm working through one of his associates. They both want fresh IDs as fast as possible."

"Who was the associate?" Taylor asked.

"A woman," Koda said. "She said her name was Natasha Prince."

"Mid-twenties, average height, blonde?" Taylor asked.

"Yeah, that's right," Koda said.

"Show me what you've got," Taylor said.

Koda eyes narrowed. "You a cop?"

"You wish," Taylor said. "And the less you know, the

better. Now, talk."

After that, Koda was a veritable font of information, and it didn't take long for Taylor to find out what he needed to know, including showing him digital versions of passports.

"You stay here until I contact you, or so help me, I'll track you down and bury you somewhere remote," Taylor said, taking a quick snapshot of him with his phone. "And don't talk to anyone, either. Got it?"

The man nodded and looked scared enough to promise Taylor his first-born child.

Taylor's phone rang just as he exited the run-down apartment building.

"Yeah, Taylor here," he said.

"It's Keane," Keane said. "Get over to Naughware's place fast. Sniper on site and two FBI agents are down. I'm on my way there now."

"Got it!" Taylor said, already in a dead run toward his car.

CHAPTER 20

The air was tinged with the scent of sulfur as a tremor reverberated through Naughware's body. It felt the same as when he was investigating the warehouse earlier that day.

He stood at the ready near the metal stairwell door that exited to the building's topmost floor. He tried wiping his hand against his pants and adjusted the still-bloodied grip on his revolver as he reached for the door handle.

A strong electrical-like charge coursed through him as he leaned against the door and thrust it open, to which a strong sulfuric smell assailed him.

The corridor appeared clear until he caught movement in the reflection of a nearby brass light sconce.

Before he could react further, his pistol was knocked from his hand by the butt of a rifle.

He dropped and spun just as the silenced rifle fired, sending a bullet whizzing past his face.

Naughware grabbed the rifle's barrel and jerked it forward and free from his attacker's grasp, momentarily causing him to lose his own balance.

As Naughware recovered, the man pressed forward as the blade of a combat knife flashed downward out of his peripheral vision.

The blade swept upward at him, and Naughware trapped his attacker's arm, attempting to redirect the blade back inward toward its owner.

A strange sensation of strength washed through his body, even as his muscles felt heavy.

Naughware's attacker kneed him into the chest, and shock ensued as Naughware flew through the air and against the wall. He bounced off it, and though painful, he miraculously managed to regain his balance.

As his attacker rushed him, Naughware desperately punched at the guy's solar plexus. Strange energy ran down his arm, and his fist felt strangely heavy while impacting the man's body.

To Naughware's amazement, there was a momentary blue-hued flash before his attacker flew backward down the corridor and rolled onto the floor many yards away!

"What the—"

Naughware gaped at his fist, even as an electric sensation coursed through his body and back down his arm.

His thoughts raced as he looked at his attacker, who regained his footing and stared back at him with a bewildered expression.

Even more surprising, he could have sworn that the man's eyes flashed yellow for a split second.

"Freeze!" Naughware yelled as he reached for his other revolver.

The man ran down to the end of the corridor and around the corner.

Naughware pursued him, pistol in hand.

***

Detective Keane and Evan Taylor arrived outside Naughware's apartment building within mere moments of each other.

They both headed for Captain Gunderson, who stood in the middle of the street trying to bring order to a chaotic scene. A mixture of FBI agents, uniformed police, and SWAT tactical team members scrambled throughout the area.

"Where's Naughware?" Taylor demanded before Keane could get a word out.

"Not sure," Gunderson said. "We found his phone on the floor in his apartment, as well as Agent Warwick and a fellow agent. Officers are canvasing the area now."

Keane scanned the area. "Where should we—"

A gunshot sounded, followed by someone shouting.

"Up on the roof, there!" shouted a tactical team member as he pointed to the roofline of the office building across the street.

They saw someone pursuing a figure along the edge of the roof.

"That's Naughware!" Keane said.

Another shot was fired.

Gunderson spoke into the portable radio unit she held. "Anybody have a clear vantage onto that roof?"

Taylor pulled one of his revolvers and ran toward the building.

"You two with me!" Keane shouted at two officers standing nearby as she trailed after Taylor.

* * *

A crashing sound echoed from ahead, and Naughware slowed to carefully peer around the corner of the corridor.

Halfway down the short length of corridor, he saw a set of double doors nearly hanging off their hinges, and he hurried toward them.

He paused and peered past the door jamb into what appeared to be a large maintenance service room. There was no sight of his suspect.

Sirens accompanied crunching noises from the back of the maintenance room. It was then he noticed a metal door, left ajar, leading out onto the roof.

Electrical sensations pulsed through his arms as the faint scent of sulfur wafted past him.

With a swift motion, he swept the door inward. Holding

his revolver at the ready before him, he ventured outside as small bits of gravel crunched beneath his shoes.

He paused to listen, but heard only sirens and crowd noise at street level below.

The hairs on the back of his neck stood straight up as he scanned the roof. Between the air handling equipment, turbines, and other assorted structures, there were plenty of places for him to get ambushed.

"Come out with your hands up," he said.

No response.

Not even a telltale sound of movement.

As he carefully ventured around to his right, a trembling sensation progressively increased in his body, like small waves of current.

Sulfur assailed his senses.

He spun in time to avoid the downward slice of the assailant's combat knife, and fired his revolver.

The pistol round propelled wildly through empty air into the night as the suspect practically changed directions in one fluid blur of motion.

"Freeze!" Naughware yelled before pursuing the man across the short span of roofline leading to the edge.

At the last moment, the man launched himself off the edge of the roof cap, hurtling forward.

Naughware skidded to a stop just short of the roof's edge as the suspect sailed through the air and onto the shorter height of roof of the building next door.

The figure rolled once and came up crouched onto the balls of his feet.

"What the fuck—" Naughware mumbled as he leveled his revolver to fire.

The suspect looked back over his shoulder, and his eyes flashed yellow before he sprinted across the other roof.

Naughware felt surges of current down his arm as he steadied his aim and fired. A strange sizzling sound accompanied the bullet whizzing down range, hitting his target in his back, on the upper left shoulder.

The suspect pitched forward from the bullet's impact, but incredulously kept running, seemingly unabated by his wound.

"Shit," Naughware said, watching helplessly as the figure disappeared into the night.

* * *

"I shot that bastard," Naughware said as the captain, Taylor, and Keane all pressed in around him. "And he ran like it was nothing."

Naughware opened his palm to gaze at the empty shell casing, wondering why the round had sounded as strangely as it did when he'd fired it.

"Adrenaline, you think?" Taylor asked.

"Or maybe he was high on something," Keane said. "PCP?"

Naughware looked up at her. "A deadly accurate sniper high on PCP?"

"Yeah, that sounds stupid," Keane said.

"Perimeter report," Captain Gunderson said into her radio.

Various officers responded negative findings, to which Gunderson said, "Extend the search in all directions. Go door to door."

"You can look but he's long gone," Naughware said.

"Probably," Gunderson said. "For now, tell us what happened."

Naughware recounted all that had transpired.

"He was gunning for you," Keane said.

"Doubtful," Naughware said. "I'm pretty sure it was Warwick he wanted."

"Any idea why?" Gunderson asked.

"Can't be certain," Naughware said. "But I think he's following the trail of pieces, and people, around Jenny Vance. We know that she was a survivor from the Bouquet Corral shootout, which everything appears to revolve around."

"All right, but then, why shoot Warwick?" Keane asked. "I'd expect her more likely to lead him to Vance eventually."

Naughware nodded. "Perhaps. Unless he's just cleaning up loose ends."

Taylor stared back at him and nodded. "Huh. It's a sizable hunch, though I'll take long odds on that."

"You think Vance hired him?" Keane asked.

"Unless we're vastly underestimating Jenny Vance, I can't imagine a fugitive on the run ordering professional hits of that kind," Gunderson said. "Though perhaps Warwick could shed more light on the subject, if she survives."

"What's the latest on Warwick?" Naughware asked, once again trying to wipe the dried blood from his hands by rubbing them against his jeans.

"She should be in surgery by now," Gunderson said. "It's a near-mortal wound, but your quick actions gave her a fighting chance, at least."

Detectives Vigoda and Levitt drove up together on scene and walked over to them.

"Well, well, if it isn't a suspension and a retiree, all in one place," Levitt said, folding his arms before him. "And trouble followed with them, it seems."

"You're up awfully late, Taylor," Vigoda said. "I thought this was well past bedtime for you old folks."

Captain Gunderson gave both of the detectives a hard look. "Stow that crap right now, gentlemen. I'll meet with both you and the tactical commander over by their command vehicle."

Vigoda and Levitt exchanged sheepish looks.

"Yes, Captain," Vigoda said.

Gunderson waited for the two detectives to walk away before turning to Naughware. "You need sleep, but you need to stay somewhere else tonight," she said. "Maybe with Father Thomas?"

"Not with a sniper on the loose," Naughware said. "At least, not until I figure out if I was a target or not."

"I'll set you up in protective custody, then," she said.

"Too confining," Naughware said. "I'll try the local hotels … maybe even stay just outside of town."

"Screw that," Taylor said. "Naughware's staying with me."

Naughware started to disagree, but Taylor gave him a hard look.

"I'll stay at Taylor's place," Naughware said.

"You both be careful," Gunderson said.

"Don't worry, I'll look after him," Taylor said.

"You want some uniforms parked outside?" Gunderson asked.

"Nope," Taylor said. "We've got things to do before our deadline's up."

Naughware looked at him curiously but remained silent.

"Well, I'm not going to just stand around," Keane said, hiking her hands atop her hips.

"You're not, Keane," Gunderson said. "You're going to run the leads that we have and help gather evidence here."

"What about Chip and Dale over there?" Taylor asked, gesturing toward Vigoda and Levitt.

"Not to mention the feds," Naughware said. "Two of their own get gunned down in my own apartment, and you'll bet they'll want to talk to me at least once … probably more."

"You let me worry about them," Gunderson said. "I'll keep both the Detective Sergeant and the feds busy and off your back until some time tomorrow. You and Taylor get some sleep and then get back on this in the morning."

"Captain, aren't you concerned about the FBI's objections?" Keane asked. "We were ordered off the case. That can't make the DA or the mayor happy."

"I'm not bothered by either right now with a gunman running around my city," Gunderson said. "Besides, everyone's going to be running amok for at least the next twenty-four to seventy-two hours."

Naughware frowned. "Maybe that's precisely what someone wanted."

"Maybe," Keane said. "But *who* exactly?"

"Listen, we'd better get going so I can get this kid safely back to the house," Taylor said, pulling Naughware by the arm away from them.

"Hey, what gives?" Naughware asked.

"Get back upstairs and grab some things fast," Taylor said in a lowered voice. "I've got a solid lead on Jenny Vance, and you and I can't afford to screw it up."

* * *

After Taylor shared all that had happened during his investigations that night, Naughware took a shower at Taylor's home and changed into a fresh set of clothes. He watched as his former partner dug out some spare pillow and blankets out of a closet.

"Hey, shouldn't we be leaving to stake out Sham Koda's place?" Naughware asked.

"What do you think we're doing?" Taylor asked. "There's no reason we can't be comfortable on stake out."

Naughware grinned. "You've changed since retirement."

"Shut up."

"What if Koda decides to bail and skips town on us?" Naughware asked.

"He wouldn't dare. I put the fear of God into the little shit," Taylor said. "Don't worry, he'll come through well enough."

"All the crap aside, it feels just like old times to share a stakeout again," Naughware said.

"Yeah, well, don't get too comfortable with it," Taylor said. "After this, I'm headed back into retirement. Already, I'm reflecting on how much better a mattress feels at the end of the day versus a car seat."

"You know, if that sniper has me on his hit list, you're putting yourself in the target reticle for no reason," Naughware said.

"A shit load of good it would do you to get pinned down with no backup," Taylor said.

"And what if he shoots you?" Naughware asked.

"The sonofabitch wouldn't dare."

Naughware cracked a smile, despite himself.

Taylor drove them to Koda's apartment building, but parked just far enough up the street as to not appear obvious while still having ample visibility to the entrance.

They each placed a revolver across their lap as Taylor described Koda to Naughware, as well as showed him Koda's photo from his phone.

"Any reason you didn't tell Gunderson about any of this?" Naughware asked.

"Yep. So far, this case has more holes than a golf course," Taylor said. "Something tells me there's a leak somewhere. Otherwise, how else would we be one step behind all this time? Not to mention, I didn't exactly follow policy or procedure in what I did to get us to this place."

"You don't need policies anymore, you're retired," Naughware said as he used a phone app to access police records.

Taylor chuckled.

"Quite a find you made in Koda," Naughware said. "Guess what? He has no priors. In fact, his record is strangely spotless."

"Well, I'll be damned," Taylor said. "I discovered a new criminal in Abaddon."

"Speaking of which, what do we do with Koda if this pans out for us?" Naughware asked.

"Maybe he can cut a deal with the feds. Eh, worry about that later," Taylor said. "Get some rest, and I'll take first watch."

Naughware covered up with a blanket and leaned his head back against the seat. He closed his eyes and tried to rest, but the strange aspects of the sniper, as well as his own body's odd manifestations kept cycling through his thoughts.

He wished for about the millionth time that he could risk confiding in anyone else about everything he felt and experienced. He scarcely believed his own faculties, much less the idea of convincing anybody the truth of what had happened.

As he mulled things over, he realized that it was his thirty-third birthday and the Bouquet Corral case that marked the beginning of it all. However, the revelation did little to expand his understanding of what was happening to him.

It bothered him that he could fill an Olympic-sized swimming pool with everything that he didn't know or understand.

His thoughts drifted back to the case, and he considered his conversation with Warwick earlier that night when another topic surfaced.

"Hey, Evan," he said. "You ever consider getting into private investigations now that you're retired?"

Taylor folded his arms before him. "The thought had crossed my mind once or twice. Why?"

"Just asking," Naughware said. "I mean, a man can only go fishing so much, right?"

Taylor grunted. "Frankly, I think I've earned the right to do a boat-load of fishing, or even just sit on my ass doing nothing."

"No argument there," Naughware said. "But you'd let me know if you ever hang out a shingle, right?"

"Don't worry," Taylor said. "You'll be one of the first I hand business cards to. I'm sure I'd need help spreading the word."

"Fair enough."

Taylor frowned. "But since you mentioned it, what makes you ask something like that at a time like this?"

Naughware shook his head. "No reason."

"Uh-huh," Taylor said. "Somebody tell you that I got a license to practice or something?"

"Do you?" Naughware asked. "Have a PI's license, I mean?"

"I did get a wild hair briefly, I suppose. Got it approved a few months ago, as a matter of fact," Taylor said. "Then I just filed it away in a drawer and haven't thought much about it since."

"Any particular reason?"

"Any reason that I did or shouldn't?" Taylor said. "Listen, what's with all this PI talk all of a sudden? Where did you hear something like that?"

"Maybe someone mentioned it in passing during a conversation," Naughware said.

"Yeah? Who exactly?"

"Agent Warwick."

Taylor paused and then shook his head. "Those damned feds have been investigating us, haven't they?"

"Watching," Naughware said. "At least, that's how Warwick framed it to me."

"Bah," Taylor said. "Watching. Damned load of good that's doing anyone. It sure hasn't helped break open their case, has it? Hell, Warwick's lucky if she doesn't die on the operating table tonight."

"True enough, I guess," Naughware said.

Taylor sat in deep thought for a time, staring out the car window at the apartment building they were watching.

"Listen, kid," Taylor said. "After nearly thirty years on the force, it sort of gets into your blood. It's a hard habit to break, no matter how much it weighs down on you … ages you.

"Someday, if you stay a detective for as long as I did, or even longer, maybe you'll understand," Taylor said. "Twelve years in the Marines and twenty-eight years on the department … well, that's a damned long time to have something dangerous to occupy my waking moments.

"Then, almost before you know it, things just stop," he said, snapping his fingers. "You sign a stack of paperwork, and suddenly, you're retired. And afterward, it's a bit of a shock, no matter how much you boast about being out of the firing line, not to mention having all that freedom and spare time," he said, staring out past the dash.

"You realize that maybe it wasn't just a job or a steady paycheck," he continued. "In fact, it's grown into something that's part of you, or maybe you're part of it, too. And you just don't drop something like that without missing it, at least from time to time. A person just can't stop cold like that. Or, maybe it's just me that can't."

"Hell, I don't know," he said. "Maybe I'm just an old man rambling on about shit."

"No," Naughware said. "What you said makes sense."

Taylor looked at him. "No, Peter, it doesn't really make sense. It just is, that's all. I don't expect you to understand fully yet … you're still fairly young in your career."

In truth, while Naughware understood what Taylor was telling him, it definitely wasn't something he had personally internalized or identified with.

Still, he had his own litany of personal conundrums that weighed upon him—each unique and puzzling in its own right.

He thought about his strange audio player and the eerie Nowhere Zone. He thought about his encounter with the sniper, and the way he had sent the guy flying down the hallway. All the strange sensations he had experienced. His body had never felt like that before.

The Nowhere Zone.

It remained the biggest, looming mystery in his life. For him, it was the ultimate mind-fuck.

In addition, Taylor's earlier comment struck at Naughware in an odd fashion, and he turned it inward onto himself.

Was the Nowhere Zone part of him?

Or, conversely, was he perhaps part of it?

"Naughware," Taylor said. "You asleep, or did I just send your brain into full tilt or something?"

"Huh?" Naughware asked.

"Tilt," Taylor said. "It's an old pinball machine term—aw, fuck's sake, never mind. Try to get some shut-eye. We need to swap off before long."

Unfortunately, sleep was well beyond Naughware's grasp.

NAUGHWARE TO RUN

CHAPTER 21

Naughware lurched with a start as Taylor shook him awake.

"Your turn," Taylor said.

Naughware stretched and yawned.

"I know three hours ain't much, kid," said Taylor. "But it's longer than I thought you'd manage."

"Anything interesting happen?" Naughware asked.

"Not a thing."

As the early morning sky gained the hint of yellowish hue to the east, Taylor settled beneath his blanket and adjusted the seatback into a reclined position.

"What if Vance doesn't show?" Naughware asked.

"Then we're fucked," Taylor said. "Because, unless you've thought of something better, this is all we've got, partner."

Naughware hoped something happened before the street filled up with cars and people.

Almost an hour later, the sun began to rise. Naughware was once again deep in thought when he spotted someone he recognized entering the apartment building, and he immediately shook Taylor awake.

"W-what is it?" Taylor woke, hoisting his revolver to bear on a prospective target.

"We gotta go," Naughware said. "Now!"

"Jenny Vance?" Taylor asked, casting his blanket off into the back seat.

"More surprising than that," Naughware said, holstering his revolver. "Skeeter Rowe and two of his minions."

"Skeeter Rowe?"

They got out of the vehicle and hurried directly to the building's entrance. The old elevator's doors snapped shut just as they entered the lobby.

They saw the numbers above the elevator during its descent to the lower floor.

"Stairs," Taylor said, leading the way to the stairwell.

They exited into the lower level's dingy hallway in time to see Skeeter Rowe and two men exit the elevator.

Naughware walked down the short distance of hallway, and noticed that Rowe was carrying a small briefcase at his side.

Rowe's two henchmen reached beneath their coats at seeing Naughware's approach.

"Hold it," Rowe said with surprise, reaching backward to bar his men with one arm. "Nobody's here for a shootout with Abaddon's finest, are they?"

Taylor and Naughware stopped short of the trio.

"Gentlemen," Skeeter said. "Imagine my surprise seeing you here."

"What are you doing here, Skeeter?" Naughware asked.

"Just here on business," Skeeter said.

"And what's in the briefcase?" Naughware asked.

"That's the business," he said.

Naughware frowned. "Yeah? Business with who?"

"I'm not at liberty to say," he said. "That's *my* own business."

"Yeah? Well, what if I said liberty or death, asshole?" Taylor asked, to which Naughware glared sidelong at him.

Taylor did a double take. "What? It's been a long night."

Naughware shook his head and returned his attention to Rowe. "I'm not playing games today, Skeeter."

"You passed on your stake in any games days ago,

Naughware," Skeeter said.

Naughware stared at Rowe. "Lev Spight."

Skeeter's left eye twitched, even as he shrugged. "Don't know what the hell you're—"

"Gotcha," Naughware said, pointing his finger at him.

"You've got nothing," Skeeter said. "And find somewhere else to point that stick of a finger, while you're at it."

Naughware didn't budge an inch.

"You know, I'll bet with a little effort I can tie you directly to Spight," Naughware said. "Though now that I think on it, I thought you were digging for Midas Hyde over the Bouquet Corral affair. Does Hyde know you're here helping Spight?"

Rowe stared back at him.

"You're caught between two clients, aren't you?" Naughware asked. "But I'm guessing Spight pays better. Am I right?"

Rowe's expression turned pensive as he pressed his palms together and then abruptly drew his hands apart. "Mr. Hyde and I have parted ways on his latest endeavor," he said.

Taylor's eyes narrowed, and he looked at Naughware. "Just a damned minute. What exactly is Midas Hyde's angle in all this?"

"I'm guessing that a variety of interested parties were disappointed that night at the Bouquet Corral," Naughware said, keeping his attention on Rowe. "Hyde, the Irish Mob, Spight, and Decebal Lungu … they each share some interest in what went down that night, don't they?"

"That's dangerous speculation, Naughware," Skeeter said. "A man who throws those names around too casually could quickly end up six feet under."

"Like The Lion did?" Taylor asked.

Rowe remained silent.

"It looks to me like somebody professional is running around cleaning up loose ends," Naughware said. "Are you a loose end, too, Skeeter?"

"Not my concern," Rowe said. "And I have absolutely nothing to do with any of it. As for Lungu, sounds like bad deals of the past finally caught up with him, that's all."

"Really? You sure there's not a professional waiting to knock on your door, Skeeter?" Naughware asked. "Now that I think about it, your men looked a little too itchy to draw down when they saw us. In fact, it sort of reminds me of Lungu's men. Maybe they'd draw down on most anyone right about now."

The right hands of both men beside Rowe slowly inched toward the open folds of their jackets.

"You two should both probably run along home," Skeeter said. "If you know what's good for you, that is."

"You can kiss my ever-lovin'—" Taylor said.

"Yeah, we'll leave you alone," Naughware interrupted.

Taylor gave him an incredulous look. "We will?"

"Sure, let's just go visit our friend down the hall there like we planned, and leave Skeeter to his business," Naughware said.

"Friend?" Rowe asked.

"Yeah, you're right," Taylor said, squeezing past the men to head for Koda's apartment door.

Naughware stared at Rowe and crossed his arms before him. His fingers slowly inched beneath each side of his jacket.

The imposing mobster's expression turned stony.

"Bad idea," Skeeter said.

As Rowe's two men reached beneath their jackets, Naughware pulled both of his revolvers free from their holsters and pointed one at each of them.

"Freeze, assholes!" Taylor said, covering Naughware with dual pistols from the opposite end of the corridor.

Everybody froze in place until the silence felt deafening.

"I'm playing to win today, Skeeter," Naughware said. "I've got no other choice, and everything to lose."

Rowe stared back at Naughware and nodded once.

"Down boys," Rowe said.

The two men showed their hands, palms open before

them.

"Your play, Naughware," Rowe said.

"Let's go have a chat with our mutual friend," Naughware said.

* * *

Naughware and Taylor relieved Skeeter and his men of their weapons, and seated them on Sham Koda's couch under Taylor's watchful eye. Naughware stood by Koda, who sat on a dining room chair placed in the middle of the small living room.

"What's going on?" Koda asked. "Who are these guys?"

"We've never met, but I'll bet you know me," Skeeter said. "I'm Skeeter Rowe, and I'm representing the final business with your client, Natasha Prince."

"Yeah, I know your name, for sure," Koda said.

Rowe looked at Naughware and beamed.

"Get over yourself already," Naughware said.

"But Prince didn't say anything to me about dealing with anyone else," Koda said.

"She thought you'd say that," Skeeter said, reaching into a pocket.

"Slowly," Taylor warned.

Rowe withdrew a mobile phone and pressed a number of options.

"Mr. Koda," a woman's steady voice said. "Due to an unexpected change in circumstances, the man before you, Mr. Rowe, is now representing my interests. As soon as you provide him with the package, he will provide the payment, just as we agreed. I appreciate you cooperating with him."

The recording ended, and Naughware pointed to the phone.

"We'll take that now," Naughware said.

Rowe shrugged as he handed the phone to Taylor.

"What change of circumstances?" Naughware asked.

"After last night, you already know the answer to that

question," Rowe said. "Word's gotten around town already about a sniper on the loose."

"Where is Prince?" Naughware asked. "Under your protection somewhere?"

"If only," Rowe said. "Unfortunately, all I have is an address and a time to meet."

"Well, I've got everything ready," Koda said, holding a thick-filled manila envelope. "It's all yours, Mr. Rowe."

Naughware looked at him. "Are you kidding? You can give that to me, thank you."

"B-But I thought—"

"That we'd be accessories to a felony for you?" Naughware asked.

Koda's eyes immediately went to the briefcase at Rowe's feet.

"Yeah, not going to happen, either," Naughware said.

Koda appeared wholly dejected. He hanged his head until his chin nearly touched his chest.

"Crissake, Koda, you're a dimwit," Taylor said.

Koda provided a manila envelope to Naughware, which contained two fresh passports with photos of Jenny Vance and Lev Spight.

Naughware noted that Jenny had cut her hair shorter and darkened it, but her eyes and nose were unmistakable from other photos he had seen of her. Lev had adopted a crew cut and added an earring to his left ear.

Naughware showed them to Taylor.

"Well, I'll be damned," Taylor said. "That's top-notch work."

"There should be a finder's fee for me," Rowe said.

"In what reality?" Naughware asked.

Rowe shrugged. "Seems to me that, without my help, all you've got is a briefcase filled with cash and two passports."

Taylor grunted.

"How about you trade your pending prison sentence for cooperating with a police investigation instead?" Naughware asked.

"You can guarantee me that?" Rowe asked.

Naughware looked at Taylor.

"It's been done before. Maybe the captain can work a deal between the feds and the DA," Taylor said. "But that's if we can turn Spight and Vance over to the feds in one piece."

"Vance?" Koda asked. "Who's Vance?"

Naughware ignored Koda and instead considered Taylor's response. "Worth a shot, I suppose."

"Woah, I'm gonna need more than 'worth a shot' before I put my neck out on the line," Rowe said.

"How about not getting shot?" Taylor asked, clinching his jaw while glaring over at Rowe. "Which I can arrange."

Rowe appeared incredulous. "Man, you can't just be threatening to off people like that. Who you trying to fool?"

Naughware glanced at his watch. "Skeeter, what time is your meet-up?"

CHAPTER 22

Naughware and Taylor watched as Skeeter Rowe reached into his jacket to retrieve another phone.

Taylor frowned. "Damn, just how many phones have you got in there, son?"

"I'm not your son," Rowe said. "And the meet's supposed to go down less than two hours from now."

"Where?" Naughware asked.

"Oh, no," Rowe said. "Not until we make a deal."

Naughware's patience was wearing thin. "Look, Skeeter, I'll do the best I can. That's all I can promise you."

Rowe considered that. "Well, at least you're honest about it."

The broad-shouldered mobster wistfully rubbed his chin.

"Rowe," Taylor said. "If Naughware can't get it done, I can probably pull some strings, too."

Naughware looked at him with surprise.

"I've been at this a lot longer than you, partner," Taylor said. "And I've built up some favors over the years."

"Good to know," Rowe said.

Taylor gave him a hard look. "Not favors for you."

"What's it going to be, Skeeter?" Naughware said.

Rowe considered him.

"All right. I'll play this out," Rowe said. "But I go to the meet with you, or they'll bolt, for sure."

"All right," Naughware said. "But if I even get a hint of you bailing on us, just remember that there's not a rock remote enough for me not to find you under."

"Fine. And you let my men go about their business," Rowe said.

"If that sweetens the deal, fine," Naughware said. "But we keep their weapons, for now."

"Fair enough," Rowe said.

"Then it's settled," Naughware said, withdrawing his mobile phone from a pocket. "I'll call Keane and Gunderson."

"What about me?" Koda said. "Don't I get anything for my troubles?"

Taylor gave him a wry look. "You mean, other than five years or more in prison, if you're lucky?"

Rowe chuckled. "I just love newbies."

Koda's shoulders drooped forward. "Aw, man. That's just wrong."

* * *

Once Naughware called Captain Gunderson, the political wheels were set into motion between the district attorney, the FBI, and Abaddon's police commissioner on negotiating the details for staking out the meeting with Jenny Vance.

Normally, the process would be painstaking. Fortunately for Naughware, time wasn't on the side of the bureaucracy.

Naughware, Taylor, and Rowe met Gunderson, Keane, a small contingent of police support, and some FBI agents at a safe house not far from where the meeting was scheduled to take place. The group quickly filled up the two bedroom apartment.

A self-important-looking man wearing a business suit walked over to where Naughware and Gunderson were talking.

"Detective Naughware," the man said. "I'm Special Agent in Charge Joseph Purvis. Given Agent Warwick's injuries, I'm taking over as lead on the case. Maybe we'll finally start making robust progress that's been absent to this point."

"Agent Purvis," Naughware said with a nod.

"Detective, we're delaying the meeting with Vance until we can get more resources on site," Purvis.

"Hold it," Rowe said, holding up his hand. "There ain't no putting off this meeting. I've only got a time and location, and no ability to contact the client."

Naughware smiled. "You see, Purvis, it's better if you let us handle this."

"Come on," Gunderson said. "Let's move it, folks."

"Now, wait just a damned minute, Captain," Purvis said. "This is a federal matter, and as Special Agent in Charge, I'll say who moves and when."

Gunderson started to protest, but Naughware walked up to Purvis and stared him straight in the eyes. "You listen to me, Purvis. Right before she was shot, Agent Warwick and I came to an arrangement about my taking lead on this case if I kept her informed. I've made sure to inform both the FBI and my Abaddon superiors. I've kept up my end of the bargain."

Purvis appeared unimpressed. "A bargain that I don't have knowledge of. And, unless I'm mistaken, the only other agent in the room who could corroborate your story is dead."

"Boys, we're running out of time," Gunderson said. "And Agent Purvis, you're walking into a case that's already matured prior to your arrival. So, unless you want the FBI's entire case to fail, and it be entirely on your shoulders, you'll let us take lead on this. At least then you'll have a viable scapegoat, and your resume won't be entirely ruined."

Purvis turned to look at Captain Gunderson.

"You may have a point, Captain," he said. "This case crosses multiple agencies, as well as jurisdictions."

"My agents will accompany Mr. Rowe to the meeting—" Purvis said. "If we're doing this, it's best with the FBI taking lead."

"These FBI agents? Hard pass on that," Rowe said. "If this lady you're seeking is a fed, these guys will get made on the spot."

"He's right, you know," Gunderson said. "If Vance is half the agent you claim, she'll make them before they even exit the vehicle. Then you may lose her forever."

"I'll go," Keane said.

"I'll accompany Keane," Naughware said.

"Vance may already know you," Keane said. "And besides, your look doesn't exactly shout 'I'm somebody from the hood,' you know."

"She's right. We need people that look like they belong with me," Rowe said, pointing to Keane. "Like little sister here."

"I'm trying really hard not to feel offended right about now," Keane said.

"Aw, that was meant as a big-time compliment," Rowe said, laying on the charm.

"Barking up the wrong tree, Sparky," Naughware said to him. "But Rowe's got a point about blending in."

Keane shrugged. "So, I'm in."

Rowe smiled with an approving expression as a police technician walked over to everyone.

"Apologies, but we need to get Mr. Rowe wired now," the tech said.

"Wired?" Rowe said. "I don't care about a wire; I want a vest in case things go south."

"Fine. Get the man a vest," Naughware said.

"Um, there's no spares," a nearby tactical team member said. "We only stock a handful in the tactical vehicle."

"For fuck's sake," Naughware said, stripping out of his vest and handing it to Rowe.

"Are you out of your—" Gunderson said.

"It's fine. I'm going to be behind cover with the feds," Naughware said.

"Don't worry, Captain. We'll look after the detective," the tactical officer said.

Rowe winked at Keane. "Can't wait to have you at my side, my dear," he said before following the tech into a nearby room.

"But you still need a second person to accompany Keane and Rowe," Purvis said.

"I've got someone in mind who should work out just fine," Gunderson said.

* * *

Detective Mateo Garcia, a twenty-something officer from Abaddon's gang and narcotics unit, partnered with Detective Keane to accompany Skeeter Rowe to meet with Jenny Vance. Garcia had a hardened look about him, which looked convincing enough for the task at hand.

The meeting was designated in a relatively abandoned part of the south side of the city outside a rather seedy-looking motel. Captain Gunderson and SAIC Purvis remained in a SWAT mobile command vehicle parked in an old warehouse well outside the area, so as not to attract attention. Unfortunately, Taylor had to remain with them, as he was no longer an actively serving detective.

Naughware insisted that other law enforcement personnel remained a half mile or more away from the location, while he, two police tactical team members, and a couple of FBI agents crouched in the first floor of an adjacent two-story building hosting an upholstery service, though their view of the actual meeting site was severely obscured.

The only other buildings adjacent to the property were a paint and body shop, a Bargain Hunter retail store, and a four-story apartment building with first-floor shops comprised of a run-down laundromat, a sandwich shop, a quick cash loan service, and a hair and nails styling shop.

"What's the latest update on Agent Warwick?" Naughware asked.

The two FBI agents glanced at one another.

"Critical condition," said one agent. "But at least she made it through surgery."

"Word is that few people survive a wound like that," said the other agent.

"Well, I hope she pulls through okay," Naughware said.

The minutes felt like hours, and Naughware absently took out his digital player and inserted the earbuds.

He clicked on the random song feature, and immediately regretted it as Creedence Clearwater Revival's "Bad Moon Rising" started to play.

"Aw, shit," he muttered under his breath, clenching his fist.

"Huh?" asked the FBI agent closest to him.

"Nothing. I just forgot to wear my lucky underwear today," Naughware said.

The agent gave him an odd look while Naughware caught a glimpse of Rowe's black Cadillac pulling into the motel's parking lot and stopping.

"Here we go," Naughware said, removing his earbuds and slipping the player into his shirt pocket.

Detectives Keane and Garcia exited the vehicle, followed by Rowe, who held the telltale manila envelope in his hands.

Jenny Vance appeared from a small corridor near some of the motel's vending machines and tentatively approached the trio. From Naughware's vantage, a bulge beneath her leather vest in the small of her back suggested she was armed.

One of the FBI agents crouched beside Naughware discreetly stayed below the window level as he made his way over to a nearby door that exited outdoors around the corner of the building, well out of view of the action taking place outside.

They watched as Rowe approached Vance with the envelope.

Vance's right hand went toward her back pocket as she reached out with her left hand toward Rowe.

Garcia and Keane subtly changed to forward-leaning stances.

"Get ready," said the FBI agent who had moved to crouch next to the door.

He cracked it open, and a breeze of outside air wafted into the room as Naughware and the others moved toward it. One of the tactical team members remained near the window with an assault rifle readied.

As Naughware neared the door, his eyes widened as he detected the unmistakable scent of sulfur wafting in from outside.

"Shit," he said, pulling one of his revolvers free of its shoulder holster.

"What?" asked the agent close to the door. "What's wrong?"

"We gotta get out there, right now," Naughware said.

"But your officers haven't acted yet," the other FBI agent said, though the other tactical team member readied himself behind Naughware in support.

Naughware shouldered past the agent with the tactical team member close behind him.

"Everybody down!" Naughware shouted as he came around the building's corner.

Detective Garcia pulled his weapon and yelled, "Freeze, police!"

A surprised-looking Keane pulled her weapon, too.

Lev Spight appeared from inside one of the nearest hotel rooms, sporting an automatic pistol in each hand.

Naughware changed direction and rushed toward Spight.

"Get down!" he shouted.

Spight looked at him with surprise just before a red dot appeared on the man's forehead.

As Naughware sprinted forward, he spun around to block the sniper's shot.

Something shifted in his pocket immediately before something hard and fast hit him squarely in the chest. The force of the impact propelled him flat on his back onto the pavement below, and he smacked the back of his head against the pavement.

"Sniper!" a tactical team member shouted.

"Naughware!" Keane yelled. "Officer down!"

Nearly losing his breath as a wave of pain coursed through him, Naughware heard a bullet whizzing above and past him.

He craned his neck enough to see Spight lurch backward onto the asphalt not far from him.

"NO!" Vance screamed.

Chaos ensued around him, including Vance crying uncontrollably somewhere behind him, followed by the sounds of people's feet stomping on the pavement.

"Stay down," Keane ordered as she tackled and shielded Vance.

Naughware heard urgent-sounding voices abound, as well as radio traffic and the distant sounds of sirens, even as pain pulsed and seared through his chest.

"Fuck," he groaned.

Despite his agony, he strained to raise his gun-wielding arm and scanned the façade of the apartment building before him where the shots likely originated.

He spotted the sniper firing a rifle from a window on the third floor, and he felt an electrical charge flowing through his body and into his hand as he struggled to steady his aim.

He fired twice amidst strange sizzling sounds that discharged from his weapon.

The first round impacted the window frame with a blue-tinged flash.

The second round hit the sniper with a whitish flash.

The sniper jerked backward but quickly recovered his poise and grinned as he leveled his rifle at Naughware, who could have sworn the man's eyes glinted yellow.

This is it, Naughware thought.

Multiple gunshots and rounds impacted the window and the surrounding brick before a louder sizzling sound whizzed above Naughware, causing the sniper to lurch backward into the apartment.

Naughware frowned, and felt a strange sensation urging

him to look somewhere behind him. He craned his neck to see back and to his left.

He saw the chiseled features of a dark-clad woman holding a long rifle and standing before the open doorway of a second-floor motel room. The edges of her mouth upturned slightly, and she winked at him. Then she gave him a small, offhanded salute.

Keane's panicked-looking face appeared over him, blocking his view.

"You're going to be okay," she said. "Help's on the way, partner."

"That woman—" he managed to say, before the effort sent a wave of pain through his chest and lungs that quickly silenced him.

Keane ripped open his shirt, then looked down at him in shock.

"Wait," she said. "You're not even bleeding."

CHAPTER 23

Naughware sat up in a bed at Abaddon South Municipal Hospital as Dr. Sal Morrison sat beside him, swiping across a series of images on a digital tablet.

Captain Gunderson, Taylor, and Keane watched with interest.

"Detective Naughware," Dr. Morrison said. "You're a very lucky man. You have a couple of bruised ribs and some serious chest contusions, but other than that, there appears to be no critical injuries."

"Incredible," Gunderson said.

"If the bullet hadn't impacted your little device, you'd likely be dead," Morrison said. "Frankly, I've never seen anything like it. You lead a charmed life, Mr. Naughware."

"Which is odd, because he's never been overly charming," Taylor said, to which Keane laughed.

Naughware looked over at Taylor, who had a good-natured grin on his face.

"Thanks, Doc," Naughware said. "But when can I get outta here?"

"Not until Father Thomas stops by," Gunderson said.

Naughware visibly winced. "You told Thomas?"

Gunderson's eyes widened. "I suppose you think he wouldn't have heard, if I hadn't told him? The press is all over this already."

Naughware pinched the bridge of his nose between his thumb and fingers.

"And then where would I be?" Gunderson asked. "He's your father, Peter. Besides, I can't afford to cross any priests, especially such a civically engaged and respected one who could make my life a living hell."

"My thoughts exactly," Naughware said. "Though for different reasons, I suppose."

She arched her brow at him. "Be nice. Father Thomas is a good man."

Naughware gave in and instead looked back at the doctor. "You were saying about my release?"

"Actually, I'd like to keep you overnight for observation, if that's okay," Dr. Morrison said. "With chest wounds, it's just a precaution, you understand. We want to make sure we haven't missed potential internal hemorrhaging."

"Please, keep him as long as you want, Doctor," Gunderson said. "He's left me with a hell of a bureaucratic mess to unravel. And frankly, I'd appreciate anything you can do to keep him out of my hair."

Morrison smiled. "I'll leave you to visit and rest, and then check back in on you before I go off-shift."

As the doctor exited, Naughware looked back at Gunderson. "Today was a failure."

"Hardly," she said. "You saved most of us. If you hadn't spotted that sniper when you did, he could've taken most of us out before we got a shot at him."

Naughware looked past her at the wall. "It didn't help Lev Spight."

Gunderson gave him a sympathetic look. "Peter, you know very well you can't always save everyone."

"I made a promise to his mother," Naughware said.

"That's the lesson, then," Gunderson said. "You have to temper your promises."

His eyes took on a distant look.

"You're a really good detective," Gunderson said. "But you're not a superhero. None of us are."

He stared into her eyes. "Then why do I still feel so guilty?"

Gunderson remained silent.

He looked at his lap and frowned before looking back at her. "Did you see—or did anyone report about—a female sharpshooter on the scene? I think she was on the tactical team or something."

Gunderson's eyes narrowed. "Not that I recall. However, it's still a fresh scene," she said. "Both the feds and us are actively processing evidence and doing field interviews. However, no, nobody thus far has mentioned anyone like that."

"Maybe another fed who we weren't told about?" he asked.

She frowned. "As far as I know, no. Are you sure you're remembering things clearly? You took a good fall onto hardtop after being shot," she said. "Maybe you've got a slight concussion or something."

"I know what I saw," Naughware said. "There was something odd about her. She—she even winked at me."

"Winked?" Keane asked. "Now I know you're loopy."

The captain looked over at Keane with an unspoken question in her eyes.

Keane shook her head. "No, Captain, I didn't see any female snipers … only the male suspect who was shooting at us," she said, noting Naughware's growing look of frustration. "But I had my hands full at the time trying to cover Vance. That's not to say that somebody else didn't see her."

"Maybe once the autopsy's completed on the sniper, the bullets inside him can—"

The captain held up her hand in a halting gesture. "Let's leave that for another day."

She gently placed her hand atop his shoulder. "Listen, I'm just relieved you're alive and in one piece. Now just focus on getting some rest."

"Yeah. All right, Cap," Naughware said. "I'll see you in

the morning."

She gave him a cross look. "Like hell. I'll see you in no less than a week … or else."

He started to protest, but Gunderson turned her back on him to leave.

"That's an order, Detective," she said. "Please, do try to follow one for a change."

"Oo, burned," Keane said, and then looked at her watch. "Speaking of burned, I'd better get started on the field reports ASAP. Otherwise, I'll miss my dinner date tonight with Brooke … and then I'd get burned."

"Date?" Naughware asked. "Just how long have you two been a couple, anyway? Wait, don't you both already live together?"

She gave him a wan look. "Naughware, it doesn't surprise me that you don't know the first thing about nurturing a happy long-term relationship. Rule one is, you've gotta keep wooing them to keep the romance alive."

"I'm pretty sure that nobody actually says wooing," he said.

"Nobody male, I'd imagine," she said.

"Yeah, well, I've never heard any lesbians say that, either," he said.

"Then you're not asking the right lesbian," she said with a smug expression. "Ciao."

With that, she promptly strolled out of the room.

Naughware looked at Taylor with a perplexed expression.

"Don't look at me. I'm not even going to touch that," Taylor said, walking over to stand beside him. "The doc was right, though. You were damned lucky."

Naughware opened his palm to look at his digital device, still clasped in his hand. "Maybe too lucky."

Taylor frowned. "What do you mean by that?"

He could have sworn that he'd felt something move inside his shirt just before he was shot. In fact, he was convinced it was his player.

But on its own?

He was bothered enough about it that he wanted to tell Taylor, but then thought better of it.

"Ah, nothing," he said. "I guess I'm just feeling a bit exhausted after everything, that's all. Been a long day."

"Well, probably not surprising. Like the captain said, get some rest," Taylor said. "After all, I figure you're going to need to work a lot of overtime in the near future."

"How's that?"

"Since I'm on nobody's payroll for this little adventure, you owe me about twenty different dinners," Taylor said. "And no less than fifteen or so different bar tabs."

"Hey, we're friends," Naughware asked. "At the very least, haven't you ever heard of *pro bono*?"

"Or, as I call it, pro no-no."

"You're all heart, Evan," Naughware said.

Taylor mussed up Naughware's hair with one hand before turning to leave. "And, after today, you should probably feel happy that you've still got one, kid," he said as he pulled opened the door.

Naughware watched him depart and then rolled the digital player over in his hand. There was a small indention in the metal casing where the bullet had impacted it, but nothing more. The black metallic surface wasn't even marred.

Naughware's eyes narrowed. "How is that even possible?"

He considered that a large-caliber bullet like the one the sniper used should have gone right through the thing, as well as completely through him.

"As if you're not already full of surprises," he said, rolling the device over in his hand again.

A few moments later, Naughware felt a presence nearby and turned to look at the door.

The looming figure of Thaddeus Prescott stood just inside, clasping his hands before him.

"You up to seeing visitors?" he asked.

"I didn't know The Monk made house calls,"

Naughware said.

"I don't," Prescott said as he entered the room. "This is a hospital."

"To what do I owe this unexpected visit?"

Prescott shrugged. "Word got around about your miraculous survival from a sniper's bullet. How are you doing?"

"Doc says I'm going to be okay," Naughware said. "The word 'lucky' has also been used a lot recently."

"Hm," Prescott said. "I think less so."

Naughware looked up at him. "Oh?"

Prescott held out his open hand toward him. "Would you mind a quick handshake?"

Naughware swapped the player into his left hand and reached out with his right. They meshed palms to shake, and Prescott clasped his free hand over the top of Naughware's. Then he drew his eyelids closed.

A strange sensation went up Naughware's ulna and into his shoulder, and his face registered with surprise.

"The storm has arrived," Prescott said, opening his eyes to stare at him. "And you, Naughware, are the eye of it."

Naughware withdrew his hand, and the sensations in his right side abated.

"What's that supposed to mean?"

Prescott stared down at Naughware's left hand. "Consult your talisman and find out."

"Talisman?"

Naughware followed the man's gaze and opened his palm. The device's LCD display was pulsing slightly.

"Now what?" he asked, staring at the display.

He felt a slight shift of air, and when he looked back up at Prescott, the man was no longer standing there.

"Hey," he said. "Where the hell did you go?"

The player grew increasingly warmer in his hand.

He grasped the set of earbuds lying on the small stand beside his bed and plugged them into his player. Then he inserted the earbuds and pressed play.

"The Gospel of John Hurt" by alt-J began to play.

He lay his head back onto the pillows with his eyes closed and listened to the song.

CHAPTER 24

By the following morning, Naughware had a couple of interpretations to the lyrics in the alt-J song, though the few insights he gained were less than hopeful sounding in their tone.

Was something breaking out of him?

Though fantastic in scope, it might reflect the increase of strange sensations and experiences he had since his birthday over a week ago.

Still, he wondered why that particular birthday—thirty-three—was noteworthy.

He was definitely in uncharted territory, and that was saying something considering his already bizarre life to date.

Conundrums aside, at least the hospital had released him to go home.

Home.

Father Thomas kindly drove him to his apartment building.

"You want me to come up with you?" Thomas asked.

"Nah, I'm fine," Naughware said, reaching for the door handle. "Thanks again, Thomas."

"I'll bring dinner by tonight for us," Thomas said. "How's that sound?"

Naughware nodded. "Sounds good. Thanks."

He exited the car and watched Thomas drive away.

When he arrived at his apartment, his door was crisscrossed with strips of crime scene tape, which he knocked down with a single swipe, only to feel pain shoot through his chest and shoulder.

"Mr. Naughware?" asked a man from behind.

Naughware spun around, and the seventy-something-aged man before him looked like he was ready to jump out of his skin.

"Mr. Holder," Naughware said. "Ever the prompt landlord."

"Well, I just happened to see you through my window as you arrived," Holder said.

"You sit by your window a lot," Naughware said.

"It's the only way to see what's going on," the old man said.

"Ever thought of taking a walk, instead?"

"Of course," Holder said. "As I was saying, since I caught glimpse of you arriving, I wanted to talk to you about the … well, the scene inside."

Naughware unlocked and opened the door, only to see the dried blood and viscera caked on the wall to his left.

"Oh, yeah," he said. "This scene."

Suddenly, he recalled that Thomas intended to come by for dinner that night. He withdrew his phone and prepared to dial him.

"Yes, well," Holder said. "I can contract some repairmen and painters in the next few days, if you're agreeable. Although it's somewhat outside the normal wear-and-tear clause in the rental agreement—"

Naughware raised his hand to halt him. "Don't worry, I'll cover any additional costs. And if you need, I'm sure the department has a list of reputable services for cleaning up things like this."

"Are you sure you don't mind?" he asked. "It's just that, we've never had anything like this happen before, and I'd hate for the other tenants—"

"Yeah, I get it," Naughware said, stepping inside his apartment and slowly closing his front door on the man. "Just bill me. Thank you, Mr. Holder."

Naughware didn't wait for a response as the door clicked shut. He turned and saw the dried blood on his living room floor before the chair where Agent Warwick had been sitting.

Where he had nearly been shot himself.

He lightly rubbed at his chest and stared at the dried blood again.

"Crap," he said as he auto-dialed Thomas.

After changing the location for dinner plans with Thomas, Naughware lay atop his bed in his apartment, staring at the ceiling in deep thought.

Time passed.

At the sound of knocking, he jolted awake, only then realizing that he had dozed off.

The light through his window was waning, suggesting late afternoon.

The knocking resumed on his front door.

"Just a minute!"

His chest hurt, and he groaned as he pivoted off the bed to stand.

His entire body ached as he walked to the door and peered through the peephole.

It was Constance Spight.

"For fuck's sake," he muttered under his breath.

Despite an inclination against it, he nevertheless opened the door.

"Mrs. Spight," he said. "What a surprise to see you here."

"Detective Naughware," she said in a cold tone. "May I come in?"

He widened the gap of the door enough to permit her to enter, and she walked past him, only to stop cold in her tracks as she stared down at the living room floor.

"You seem to leave a trail of blood wherever you go

these days," she said.

As he closed the door, she turned back to him, only to go wide-eyed at the sight of the dried gore on his wall.

"You'll have to excuse the apartment," he said. "It's been through a lot lately."

She quickly regained her composure but said nothing.

"Mrs. Spight, I must tell you, I'm so very sorry about Lev," he said.

"*You promised me*," she said, raising her index finger before him. "You said you'd bring him back to me, but I never expected it would be as a *corpse*!"

"Yes, and I did my best. I really did," he said. "I even took a bullet to try to save him."

"I don't doubt that you tried, though you look surprisingly well for a man who's just been shot," she said. "But, no matter. In the end, you failed … quite miserably."

Amidst the aches and pain, he felt an immense wave of weariness flow through him. His guilt-laden mind felt nearly too heavy to keep his head aloft, while his body was physically beaten to near exhaustion.

"Yes," he said. "I'm afraid I did, at least as far as Lev was concerned."

"He was my *only* concern, Naughware," she said. "A mother will fight to the grave for her children."

He had nothing to say to that.

"Now, you're going to have to carry that failure, and the shame of it, with you forever," she said. "It's *your* personal burden … and my curse upon you."

While he could hardly deny a grieving mother her right to express herself, he was quickly reaching a limit to his forbearance.

"I carry a helluva lot of burdens," he said. "Perhaps this isn't the best time for either of us to—"

"I've said what I came to say," she said. "Except to add that I'll never forget this. And, if it's within my power, neither will you, Detective."

Naughware's features hardened, but he said nothing.

She stared coldly into his eyes, and then turned to leave.

At least, he retained enough cognizance of manners to hold the door open for her.

"Goodbye, Mr. Naughware," she said before turning to march down the hallway.

He quietly closed the door and stared at the dried blood on the floor.

* * *

Naughware was appreciating a hot and steamy shower when his smartphone rang.

It was Eva Shyne.

He turned off the water and answered.

"Hello?"

"Detective Naughware?" she asked.

"Yep, it's me."

"I hope I haven't called at a bad time," she said. "What with everything I heard on the news."

The edges of his mouth turned up. "Oh, not at all. Actually, it's good to hear from you."

"I'm pleased to know that," she said.

He could almost picture her smiling.

"The reason I'm calling is, I have some really interesting information to share with you," she said. "It's about the things we discussed yesterday at the shop."

"What have you learned?" he asked.

"Well, given everything, it's probably better if I can show you some things in person while I fill you in," she said.

"Okay," he said. "How about an hour from now?"

"Yeah, that's perfect," she said. "I'm still here at the shop."

* * *

Naughware was sore, tired, and operating on no small amount of residual adrenaline and willpower when he walked into The Spooky Word. But the moment he saw Eva standing at the counter with an array of papers and books before her, he felt a strange renewal of energy and enthusiasm.

She looked up when she heard the shop door open. "Detective, I'm glad you could come here on short notice."

"Good of you to call, Ms. Shyne," he said.

Naughware walked over to her, and she smiled at him in a warm way that made him smile in return.

"Ms. Shyne," she said, subtly shaking her head. "You make me sound so mature, somewhat like my mother. And besides, surnames are so formal. What if I asked that you just call me Eva instead?"

"Okay," he said. "Only if you call me Peter."

"Done," she said. Then her eyes took on a playful glint. "Ah, but are you a Peter or a Pete?"

"Friends and family call me Peter," he said. "But sometimes my friend, Glenn, calls me Pete."

"Mm. Peter then," she said.

He looked down at the items arrayed atop the counter while absently rubbing at his bruised chest. "You look as though you've been busy."

She began shuffling the papers and books into a more orderly fashion.

"Busy, yes, but I love doing research," she said. "Especially into topics like this."

"I didn't expect to hear back from you so quickly, to be honest," he said. "In fact, I sort of feel as if I sent you off on a wild goose chase."

"I like geese, too," she said with a twinkle in her eyes.

A wave of amusement flowed through him. "What did you discover, oh-accomplished-researcher?"

She walked around and to the outside of the counter to stand beside him.

He caught the faint scent from her perfume, which he liked.

"That's a nice scent on you, if you don't mind me

saying," he said.

She smiled and looked up at him. "What?"

"Your perfume," he said. "I like it."

Her expression turned quirky. "But I'm not wearing any."

He frowned and felt his cheeks flush with heat.

"No worries," she said. "I'll bet it's just the incense that I sell at the other end of the shop."

"Okay," he said, feeling a bit confused, as the scent grew stronger as she stood beside him. "Maybe share with me what you've discovered," he added, eager to change the subject.

"Sure," she said, pointing down at one of the books before her. "So, you told me about a number of substances."

"First, let's go over the human bone powder, serpent bone powder, and ground rose thorn," she continued. "These are components commonly used for spells or incantations and the like, mostly to either increase, strengthen, or focus the other properties of the spell."

Naughware didn't particularly find that useful. "Increase, strengthen, or focus the other properties," he said. "I'll keep that in mind."

The problem was, he had no earthly idea how to apply that sort of information, much less where to start searching.

"What if someone added it to something?" he asked. "A street drug, for example."

She stared back at him. "Seriously?"

"Hypothetically, of course," he said.

She considered that. "Well, that's an interesting prospect, to say the least."

"Do tell."

"Well, let's just suppose that someone wanted to focus a lot of ambient energies to increase the power of a spell," she said. "But—"

"Yes?"

"That would take someone who was planning on leveraging an entity or Power," she said. "I've never heard of that being attempted on a large scale, much less being successful."

"What might it do, if it were successful?" he asked.

"Without more information, one could only guess how it might affect a given incantation or spell," she said. "Think of it like trying to power a light bulb with a host of ambient batteries around you. The light bulb requires a minimal level of power to light at all."

"But suppose that bulb had further capacity, based upon folding in more voltage," she continued. "Imagine how much brighter the illumination might grow with additional energy funneled into it, given the bulb didn't burn itself out beforehand, of course."

He nodded. "Now, that's an analogy I can wrap my mind around."

She momentarily sorted through her notes.

"As for the sulfuric powder residue you mentioned finding in a circle," she said. "Most of the references point to a summoning process of one kind or another."

"Oh, and there was a pungent smell around it," he said. "Reminiscent of burned sulfur, but different somehow, and much stronger."

"I'm willing to bet you smelled brimstone," she said. "Well, that helps narrow it down further."

"Brimstone," he said. "As in, hell, fire, and brimstone?"

"Yep," she said.

He mulled over the ominous prospect of that.

She thumbed through another book that had multiple tabbed pages. "The strongest scents reflect the most potent and powerful powders. In fact, this book refers to such a substance as Elouthrektar, and—"

"Wait," he said. "What the hell would someone try to summon with that?"

She read further and stopped to look at him with a wry expression.

"Yes, hell," she said. "A very apt reference, Peter."

He certainly didn't like the sound of that.

"Based upon lore, such a substance could be used as a

conduit in order to summon a Marquis of Hell," she said. "From what I read, the most detailed accounts reference the demon Marchosias."

His eyes widened. "Marchosias … who is a—"

"Marquis of Hell," she said, pointing to a drawing in one of her books. "According to this, he's a fire-spitting demon; one of the worst that you might run across, if that were actually possible in the first place."

"That's mere fantasy," he said. "Like all those angels mentioned in the Bible."

"Well, I've never encountered anything either that magnificent or malevolent," she said. "But I believe that Powers and Principalities are legitimate."

Naughware didn't quite know what to say.

Then the conversation that he had a few days ago with The Monk came to mind.

"Powers and Principalities again," he said.

"Frankly, I have to give you bonus points, in one respect, for neither laughing or cursing at me outright," she said. "And two, for not walking out of here already. Most ordinary people would've left by now."

He looked down at the drawing. It was a hideous-looking beast; the stuff of nightmares.

"If there's one thing you need to know about me, it's that I'm not what you'd classify among *ordinary people*," he said.

"I had a feeling that might be the case," she said.

He grinned at her and then looked back at the image of the demon.

The sniper-assassin didn't strike him as overly malevolent—merely strong and surprisingly accomplished in his skills. Although the flash of yellow to the assassin's eyes appeared otherworldly.

"He wasn't like that drawing at all," he said.

Her eyebrows rose. "Wait, you're not saying that you've actually seen something resembling that?"

"Thankfully, no," he said. "Just a rather unique man. A

suspect."

She considered that. "Then maybe he was just attempting to channel some of the demon's power. Trying to enhance his own abilities, perhaps."

That caught Naughware's interest.

She looked down at her notes. "Most texts call the sulfuric powder accersito, which is used to summon powers and entities in general."

He looked back down at the illustration in the book and pointed to the demon. "Those books didn't say anything about how to battle a creature like the one pictured there, did they?"

She flipped through a few pages of the book.

"If what's here is actually true, it says that it's vulnerable to cold or lightning," she said.

"Lightning?" he asked.

His mind reeled.

Electricity.

He recalled the distinct sensations he had felt when in proximity to the powder, as well as those experienced when fighting the sniper hand-to-hand.

That experience alone had been mind-numbing.

Channeling.

"Shit," he whispered looking at his hands. "No way."

"You okay?" she asked, touching his elbow. "You look like you just saw your own ghost or something."

"Huh?" he asked, starting. "Uh, nothing. Just processing everything."

She frowned. "O-kay."

"You ever hear of anyone—" he said, then stopped. "Anyone who could manifest things like electricity without using those other components we first spoke about."

"Oh, I never said anyone could do that," she said. "Just channeling or focusing spells and incantations. To summon elements such as fire, cold, or energy … that's way outside anything I've ever heard of. Of course, maybe if a Power or Principality channeled through a person to harness those abilities, but—"

"But what?" he asked.

"Well, I'd venture someone would have to channel most of that Power or Principality into themselves, and that's—wow. Suffice to say, most people would probably just get consumed by the entity first."

"You mean, possessed?" he asked.

"To say the least, I would think," she said. "Probably more like burn through someone, much like grabbing onto a high-power transmission line."

He tried to fathom that, and wondered if that was what happened when the electric sensations spanned through his arm and hand.

"Could a person channel those things by accident?" he asked. "That is, unconsciously?"

"Do you mean, without forethought?" she asked, quirking her lips. "That would imply the wielder was unaware, and yet able to channel energies."

He noted her look of deep contemplation. "Yeah. Is something like that possible?" has asked with a hopeful expression.

"I wouldn't think so," she said with a pronounced look of puzzlement.

"Well, it was just a thought," he said disappointedly. He was grasping at any explanation, and felt stymied at each turn.

"But understand, that's not really my specialty," she said, noticing his dejected look. "I could check into it further … call around to a few people, if you're interested. Might take me some time, though."

"No, don't bother," he said. "I sort of wrapped up the problem anyway."

"Problem?" she asked.

"Uh, the case, I mean," he said. "We stopped the suspect who was using the sulfuric powder."

"Oh," she said. "That man you mentioned?"

He nodded.

"Can I ask?" she asked. "What was he like?"

"Well, he was surprisingly strong," he said before noticing her rapt attention. "But he's dead now. We weren't able to take him into custody."

"I see," she said. "Wait, from that place where you were shot?"

"I'm sure the press would've mentioned that," he said.

Her expression turned sheepish. "Well, I wasn't exactly sure which cases you were working on."

"Sure, that makes sense," he said. "I suppose I seem pretty cagey. It's all part of the job, you see. People might innocently misrepresent critical information, which could jeopardize a case."

"Oh, I understand all about misrepresentation in my line of work," she said. "For one, people outrageously misrepresent Wicca and the Wiccan community."

He nodded and had the feeling there was more to her sentiment than she was saying. However, when she said no more, out of respect, he didn't press her for further details.

"Thank you so much for your assistance, Eva, but I'd better get going," he said. "It's been a bit of a slog today."

She smiled. "Sure. Happy to help, Peter."

Before he reached the door to leave, she hurried over to him with a business card. "If I can be of further help with anything else, just let me know. Text or call … I wrote my personal mobile number on the card."

He noticed her handwritten number. "Absolutely. Thank you."

"Regarding the topics we discussed, there's a lot of misinformation out there, and I'd hate for you to be misled," she said.

He smiled. "Why, Eva, who else would I ever consider asking?"

CHAPTER 25

Despite Captain Gunderson's warning not to return to work for a week, Naughware rose later the next morning and went to the precinct for his interview with the FBI.

It went as well as could be expected, though he had the distinct impression that they found his innate detection of the sniper to be uncanny, at the very least.

After his interview, he stopped in to see the captain and inquire further about the case.

"What can I tell you?" she asked. "There's still so much information coming in. You know how this works; we won't have all the details together for some time yet."

"Sure. I get it," he said, staring at the clock hanging on the wall to his left.

She sympathized with his expression of disappointment, and she realized how much he had given in service to the case.

"Hey," she said, to which he looked back at her. "Maybe I did hear a couple of things that I could share, but strictly in confidence and off the record."

He nodded. "Done."

"Word has it that Jenny Vance is talking," she said. "Agent Vance, though I'm certain that's not her real name, was deep undercover and collaborating with the dead DEA agent, known only as Julio Bonilla. Apparently, Vance and

Lev Spight fell in love while she was operating in Abaddon, so your instincts were correct there."

"Good to know," he said.

"The warehouse gathering was a result of 'drugs for cash in exchange for immediate money laundering' gone bad," she said. "Add the ulterior motives of Spight and Vance to steal the untraceable portion of the money, and you've got carnage on an epic scale."

"That's a shitshow example of multitasking if ever I heard it," he said.

"There's more," she said. "When Vance and Spight wanted to go off the grid together, they leveraged some of Decebal Lungu's men to pull off a heist of the pre-circulated cash. However, things went down badly, and only Vance and Spight made it away alive with the cash."

He nodded. "And, naturally, they left the new cash behind because the bills were sequenced, and they thought it'd be more readily traceable. That's just money laundering 101."

"True enough. The problem was, they needed to change identities in order to make it out of the country," she said. "So, Spight leveraged some local contacts to find someone who could put together new identities for them."

"Sham Koda," he said.

"That's right," she said.

"Lev Spight already had access to money and power," he said. "Why did he abruptly drop off his parents' radar like that?"

Gunderson appeared reflective. "That's a key question, though Vance won't say, and the Spights aren't talking, either."

"Doesn't that strike anyone as a bit suspicious?"

"I'm sure," she said. "At least, it looks that way to me. But, lacking further evidence or probable cause, we'd be opening up both a political and legal firestorm. Viktor Spight isn't the sort of person to take uninvited scrutiny lightly."

"I think there's something nefarious going on with

Spight," he said. "Otherwise, why would Lev have such ready access to Lungu's men in the first place?"

She shrugged. "I don't disagree with you, but it's not my call," she said. "At least, barring something more substantial to go on, I'm not prepared to press further against Spight right now."

"What about the sniper?"

She frowned. "That one's more problematic."

"How so?"

"He's a ghost," she said. "No identity, not even fingerprints on file with state or the federal databases … not anything."

"That seems unlikely in his profession," he said. "Foreign national, maybe?"

"Perhaps European, based upon his features," she said. "Though Interpol didn't have anything yet, either."

"Are they performing an autopsy on the body?" he asked. "Maybe the round that killed him could provide some leads on the mysterious sharpshooter I saw?"

"I understand an autopsy's pending," she said with a perplexed expression. "Though I understand that the entrance wound appeared as if the bullet burned its way straight through his head, like a lightning strike or something."

He frowned. "What?" he asked. "How's that possible?"

"It may only be hearsay," she said. "Like I said, they'll know more once the official autopsy is complete."

"Huh," he said. "Do we have any idea who employed him?"

"Not currently," she said.

"What about Skeeter Rowe's part in all this?" he asked.

"Despite everything, it seems he's been granted complete immunity for his cooperation and testimony," she said.

His features perked up at that. "Anything from Rowe tying Midas Hyde to anything?"

"Nope," she said. "Though I'd keep those theories about Hyde to yourself for now. It's bad enough the Spights glare at the sound of your name. Let's not add another powerful family to that list."

"Right," he said. Despite that, he wasn't about to let that lie forever.

She stared directly at him and tilted her head down slightly, like a bull readying to charge. "Peter, this case is closed," she said. "Leave it alone. Are we clear?"

"Okay," he said. "You got it, Cap."

He absently rubbed at his sore chest as he considered everything she had told him.

"Wait a minute," he said. "Did the feds tell you all this? I'm surprised they'd share."

The corners of her mouth upturned slightly. "I have a couple of sources that I'd rather not name."

His eyebrows rose.

"Now," she said. "Get out of here, and I don't want to see you again until next week. Plan on Monday morning, bright and early."

"Say, how about mid-morning instead?" he asked with a lop-sided grin.

"Nice try," she said. "Now, go. And close the door on your way out, Detective."

"Absolutely," he said with a wink.

As he reached for the doorknob, Gunderson said, "And Peter?"

He turned to look at her.

"Be patient," she said. "Play the long game."

***

Detective Keane was in the middle of reviewing some old case files that she hoped would help with her investigation into the stolen jewelry from Karatopia when the phone rang.

She glanced over and saw that the call was on Naughware's extension. It appeared as an external call and an unlisted number.

On a whim, she decided to answer it.

"Detective Keane. South Precinct, Robbery-Homicide," she said.

"Detective Keane?"

"Yes," she said. "Who's speaking?"

"Thaddeus Prescott, at your service," he said. "My apologies. I must have misdialed. I thought I was calling his mobile."

"You mean, Detective Naughware?" she asked.

"Yes, indeed," he said.

"Well, I'm afraid he's not in the office today," she said. "Anything I can assist you with?"

There was silence.

"Hello?" she asked.

"Detective, I regret you may not be as interested as Naughware in hearing what I have to share," he said. "I can call back on his mobile, or perhaps text message him instead."

While she suspected he was correct, nevertheless she said, "Try me."

"Abaddon has unexpected visitors," he said. "Naughware may need to prepare for them."

"Oh?" she asked. "Abaddon gets lots of visitors, I'm told. Many are just passing through on their way to somewhere else, I suspect."

"Suffice to say, Abaddon's receiving visitors unlike it has experienced in quite some time," he said.

"Such as, who?" she asked.

"I'm not sure yet," he said. "But as soon as I have a clue, I'll happily share."

Keane frowned. "Well, I'll pass along the message for you."

"Thank you, Detective Keane," he said. "Pleasure talking to you again."

The call disconnected, and Keane looked at the receiver in her hand before placing it back in its cradle.

"Weird," she said.

At that moment, Evan Taylor entered the office carrying some papers and headed over to Naughware's desk.

"Taylor," Keane said. "What brings you here?"

"Just dropping off some notarized statements from me for the Vance case file," he said, dropping them atop Naughware's desk. "Even when I retire I can't get away from paperwork, it seems."

A faint smile crossed her face. "Well, I know he appreciates it."

"I don't suppose he's actually around here somewhere?" Taylor asked.

"Oh, he stopped in for an interview with the FBI a little earlier. Then the captain reaffirmed his leave for the rest of the week," she said. "He should be back in on Monday."

"Well, good for him then," he said, turning to leave. "Catch you around, Keane."

"Hey, Taylor," she said.

He turned around. "Yep?"

"You ever have any dealings with a guy named Thaddeus Prescott?" she asked.

"The Monk."

She shook her head. "Man, how I hate that nickname."

He chuckled.

"You worked with Naughware for years," she said. "Is this Prescott on the up-and-up?"

"The Monk's a different sort, that's for sure," he said. "But he seems solid enough from everything I can tell. He's been helpful on a few cases, in fact."

"Naughware and Prescott seem like big fans of each other," she said.

Taylor's expression turned reflective. "Well, there's history there."

She nodded. "Any chance you'd let me in on that?"

"That depends," he said. "You asking out of curiosity or concern?"

She considered that for a moment. "Concern."

Taylor folded his arms before him. "Mm. You ask

Naughware about him?"

She shrugged. "He didn't say much, really."

"All right then," he said. "I'll give you the short and sweet version."

She gestured toward Naughware's empty chair, and Taylor sat down.

"You know," he said, patting the arms of the chair. "This used to be my desk … my chair. Feels just like I remember it."

She waited for him to continue.

"But you asked me about Prescott," he said. "A little over two years ago, Naughware and I got caught in the middle of a city street in a shootout with a couple of robbery suspects that we tracked down."

"It was a real shitshow. Busy street with people everywhere," he continued, shaking his head. "There was a woman with her young son nearby, and they were directly in the line of fire. Naughware jumped up and took two rounds shielding them and getting them safely under cover."

Keane's eyebrow rose, and she leaned across her desk. "No shit."

"I thought I lost Peter for sure that day," he said. "You see, there's something you've got to understand about him. He's the sort of person who considers a hail of gunfire as a personal invitation."

"I'll try to remember that," she said.

"Fortunately, Peter had a vest on, but still cracked some ribs for his efforts," he said.

"Thank you for sharing that with me," she said. "It says a lot about the sort of man he is."

Taylor nodded and gave her a meaningful look. "Yes, it really does."

"But where does Prescott come into play?" she asked.

He pursed his lips. "Turns out, that woman and child were his wife and son," he said. "Apparently, Prescott applied two life debts to Naughware's scorecard for saving them. At least, that's how I recall Naughware once describing it."

"What does that mean, exactly?" she asked. "Life debts. Scorecard."

He shrugged. "Damned if I understand it thoroughly, myself. Suffice to say, Prescott's never hesitated to assist Naughware when he asked for help on a case," he said. "And, like I said, Prescott's been helpful in a number of ways. Or, at least, in his own unique way, which again, I don't claim to fully understand. And how long that 'debt' continues is between The Monk and Naughware."

"Hm," she said. "I appreciate you sharing that, Taylor."

He rose from his seat. "Glad to help."

She watched him leave and then reached into the desk drawer to retrieve a completed department request for transfer form. All that remained before turning it in was her signature.

Keane stared down at the form in quiet reflection and then looked over at Naughware's empty chair.

After a few moments, she folded request in half and tore it into pieces, dropping them into the recycling container by her desk.

CHAPTER 26

Naughware was no stranger to the mysteriously vacant Nowhere Zone.

And yet, each time he ventured there, he hoped he would find something new or different about the surroundings. And on each occasion, he was sadly disappointed.

However, for all that it was a dark, empty void, at least it was peaceful.

Using a flashlight, he strolled along in the quiet, his footsteps muted against the strange, non-descript surface. As he walked, he contemplated the array of circumstances and feelings he had experienced in the short time since his thirty-third birthday.

After a time, he withdrew his digital player and inserted his earbuds. Then he navigated to the root directory and selected a song; one of the original eleven that came preprogrammed in his device.

Triumph's "Fight the Good Fight" began to play.

It felt appropriate given all that had happened recently.

While the Bouquet Corral case—he swore that was the last time he would call it that—was effectively complete, he still felt no sense of closure for it.

Sure, Jenny Vance had been located and taken into custody, and even the disappearance of Lev Spight had been resolved; albeit fatally. Some of the participants, chiefly Decebal Lungu, had been murdered for their part in the case.

While it was true that numerous elements of the case had yet to come out, including any additional information the feds might learn from Jenny Vance, many pressing questions remained unanswered.

First, there was the matter of Lev Spight. How deeply had he been connected with Lungu prior to the Bouquet Corral shootout? Were any other members of the Spight family also involved?

Then there was the sniper. Who was he? Who had hired him?

And was he merely boosted by some substance, medically enhanced, maybe possessed … or worse?

More to the point, who was the mysterious woman Naughware had seen at the motel who had taken the killing shot on the sniper?

And as if hopeful insights couldn't be more convoluted, The Monk's portents continued to present an exercise in both philosophy and mysticism for him.

Was Prescott being intentionally vague, or did it reflect limitations to the man's abilities?

Were those abilities even real?

Something ominous lurking in the back of his mind tugged against his inclination to dismiss The Monk out of hand. In truth, the man had been remarkably helpful to him in the past.

And, as if that weren't already enough, he and Keane still had an unsolved jewelry robbery case to solve, including the hopeful recovery of the stolen merchandise.

He paused, focusing on the song's closing lyrics, and noted they were, indeed, both hopeful and helpful. His mood had markedly improved.

Once the song ended, Naughware stopped his player, withdrew his earbuds, and returned the device to his pocket.

Unfortunately, the host of quandaries plaguing him were topics that would have to wait for another time. Though he had few ideas of where, or how, to procure the answers he needed, much less who to seek out for those insights.

Then he thought of Eva Shyne, and smiled.

"Okay," he said, to nobody in particular. "Maybe there's one person."

However, he had only just met her, and he knew little about her background, much less her level of trustworthiness.

Perhaps it was simply that she validated concepts that most anyone else in his life would either frown upon, or openly rail against.

Still, the fact remained that he was attracted to Eva, liked her, and wanted to get to know her better. And, in truth, he wanted to further leverage her expertise and knowledge of the more paranormal or mystical aspects of the quandaries he was working on.

Certainly, there was Thaddeus Prescott, but he still felt a bit unnerved being in the man's presence. Maybe it was his uncanny portents, though perhaps it was the strange way he seemed to look into Naughware's soul.

"Or, was it my chakra?" he asked, thoughtfully rubbing his chin.

Granted, his interactions with The Monk felt both genuine and on the level.

But what bothered Naughware, was that, in all that time, The Monk was difficult to read, like a closed book. Add to that, Naughware wasn't entirely certain he understood the full scope of Thaddeus' personal agenda, if he even had one that could be determined.

Time would tell, he supposed.

He shined his light to and fro and turned around in a complete circle, all the while sweeping a beam of light until it ended, disappearing into the nothingness.

"You know," he said. "This would be a helluva lot more interesting place if there was actually something here!"

He paused to listen for a response, or even a small sound.

Nothing.

"Nothing in a place that goes to nowhere," he muttered.

He turned to continue his ambiguous stroll, but a few steps later nearly tripped on something. He spun and shined his light down to see a small metal flashlight lying on the surface.

Frowning, he picked it up to examine it more closely.

It was of a very old style with a cheap metal tube, a hard, red plastic bezel, and sliding-style power button.

Most of all, it looked oddly familiar.

He looked at the end cap and saw something crudely scrawled onto the back of its metal surface.

Peter N.

"Shit."

His heart palpitated as his throat muscles tightened and his mouth suddenly felt dry.

Memories washed over him like it was only yesterday.

It was the flashlight that he had dropped when he had aimlessly wandered the Nowhere Zone back when he was only eleven years old.

He recalled it had been during one of his early visits to the void. He could almost still sense the feelings of terror he had felt, running around in the darkness, desperately seeking an exit.

It was before he had fully trained himself to focus his thoughts in order to successfully return to the "real world" again. To his dismay, it hadn't always worked on the first or second attempt.

He recalled those terrifying hours of crying and desperation before finally collapsing onto the hard surface in futility. Only after tightly shutting his eyes and daydreaming about his home did he eventually feel his own bed beneath him.

One of many hard lessons he had made all on his own.

He switched the flashlight on, though nothing happened. As when he had dropped it all those years ago, the batteries were dead.

"Just how big is this place?" he asked, staring into the

darkness.

In a way, it almost felt as if his journey in the Nowhere Zone had come full circle.

He contemplated that for a moment.

The more he thought about it, the more he desired a less ominous distraction, if only for a brief period of time. He wanted—no, he needed—a respite from his cases, the Nowhere Zone, and the host of other conundrums that plagued and puzzled him.

With a smooth motion, he lay down flat on his back on the surface, closed his eyes, and concentrated on the impressions of his bedroom and of lying atop his bed.

Moments later, he felt a whirling of disorientation, and he disappeared from the void.

Complete silence and utter darkness reigned once more, unabated.

The stillness was broken by the sound of a distant rumbling, like thunder coupled with the shifting of stone against stone that resisted being moved, but in the end, slowly parted.

A deep, ominous chuckle followed.

Then, once more, silence reigned.

CHAPTER 27

Naughware's momentary disorientation ended by settling atop a mattress. He opened his eyes to view his familiar bedroom surroundings.

He promptly sat up and dialed his mobile phone.

"Miss Millie's House of Perdition," said a husky-voiced woman. "I'm Trudy. How can I assist you?"

"Hi, Trudy," Peter said. "It's Peter Naughware."

"Oh, hello, Mr. Naughware," Trudy said.

"Listen, I know it's short notice, but any chance there's an opening available with Becki tonight?" he asked. "I've been meaning to reschedule, but things—well, things have been busy."

"Certainly, Mr. Naughware. I'm certain we can make an accommodation for *you*," she said. "One moment while I check her schedule."

* * *

Night had fallen as Naughware continued his drive on the county road outside of town while listening to alt-J's "The Gospel of John Hurt" and further pondering its meaning.

He had the eerie notion there was a reason the song had appeared for him on his birthday. But was it reflecting something about him that was going to happen, or had it already occurred?

The memories of his altercation with the sniper washed over him. He recalled the powerful sensations he had felt while punching the man, who shockingly sailed down the hallway.

The song's chorus played again.

Maybe something has burst from me, he thought. *Or through me.*

If so, was there more to follow?

As he turned his vehicle onto Miss Millie's wooded sixty-acre property, his digital player abruptly switched tracks to "House of the Rising Sun" by The Animals.

"This is getting really old," he said. "You do this every single time."

He slowly proceeded up long, narrow stretch of asphalt driveway that wound deeper into the property.

The driveway opened up to a concrete parking area set before the estate, where he parked his car near the handful of those already present.

The sprawling mansion was nowhere nearly as massive or posh-looking as the Spights', but its early-twentieth-century design gave it a quaint nostalgic appearance of days long gone by.

He exited his vehicle carrying a small gym bag, and used his key remote to lock the doors.

As he started to walk away, the car stereo came on and blared the song again.

"Shit!" he exclaimed while rushing back to unlock and open the door. He jerked the player free from its cable connection to the stereo.

He stared down at the device in his palm and noticed with surprise that the prominent dent from the sniper's bullet impact was gone, and the surface was once more smooth.

"How the fuck—" he muttered.

That was doubly impossible.

"What the hell are you?" he asked.

He looked heavenward into a sky that appeared like a vast black curtain filled with countless celestial bodies.

Having escaped the big city's light noise, he marveled at the scene arrayed above him.

"For that matter, precisely, who the hell am I?" he asked. "I mean normal people can't go to the—to a—Nowhere Zone."

He pondered and watched, feeling no small degree of foolish as he stood there.

"There's probably nobody even up there, much less anybody willing, to answer me, is there?" he asked.

The sounds of crickets continued until, finally, he inhaled a deep breath of fresh air and slowly let it out.

"Yeah, figured as much."

He looked back down at the player in his hand, a device that had been like a trusted companion since it had mysteriously appeared on his twenty-second birthday. It had seen him through a tour of duty overseas with the Army, as well as through many other adventures as a police officer and now a detective.

"All right, you can come along then," he said, dropping the player into his jacket's inner pocket. "But don't make a scene."

He slowly ascended the steps leading up to the estate's expansive and well-lit front porch and rang the doorbell.

* * * *

ABOUT THE AUTHOR

Jaz Primo: Delving into flights of fancy and realms of imagination; eagerly sharing with you.

Jaz lives in the Great American Midwest where he writes paranormal romance, sword and sorcery, urban fantasy, and young adult literature. He's a history aficionado, Dungeons & Dragons enthusiast, Doctor Who fanatic, "pun-master", an all-around fan of vampires, and a caregiver to the world's most endearing cats.

Visit Jaz's website at jazprimo.com where you can also find his blog and links to Jaz's other social media platforms.

Sunrise at Sunset: Revamped

Sunset Vampire Series, Book 1

(Second Edition)

by Jaz Primo

The Sunset Vampire Series achieved Third Place in the Reviewer's Choice Award for Best Paranormal Series of 2012 (Paranormal Romance Guild).

This new, second edition of the original, has new never-seen-before material, *Revamped* includes a forward by Jaz explaining how this version improves over the original. Additional bonus material includes a new bonus chapter that bridges events between the first novel and the sequel, *A Bloody London Sunset.*

When is a bloodthirsty predator the best protection against a psychotic killer?
When the predator is both a vampire...and the woman you love.

Caleb is bravely overcoming a dark past while having no memory of the beautiful vampire that saved him. Despite a promise to stay away, Katrina is compelled to return to him.
However, a vengeful rival from her past has dire plans for both of them.

Available in trade paperback and all major eBook formats.

Go to http://jazprimo.com/books for purchasing links.

Winner of the Paranormal Romance Guild's Reviewer's Choice Award for Best Young Adult Novel of 2012!

Gwen Reaper

A Young Adult Paranormal Romance

by Jaz Primo

Boy meets beautiful and mysterious, yet reclusive, girl who harbors a potentially-lethal secret.

"A thing of beauty is a joy forever: its loveliness increases; it will never pass into nothingness." John Keats, English romantic poet.
I never thought that my first exposure to real beauty would be tinged with the threat of oblivion…

~ ~ ~ ~ ~

When high school junior Scott Blackstone is forced to move from his childhood home in Springfield, Illinois to small-town Custer, South Dakota, he expects nothing less than to languish in complete disappointment. Instead, he discovers a beautiful and mysterious seventeen-year-old girl named Gwen, who captivates him from his initial, adrenaline-laced sight of her on the shores of Stockade Lake. Scott's pursuit of the elusive Gwen sweeps him into the midst of a potentially lethal family heritage that was birthed in hope, only to be passed into a legacy of guilt and death.

Scott engages in a journey of discovery, tinged with both angst and danger. Like many dire legends throughout history, he is unprepared for the untimely revelation that both love and despair are often two sides of the same coin.

Gwen Reaper
(A Young Adult Paranormal Romance)
is available in trade paperback and all
major eBook formats.

Bringer of Fire

***Logan Bringer* Urban Fantasy Series, Book 1**

by Jaz Primo

The twenty-first century has arrived, but the world is a darker place where international superpowers tenuously jockey for both political and economic supremacy. It's a time when the rights and interests of the individual carry little weight. But a medical breakthrough spontaneously blossoms telekinetic abilities within the body of one man, altering humanity's evolution and threatening to tip the world's balance of power. That man is Logan Bringer.

When humankind's greatest achievement leads to a race for its control, some will bring political and economic powers to bear.

Others unleash an array of assassins and weaponry.

However, when Logan's family is directly threatened, he unleashes himself.

He is...the *Bringer of Fire.*

Available in trade paperback and all major eBook formats.

Go to http://jazprimo.com/books for purchasing links.

www.ingramcontent.com/pod-product-compliance
Lightning Source LLC
LaVergne TN
LVHW091116080826
845145LV00008B/1940

* 9 7 8 0 9 9 6 8 8 1 3 1 9 *